BELOVED INTRUDER

BELOVED INTRUDER

A Romance Novel

Tania Park

Tania Park Publishing

A catalogue record for this book is available from the National Library of Australia

ISBN: 978-0-6485565-6-5 (Paperback)
ISBN: 978-0-6485565-7-2 (Ebook)

Printed & Channel Distribution: Lightning Source | Ingram (USA/UK/EUROPE/AUS)
Cover Designed—Laila Savolainen, Pickawoowoo Publishing Group
Publishing Consultants/Interior Design—Pickawoowoo Publishing Group

Tania Park Publishing
For enquiries, write to: rights and permissions via publisher.

First Printing, 2022

This is my first purely romance novel. It was Penny Swingler, a writing group member, who convinced me to join Romance Writers of Australia several years ago. Every year since, I have entered a manuscript in one of their competitions. My stories seemed to hover mid-way in the results chart until Beloved Intruder was a finalist and ultimately won third place. If the judges enjoyed my words, then maybe other readers would also enjoy the story but third place meant the manuscript needed some work. This is the result of a major re-write. Thank you Penny. Maybe I should now publish all of my romance novels.

Mistaken: 2015

He never got around to telling me why he wanted me dead.

Retribution: 2015

Amy spends the next week hiding while planning to escape the clutches of Rico and his family crime gang.

Blind Justice: 2016 – Commended *2016 Christina Stead National Literary Awards.*

Panic turned to terror at the sudden on-rush of two sets of feet. A rough hand clamped over her mouth to silence her.

Road Trip: 2016

Something inside her broke apart, leaving an intense sensation of emptiness. It was like he'd taken a huge chunk of her heart with him and he was only her brother.

The Swan: 2018 - Finalist 2020 *The wishing shelf International Awards.*

I was seven years old. Do you honestly think I would tell the truth so that I could get beaten again the minute the police left.

Stalked: 2019 – Long listed *2020 Davitt Awards.*

A triumphant sneer shot from the corners of his mouth at the thought of one way he could leave his mark to let her know she belonged to him.

Double Cross: 2020 – Long listed *2021 Davitt Awards*

The weekend was awesome, right up until I murdered a man.

The Chest: 2021

The surprises kept coming, disconcerting her more each day. It felt as though she had been transported to some alternate world.

One

'This feels so wrong.' Wrapping both hands around her thigh, Abigail Sharpe lifted her weak left leg over the lip of the car doorway. To gain the support she needed to alight, she planted one outstretched hand on the armrest of the door and the other on the glove box before locking her arms straight to hoist her aching body from the seat. After settling both feet on the ground and finding her balance, it took a few moments before she released her death grip on the car door and huffed out a long breath. At least she was upright even though her legs had turned into overcooked spaghetti.

'It's okay, Abby. I left at least a dozen messages for Paul.'

'But does he know yet?' Abby shuffled around in a half-circle to face Grace but had to close her eyes against the shaft of sunlight which hit her retina, but boy, it was so good to feel real warmth from the sun after so many months of being cloistered inside hospital wards.

'He will ring me back when he can. Communications are not so hot in Kabul.' Grace Sanders moved around to the back of the car and unlatched the boot, the car jerking when it lifted.

'This is why it isn't right for me to be living in his house.' After she managed to get her eyes to adjust to the brightness, Abby stared at the hospital volunteer who had become a close friend – her only friend now. When Grace's head dipped below the top of the car, Abby glanced towards the cute house built from fresh painted weatherboards and calculated the distance from the kerb to the front door. It looked so far. Would she be able to make it without falling?

'He won't mind in the least. Besides, he's not due back for another four weeks.' There was a rattle as Grace pulled out a pair of aluminium crutches and hurried around to the passenger side. 'Here we go.' She held the dreaded silver sticks in front of Abby.

Turning to the older woman Abby shook her head. 'No, I don't need them. I can make it.' The smile she plastered across her face was all for show for she certainly didn't feel at all fine. Not used to sitting for such a long time, the two hour car journey had taken a toll on her mending injuries. All she wanted was to reach the darn door, get inside and stretch out horizontal on the first bed she could find.

Abby bit her lip, annoyed at Grace when she hovered like a bee over a pollen-laden bloom while Abby took one slow step at a time until she reached the white picket gate. She slumped against it to catch her breath. The deep concentration needed to tell her brain which muscles to use to take each step, took a lot out of her until her muscles warmed up and began co-operating.

After giving herself a minute to rest, she was confident she could continue, so reached over, unlatched the gate and shoved it open. The crazy paving leading to the front veranda, suited the cottage-style house but despite the smoothness of each odd-shaped paving stone, the mosses and Mondo grass growing between each slab made the path look uneven and downright impossible to traverse. This was going to be a challenge. All the surfaces she had walked on over the past few months had been flat and smooth and she wasn't at all sure she could manage to lift her feet high enough to avoid tripping.

'Are you sure you don't want your crutches?' Grace asked.

Abby released a half laugh, half sigh. 'If I am going to stay here I need to get used to it. I can make it my goal for the week: walk the front path without falling.' She stared at the daunting path. All of a sudden, her fierce strive for independence seemed to be unachievable. Closing her eyes to search for an ounce of courage, she turned her face heavenwards in silent prayer, adding under her breath, her credo for the past few months, 'one step at a time.'

On a sucked in breath she pushed her body upright from the gate pillar, found her balance, lifted her right foot from the ground and continued her slow, ungainly walk.

Grace hovered by Abby's side ready to grab her if she tripped, the same way she had done all the months of Abby's rehabilitation. Even though it had proved necessary many times, it still grated how she had gone from a fit, active sports' teacher to this poor excuse of a human, but at least she was alive.

Halfway along the path, her flat shoe caught on the edge of a paving stone. She stumbled and wavered to and fro with outstretched arms moving up and down to counteract her unsteady sway. Grace's hands poised either side of her waist, so close Abby could feel them. 'Go away, Grace.'

'I'm sorry.'

'You don't sound sorry.' Abby paused and twisted around to Grace. 'How about you go and open the front door to let me take my time. You, hovering around like a pesky mosquito, is making me more nervous than this darn path.'

'No need to get tetchy,' Grace mumbled as she sidestepped onto the garden to pass Abby before stalking towards the veranda.

'I won't get tetchy if you let me handle this on my own.' To belie her words, Abby grinned when her wobble ceased and she began the slow process of continuing along the path. With each step she became more confident and began moving faster and faster until she reached the edge of the veranda where she paused at the bottom of the two steps and released her held breath through gritted teeth. Who built steps without a handrail?

'Congratulations, you made it.'

The cheery words brought Abby's mind away from the steps. She smiled when she realised she had indeed achieved her aim. 'Yeah, I did, didn't I?' Grace stepped close enough for the two women to slap hands together in a high-five salute.

'Now there are steps.' Turning back, she stared at them. They weren't big steps and really there were three if she counted the one onto the veranda. She could climb up them with the crutches. Going down was more of a problem, one most people wouldn't realise. It was easier to keep your centre of balance when rising than it was when descending. Her mind wavered on whether or not to take the crutches still tucked under Grace's arm but since she would be living here alone, she had to be able to manage. There was no choice and she sure didn't want to spend another second in the darn hospital.

It took a few seconds to figure out the best way to tackle climbing the steps since there was no handrail. She wavered her right foot millimetres above the ground, lifted it, eased it on the first step and pushed up. As soon as she was high enough, she dragged the weak left foot next to her right. Success, even though she had to wriggle her hips to centre her balance. Next step was easier because she could reach over to grasp the post at the top and pull with gripped hands against the post to raise her body upwards and centre her weight on the next step, and the next, until she was standing on the veranda in triumph.

'Wow, Abby, three steps up without crutches. I knew this was the right thing to do. A couple of months here and your legs will be as strong as they were before.' Grace enveloped Abby in a hug but when Grace's words registered, Abby pulled away.

'A couple of months. I can't stay here when your son comes home. I thought this was only while he was away.' Mortified, Abby stared at her friend.

'I am sure Paul won't mind you staying here for as long as you need. Once he knows the circumstances and meets you he will be more than happy for you to stay. Besides, he's only coming home for a few weeks R & R before he has return to overseer his project in Afghanistan.'

Still unsure about living in a virtual stranger's house, Abby watched Grace unlock the door. Sucking in a deep fortifying breath, she wobbled across the veranda but by the time she stepped over the threshold, her legs had gone all rubbery as though they were about to give way. Certain she couldn't go much further, she headed for the nearest chair, a large, comfortable looking leather sofa, to rest her aching body. To prevent falling in a heap, she flopped down, wincing at the jolt of pain when still healing hips hit the cushion.

Grace raced forwards at Abby's small groan. 'Are you all right?' She glanced at her watch. 'It's not really time for more painkillers.'

Abby sighed. Much to her disgust she had become dependent on drugs to deaden the constant ache but before leaving hospital she had made a secret promise to slowly wean herself from the painkillers but didn't dare tell Grace of her plans. Grace wouldn't agree. Nor would the doctors. 'It's okay. I sat down a little too hard. All I need is to rest for a minute or two.' More like half an hour, she thought as she eased back against the cushion and let her eyes drift shut on a long sigh as aching bones settled into the comfy cushioned seat.

Grace lifted her legs onto the sofa. 'If you are sure, I'll get your things from the car.'

'I'm sure.' After giving Grace a little dismissive wave, Abby dropped her head on the padded armrest. Sweet mercy, how she ached. The effects of the two strong painkillers she took before leaving her private ward were beginning to wear off and her body was begging for more. Let me last two more hours, she thought. If she could lengthen the time between doses and reduce the strength bit by bit, she figured she would be able to manage the pain at the same time she began the weaning process, especially without nurses or Grace hovering over her to ensure she swallowed the dreaded tablets.

While Abby remained still, willing the dull ache to settle, she heard Grace make three trips to and from the car to bring in the various bags of Abby's belongings and enough groceries for a week. It wasn't until after a lengthy silence, she glanced up and spied Grace watching her. Even though she was desperate to be alone she didn't have the heart to send the woman who had been her mentor, friend and everything else, for the past seven months, away so soon. Somehow she would have to be more sociable than she felt. 'Show me this gorgeous house.'

After forcing her body upright without showing a wince, it didn't take her long to realise the house was larger than it appeared from the outside. Modern appliances had been fitted in a major renovation but it was decorated in such a manner, the house still kept its cosy cottage atmosphere. One bedroom on the front of the house was now a well-appointed office with the dark, rich colours indicating a definite male zone. The two guest bedrooms had more of a feminine touch with lace curtains and chintz covers while the master bedroom was painted a deep burgundy and blue – definitely male. The contrast mystified Abby.

'Is Paul married?' Abby closed the door as she shuffled back into the passage.

'I wish, but no, why do you ask?'

'Two rooms have the feminine touch while the others are so - manly.' Abby limped along the passage to the next room.

'I had a hard time convincing Paul to decorate at least some of the rooms for a woman. I pretended I wouldn't be caught dead staying in such dark rooms when I came to stay. Really, it was in the hope he would bring his latest girlfriend to stay and perhaps get married. I am desperate for a couple of grandchildren.'

'Did she stay?'

'Not to my knowledge. He was engaged – briefly. I'm not sure what happened but he was badly hurt. So much so I don't think there's been a woman since. Such a pity. I think it's why he took this job overseas: to escape.' Stepping in front of Abby, Grace swung open the next door.

'Oh, my.' Abby peered into the bathroom. It was pure luxury. As far as bathrooms went, the room was enormous with a large spa-bath set along the end wall. Above it sat a long window overlooking a shaded veranda and extensive backyard with discreet lattice and shrubs giving the room privacy. 'This is gorgeous.'

'Spectacular, isn't it? Paul outdid himself in here. And this luxury is all yours until he comes home.'

A sudden sense of misgiving swamped Abby. 'I feel as though I am invading his personal space. I don't think this is such a good idea.' With her limbs and muscles losing some of their stiffness, her steps were less stilted as she continued on down the passage into the kitchen. She gasped out aloud. It was a master-chef's dream. 'Even in all the housing magazines I have looked at, I have never seen such a wonderful kitchen. This is amazing.'

Turning in a slow circle, she studied the features, overawed by the dark blue granite benches over cream cupboards with the same cream tiles as in the other rooms covering all necessary wall spaces. The colour scheme melded perfectly with modern stainless-steel fixtures. A large window over the sink showed the same scene as from the bathroom but with a glimpse of the ocean beyond the white picket fence. It was such an idyllic property. In the centre of the room sat a polished jarrah table with enough chairs to seat a family of at least ten.

'Paul doesn't like formal dining rooms so he incorporated both rooms in one. Most visitors congregate around the kitchen table in any case so he figured he would make it big enough for a party. Do you like it?'

'I love it, but I still feel like an intruder.'

'Nonsense, dear, Paul won't mind in the least. Now, I put your clothes in the main room. The larger bed is more suitable for you. It gives you the room to spread out and do your exercises. Plus it's the closest to the toilet and bathroom so you can reach them easily during the night.' While she spoke, Grace led Abby back down the passage to show her what she meant.

'I can't, Grace. This is going too far. This is Paul's private domain.'

'Paul would insist.'

'I am still really uncomfortable about this whole thing.'

'At least use this room until he comes home. After four weeks I have no doubt you will be much stronger. Now I must go. I have a meeting to attend this afternoon and this evening I'm going out for dinner with a couple of old friends to make final plans for our holiday.'

Abby enveloped her friend in a tight hug, still apprehensive but what else could she do? She had nowhere else to go. To show she was okay, she plastered on a smile and slung one arm around Grace's waist as they moved towards the front door. 'You have a wonderful time. And thank you, for everything. I would never have been able to cope since the accident without your help and friendship.'

Standing in the open doorway, Abby kept a false smile plastered on her face and waved until Grace was out of sight. As she swung the door closed, the edge caught her on the right hip, knocking her sideways. She reached out to find something to grab when she lost her precarious balance and stumbled sideways. When her left foot caught on the leg of a small hall table she grabbed wildly, teetered and tumbled to the ground when her weak left leg didn't have the strength to hold her upright. One flailing arm managed to hook into the tightly curled cable between the phone and receiver. A resounding crash of table, telephone, a ceramic dish of knickknacks and thick telephone books echoed her cry of pain when she landed on one side.

With tears of pain and frustration welling, Abby groaned, too scared to move an inch. 'Damn it all to hell,' she muttered, daring to lift her head to glance around at the mess. 'Don't you dare cry, Abigail Sharpe,' she added at the top of her voice. 'You will not cry. You have been in bigger pickles so be a big girl and get yourself up.' Willing her tears to not fall, she rolled over, first onto her side where she rested before managing to lean up on one elbow. Terrified she had undone months of rehabilitation, she pushed with one hand to roll onto her bottom. Her breath held while testing joints and bone by tensing and releasing muscles before she managed to struggle into a sitting position.

Still on the floor, she hoisted the small table upright and after inspecting it for damage, shoved it back against the wall. Knowing it would be easier to lift the items from the floor while still down, than trying to bend when standing, she swept everything into one pile with her hands and did her best to sort them out. By lobbing each small item one at a time, she tossed them onto the table. The two heavy telephone books were more difficult but she shuffled on her bottom until she was close to the table edge and thrust them on top. She stared at the only items remaining on the floor; three broken pieces of porcelain from a small dish she presumed held the odd knickknacks and house keys. With her right leg, she shovelled the pieces together until they were within reach. One by one she got them onto the edge of the table but had to use the handle of the front door to haul herself up onto her feet. The telephone was set back into place by reeling it upwards using the cable.

After tidying the tabletop she tested the phone to ensure it hadn't been wrecked. The sound of the dial tone sent a wave of relief through her aching body. Abby held the three shards of broken dish in her hand and wondered what to do about them. The porcelain looked delicate and old but was it valuable? She inspected the back of each piece for a hallmark and shuddered when she recognised a famous old English pottery.

'Great start, Abby. You squat in a stranger's house and manage to break his valuable dish – all within the first half-hour.' Angry with herself for her stupidity, she shoved the three broken pieces into the drawer of the hall table. How on earth was she supposed to find a replacement and how much it would cost? She didn't even have a laptop anymore, to search on-line. Desperate to ease the ache in her hips, she hobbled to the bedroom, using the wall for support. The sharp twinge told her there was going to be a substantial bruise on her thigh come morning but compared to the ones she had after the accident it would be nothing. Once there, she took her time to ease onto the mattress, experience telling her she needed at least a couple of hours' rest before inflicting any more damage on the house.

Two

The sun's rays were beginning to cool but Abby was reluctant to shift from the padded mattress of the cane lounge she had managed to drag from the shed to the centre of the lawn. It had been a long time since she felt this wonderful; a long time since she could laze in the sun to feel the warmth sink into her skin. Stretching her limbs, she luxuriated in the renewed strength of withered leg muscles. After only a week of regular walking and pushing her body to exhaustion, the muscles were stronger, not so twangy. Not only did she physically feel stronger but she was far more invigorated and for the first time, felt there was real hope she would be able to walk normally. There was still a long way to go but she now believed her physiotherapist and specialist who had insisted she would be able to discard her crutches one day. Until now there had been vague hope but she hadn't really believed them.

Turning on one side, she peered through the open picket fence set at the rear of the large property. Thirty metres to the fence, she had figured out, and beyond the low pickets was a well-worn track through low dunes, sand and joy of joys, the ocean. A smile broke out as she eyed the waves, recalling day three when she managed to reach the water rolling up the edge of the sand. She didn't know how to describe the sensation of cold salt-water eddying around her ankles or why tears had washed over her eyes; the icy sensation such a simple pleasure but something she thought would never happen, especially when amputation had been under serious discussion for a couple of weeks after her accident. After demanding no amputation there had been serious discussions about spending the rest of her life in a wheelchair, which had made her even more determined to work hard and prove all the professionals wrong. It had been an amazing sensation to stand on two feet with the water lapping until she knew the soles of her feet had wrinkled. Being able to stand so long without wobbling or overbalancing had overwhelmed her with pure bliss.

Day four, she repeated the distance three times; each time the joy had been to wriggle her toes in the cold, clear brine before sunning on the warm sand to rest before returning to the house. Day five, she made a crutch assisted waddle about 150 metres along the main road but had to search for a log to rest on for a whole hour before attempting the journey back. The trip had exhausted her to the extent she hadn't been able to find the energy to rise from her bed to prepare an evening meal. Forced to still use one crutch for her weak left leg was what she considered to be a minor hurdle but one she was determined to overcome this coming week. She had jumped the hurdle of possible amputation, crawled over the hurdle of being wheelchair bound, been through agony at the hurdle of walking again so now she could manage the hurdle of getting rid of the crutches. So many impossible-to-achieve hurdles, yet she had won all so far.

With her eyes still closed behind dark sunglasses, she planned the next week's goals. Get to the beach and back without a crutch - goal one. Goal two? She thought hard. No sedatives to help her sleep. Oh, wow, could she manage? The heavy sedatives were the only way the scary nightmares didn't disturb her sleep. She hated having to take the pills for they left her with a fuggy brain, a tongue like corrugated cardboard and her stomach nauseous. She smiled. At the moment she was surviving on half the dose of painkillers than she had a week ago. The pain was worse after pushing her body to its limits but it was lessening each day. So now, she would work on reducing the sleeping pill dosage.

Happy with her decisions, Abby hauled her body upright, paused, wiggled and swayed till she was standing and grinned at having stood without gripping onto the armrest. She lifted her sunglasses up onto her head, giving her eyes time to adjust to the brightness of the sinking sun. Yes, success. She had stood upright without aid. Elated, she high-fived an imaginary friend, and eased around to make her ungainly but unsupported way back inside.

Before climbing into bed, she cleaned her teeth and with the tap still running, automatically began unscrewing the cap of her bottle of sleeping pills. But the cap caught. It took a close inspection to realise she had somehow cross-threaded it – probably because she was half asleep last night when she took a pill. Determined to get it free, she jerked at the lid. It shot apart, spilling the contents into the sink. 'Oh, no,' she cried as her fingers grappled around trying to retrieve the dozen white pills but they dissolved faster than she could grab until she could do nothing but stare at the swirling water sucking the sodden pills down the drain. She snorted. One problem solved, she thought as she threw the empty container into the small rubbish bin by the side of the vanity. With no choice but to sleep without the aid of sedatives, she figured tonight would be a real test.

On her return to the bedroom, she settled back onto the pillow, drew the quilt up around her shoulders and as with every night, physical exhaustion dragged her into a deep sleep.

Abby thrashed from side-to-side on the bed, arms flailing around above her head and legs twisting in the sheet. The pictures tumbling through her brain were in vivid technicolour, the sounds in stereophonic splendour and the aromas an abomination of her sense of smell.

Passengers screamed when the carriage shuddered as though it was rolling in an earthquake. It swayed from side-to-side, each swing wilder than the previous one. Seated between her parents on the bench seat, Abby heard her mother's suppressed screech at the same time her father reached behind Abby's back to lay a comforting hand on his wife's shoulder. Abby automatically reached out with one hand to grip the top edge of the rail behind their shoulders, the other on the seat in front. Her knuckles whitened with tension as arm muscles clenched taut in an attempt to counteract the frenzied sidewards threshing and maintain her equilibrium. She pushed her feet against the vinyl floor, tightened and released her leg muscles in rapid succession to keep her body upright on the swaying seat. There was intense pain as she thumped and rubbed against her parents and the back of the seat again and again and again.

'Dad, what's happening?' she whimpered on a gasp. Her voice thrummed in her chest in rhythm with the lurching carriage.

'We'll be right, chicken.'

Despite the forced calmness of his voice, Abby sensed her father's fear. Gut instinct told her they were not going to be all right. A surge of adrenalin burst through her veins followed instantly by her stomach muscles clenching so tight, it hurt. Terrible visions flashed through her mind. She screamed when the carriage jerked before losing traction from the rails. Other screams of terror joined hers in symphonic splendour as the train tumbled onto its side with a tremendous roar.

Continuous loud squeals and yells from panicked passengers mingled with the high-pitched grating of metal dragging along the ground at high speed. The stench of sparks, melting metal and smoke, filled the carriage and her nasal passages. Her eyes streamed but still through the haze she could make out human bodies flying like fluttering flags in all directions, juddering from side-to-side and as they were tossed in the air when the carriage scraped down an embankment and turned onto its roof in a ditch between the roadway and train line.

The pressure of being crushed between her parents, eased all of a sudden to be replaced by the sensation of soaring. The noise of terrified humans screaming in fear and pain was over-shadowed by screeches, thuds, bangs and crashes of seats being torn from their mountings, windows smashing, steel being shredded apart as though it were tissue paper and massive pieces of machinery being concertinaed together and finally tumbling over. When she landed, searing agony tore through every cell in her body. Then there was nothing.

Silence. Stillness. Blackness.

At the blood-curdling scream, Abby shot upright on the bed, wincing at the sudden stab of pain which seemed to radiate outwards from her hips to every extremity. Sweat poured from her skin, saturating her nightdress. Twisted, tangled sheets had her trapped in claustrophobic binds which held her tight as she attempted to reach over to switch on the bedside lamp. Deep sobs tore from her throat. Hot tears streamed down her face. She struggled to free her arms until one let fly as she lunged to the side, jamming down the tiny lever to bring light to her terrifying darkness. Her chest heaved as she gasped for breath. It took a few minutes before she realised her recurrent nightmare was only a bad dream. As she closed her eyes she forced her lungs to take in deep slow breaths. Only when her pounding heart had eased and her adrenalin surge had run its course did she cease the controlled breathing and lay back on the pillow staring at the ceiling.

She knew it was only a dream but it was such a detailed rehash of what had really happened. She also knew the accident had taken less than five minutes but every time she relived the horror in her nightmare, it felt like hours. The tangled sheets told her she had been tossing for longer than a couple of minutes.

When the cold air hit her saturated nightie she shivered in response, grabbed the hem, lifted her arms and tore the sodden fabric from her body. Her bones ached from the threshing, and a knife stabbed at every muscle twinge while she fought to extricate her limbs from the tangle. Even as she struggled to get upright it hurt like blazes but she managed to shuffle across the room towards the bathroom.

It was always the same. The same scenes, the same result. She would end up drenched in sweat; the bed would be a mess and she always woke at the same spot – with the darkness and stillness. She knew there was more but her mind had blanked it out. Her next recalled memory was waking up in hospital in agony two days after the accident. The paramedics had told her she had been fully aware of proceedings during the rescue but now she couldn't recall a single detail about the entire twelve hours. All she knew was she had survived but her parents hadn't.

Under a steaming hot shower, Abby attempted to block the memories by concentrating on and visualising the past week, forcing more pleasant images into her brain.

She pictured lying on a towel on the warm white sand of the beach, wading through the shallows, watching seagulls wheeling on warm updrafts and squawking over her bread crusts. Her mind turned to weeding the flowerbeds around the house so struggling blooms had a chance to thrive and attain their full beauty. She forced a smile at being free of the restrictions and clockwork timetable of the hospital. The smile widened as she imagined enjoying the aromatic smells of home-cooked meals instead of the sterile antiseptic of ultra clean wards and vapid taste of pre-prepared food.

After rubbing the moisture from her body with a fluffy towel and dumping her wet nightie in the clothesbasket, Abby stared at the basin drain. One tablet. All she needed was one tiny white sleeping pill. A half would do or even a quarter. Surely it wasn't too much to ask? Why didn't she use her tongue to suck in sodden residue? Even a small amount would be better than none. A smattering of grains might have given her a deep enough sleep to prevent the nightmare.

Hmm, maybe Paul Sanders had some type of sedatives. Hopeful yet doubtful, she opened the cupboard doors under the vanity. Guilt surged as she searched the contents, pulled out the few packets to scour the labels, shoved back the painkillers and cold tablets but pounced on an unopened box of what looked to be over-the-counter sedatives. 'Oh, wow,' she said as she stared at the box in her hand and read every word. They were sedatives she was sure because she'd heard the name before but couldn't picture why the name stood out, but they weren't of the prescription variety, which, she hoped, made them relatively safe. She didn't recognise any of the ingredients and had no idea what strength they were but guessed they wouldn't be anywhere near as strong as her prescription. Unsure what to do, she hesitated. Should she chance it or not? Desperate for no more nightmares, she dropped two into her hand, scooped a handful of water into her mouth to wash them down and swallowed.

Back in the bedroom she eased onto bed without bothering to find another nightdress. No-one else was here so no-one could see or would ever know. She was beyond caring. All she needed was to sleep undisturbed for what was left of the night. After switching off the light she lay back on the pillows with her eyes wide open to stare at the dark ceiling until the pills took effect and dragged her into blissful oblivion.

Three

Despite not having slept for over twenty-four hours, Paul Sanders found sleep elusive despite trying every trick he'd ever read about. For some reason, his brain cells refused to block the scenes of the melee after the bomb blast. Pink mist, they told him the raining down of minute pieces of human flesh, bone and blood, was called. He had been covered in it. Shudders wove down his body at the memory while his hand automatically began rubbing exposed parts of his flesh. Even though he had scrubbed every bump and crevice of his flesh over and over again with soap and antiseptic, he never quite felt clean. Like now, he often had the sensation of his skin crawling. It was really spooky. When he realised he was scratching already raw skin, he forced his hands to still from the unconscious act and shoved one in the pocket of his jeans and the other under his back-side. It was fortunate he hadn't suffered any more than the agony of being thrown across the road from the blast, a burst eardrum and a pounding concussion headache for several days. Twenty others hadn't been so lucky. More frazzled by the incident than he thought he would be, he needed time away from Afghanistan to recover and had negotiated returning home three weeks early for his R & R.

A crackle caught his attention. He glanced up. 'Ladies and gentlemen, please return to your seats, secure your trays and raise your seats into the upright position. We will land in ten minutes.' Paul packed up his unread book, unused pen and pad in his small backpack, folded up the tray and pressed the button to raise his seat. The plane banked. Popping his ears was difficult and more painful than usual with one eardrum not yet completely healed over. He plugged it with a finger to help equalise the pressure. To take his mind off the pain, he peeked out of the window. A shiver of delight wove across his shoulders when he recognised familiar landmarks in the lowering sun. Home. After five months away it felt damn good even though it had been equally as good to leave the place after... don't go there, Sanders.

Paul shuffled from foot-to-foot to get blood flowing while he queued for a taxi after he had collected his suitcases and cleared customs. It was a pain to be carting all of his luggage home for a mere four weeks but he didn't dare leave it behind for there was every chance there would nothing left when he returned.

During the hour-long drive across the crowded city to his coastal town, he leant back in the rear seat with his eyes closed, thinking of the peace and solitude he was going to enjoy to the full. Not contacting his mother or friends of his return had been deliberate to allow him a week of solitude to get his head together. It had been an easy decision since his mobile phone had been damaged in the blast. Lazy swims in the sheltered bay outside his back door were one of his pleasures in life and why he had purchased the cottage outside the confines of the coastal town. He smiled at the picture of his piece of paradise - home.

Hazy pictures flashed past on the journey home. His sleep-deprived brain fought to stay awake at the same time he thrust memories of the bomb blast away every time they surfaced but it seemed they were determined to run on a repeat loop through his grey matter. In a hazy stupor, Paul fumbled around for the hidden front door key, stashed in a metal container behind the garden shed. After flicking the key out, he staggered across the back lawn and along the veranda. It took several attempts to jiggle the key into the elusive keyhole with darkness and a numb brain making the tiny slot an impossible target. Once the door was open, he grappled to find the handles of the suitcases, dragged them into the entry hall and left them there.

A pressing need to rid his bladder of what felt like litres of fluid was the only pause on the pathway to his bed. Since all he needed was oblivion for at least twelve hours, there was no need to turn on any lights. He shed his clothes, dropped them in an untidy pile on the floor beside the bed. Naked, he pulled back the covers, flopped onto his back and was asleep before he even had a chance to drag the covers up over his body.

* * *

At a sudden bounce of the mattress, Abby stirred in her heavy drug-induced sleep. She turned over, rolled towards the lower indentation and snuggled closer to the source of warmth. Lying on her side, she reached out with one hand and draped it over the cushion mound. Fingers began snaking across hard dips and bumps and twirled around coarse chest hairs. A familiar fantasy flashed through her brain.

One day, a wonderful man would sweep her off her feet. They would get married and have the family she yearned for. At the visions of the tall, good-looking man, she smiled while her hand roamed further, undertaking the movements of her fantasies. Snuggling in even closer, Abby lifted her head and brushed her lips along the shoulder of her dreams. Her nostrils sniffed in the all-male odour; her hand swept across taut muscles of his abdomen and crept lower.

* * *

A woman entered Paul's dream. He couldn't see her features but he sure could feel the sensation of her creating havoc with his hormones. Long, soft fingers swept across his flesh, creating tingles of pure pleasure. The warmth of her soft lips dropped butterfly kisses across his shoulder, up his neck, down his cheek before those luscious lips settled on his mouth. He kissed her back with an equal amount of fervour. When he opened his mouth and drew in her tongue, it danced with his, playing the age-old mating game.

The hand moved lower, stroked, investigating every nuance of his groin. Gentle fingers manipulated for a while before wrapping around the growing hardness and length. Paul groaned with pleasure as he dreamt about the woman mounting his body, her mouth grinding against his in the most sensuous kiss he had ever enjoyed. His hands gripped around her waist before seeking out her breasts as she leant over him with her legs straddled over his lean hips.

There was a sudden draft of cooling air as the body lifted away. Paul groaned at the loss, sought and found the velvety warmth, and hauled her back over him. The rhythmic ride was pure, exquisite pleasure as her feminine heat wrapped around him, the silky moisture gliding sensuously up and down, up and down, dragging him along in exquisite bliss.

He woke to realise he wasn't dreaming.

Stunned, his eyes flew open as his hands stalled before gripping the woman around her waist. He could see little except her dark outline but heard her panting hard in time with him and he knew not only he, but she was also on the verge of climax. Something in the deep recesses of his foggy mind told him this was all wrong. He had to stop. But experience told him he was too close to the edge and it had been too long since he had enjoyed a woman. There was no way he was going to be able to end this sweet torture except with physical release. Two seconds later a female scream of sheer ecstasy echoed around the room and he followed suit as climax dragged him into a star-spangled euphoric bliss.

Her hot, slick body flopped across his chest. In an automatic action he dropped her sideways with his arms snaked around her waist and drew her in a tight embrace against his side. Lips met in another hot kiss.

The warm soft body stilled.

It stiffened.

He knew the instant the woman became aware. He felt her drag her mouth away and raise her head. Even in the darkness, he could make out a pair of dark eyes staring back at him.

'What the... who are you? What are you doing in my bed?' the woman screeched as she drew back even further.

'Your bed. Since when has it been your bed?' Even to himself his voice sounded like a sexy deep drawl. He winced at the thought of how he must sound as he leant up on one elbow but kept one arm across the sweat-slick body next to him.

It seemed even the air held its breath in the lengthy silence.

The woman appeared to be fighting for comprehension as though she wasn't yet fully awake. Worry niggled at his brain. Why hadn't she leapt from the bed? Why wasn't she spitting at him in anger? Why was she even in his bed? Who was she? He leaned closer to get a better look at her features.

She recoiled as her eyes popped open even wider. 'What the devil? You raped me.' She winced as she jerked away and scrambled awkwardly to the other side of the bed. There was something un-gainly about the way she got her legs to the floor and tried to stand. A grunt broke the silence when her feet thumped on the ground.

'You raped me,' she shouted again, her words echoing around the room.

Paul shot up, the accusation stirring anger. 'I have never raped any woman in my life. The boot is on the other foot. You were the one who seduced me.' He smiled at the delicious memory. 'Mind you, I'm not complaining. It has been a long time since I have been with a woman and the experience was... umm... exquisite.'

'What are you talking about? I have never... I don't even know... I took a drug... I was asleep... Who the hell are you?'

Wild gesticulating arms waved around in all directions; the dark amorphous shapes outlined against the moonlit sky showing through the window. Swinging his legs over the side of the bed Paul stood, towering over the petite woman in front of him. He could make out the hands on her hips and her angry stance. 'I own this house and I don't appreciate some drug addict using it in my absence.'

'Drug addict. I'm no drug addict.' The woman stepped forward and prodded him in his chest with one finger but his hard, well-toned muscles must have hurt her finger. She gasped in pain as she stepped back again flicking her hand in quick succession to ease the pain.

'You admitted you took drugs. Sounds like a drug addict to me.' He twisted around, leant over the bedside table, searched around in the darkness until he found what he was looking for and switched on the bedside light.

The woman blinked several times at the sudden brightness. He heard her suck in long breath at the sight of him. Still bent at the waist, he smiled as she stared at him, especially when her eyes gradually lowered. His skin prickled where her eyes examined every detail of his body and knew by the instant reddening of her entire neck and face exactly when she realised he was buff naked. Normally he didn't feel embarrassed about his nudity but this time he felt as though he should cover up. With regular exercise he knew he had not an ounce of spare flesh covering his muscular frame so wasn't ashamed of how he would look but the woman appeared to be shocked.

As he rose to his full height, her mouth gaped wide. He wasn't sure if it was because he was so tall or if she felt suddenly threatened by his size, but the look of her face seemed to be more of sheer amazement than fear. She yanked her eyes up again. 'You... you are naked. Don't you think you should put your clothes on? I'm not used to seeing...' Her mouth clamped shut. He would give anything to know the end of her sentence but by the look of her face he guessed she was about to reveal being with a naked man was not a regular occurrence. The thought pleased him.

Paul grinned at her half admission while thoroughly enjoying his own perusal. She was downright gorgeous. A little too thin but with gorgeous feminine curves in all the right places and her breasts were perfect. Not too large, pert with nipples soft and rosy. He remembered his hands cupping them. His grin widened. He figured she would about reach his shoulder and wondered what the cloud of gold hair would feel like brushing against his bare skin. Now, he was sorry he had been too befuddled by exhaustion to recall the sensation.

It suddenly dawned on him she wasn't aware of her own nudity. He grinned. 'I'll get dressed if you do. But please don't hurry. You are one beautiful woman and I don't mind you standing there for me to take in every detail of your sexy body.'

A yelp as she glanced down at her nakedness. Instant redness flew up her neck before the woman stumbled around to the foot of the bed where she grabbed a pink towelling robe he had never seen before and flung it backwards across the front of her body.

He chuckled while she wriggled her arms in the sleeves while attempting to maintain her dignity and keep her body covered. Little did she know he could see her bare butt and the smooth curve of her ivory back in the mirror behind her and he wasn't about to inform her of the fact: he was enjoying himself way too much.

Somehow, she managed to get the robe on the right way around. Once she had secured the belt in a very tight knot around her stomach, Paul took his time to walk to his pile of clothes where he reached down to the ground and pulled on the pair of jeans he had dropped earlier. He didn't bother turning his back. Only a few minutes ago this woman had made love to him, explored all the erogenous zones of his body if his dream had been real so there was little point. Much as he was took pleasure in the moment, he didn't feel so great. His conscience pricked, telling him he needed to get to the bottom of why a naked woman was sleeping in his bed. He pointed to the door.

'Kitchen. We need to discuss a few things.'

'No way, I'm not going anywhere near you. You can leave and let me get back to bed.' She edged backwards.

'Not likely, I want to know what the devil you are doing in my house.'

'Sleeping. Or I was before you... you... raped me. I should call the police.'

The expression on her face told him her brain had begun to function more clearly. He wasn't overly concerned when she stalked across the room with her chin held high but her attempt to look as though she were in charge, was negated by the swagger and sway of her ungainly walk. He recalled what she'd said about drugs and figured she was so doped up she couldn't even walk straight. Anger surged. What was a drug addict doing in his house? Dear God, he had an intruder living in his house.

He began to chase after her but paused when he heard a loud groan. She swayed, paused and staggered another two steps before stopping to reach out for the telephone on the bedside table. As she lifted the receiver to her ear she jerked when she spied him stalking towards her, causing her to stifle her threatening yawn and turn it into more like a yelp.

'Go ahead. Sergeant Shaun Walker is a good friend of mine. He knows me well and knows I would never rape a woman. But you, how well does he know you? How are you going to explain your presence in a house which doesn't belong to you? In fact, give me the phone.' Reaching over he jerked the receiver from her hand. 'I'll phone him myself and detail how you raped me, how you admitted to taking drugs and he can give you a blood test to confirm it.'

A wave of shudders wove down her body. At first he thought it was fear but her face took on the look of sheer anger.

He watched her eyes screw as she stretched up to her full height, which compared to him wasn't very high. He knew she was furious but her fury made her look even more gorgeous. A range of emotions flitted across her features before her mouth opened and closed three times as though she wanted to say something but couldn't find the words.

'I don't believe for one minute this house is yours,' she finally blurted. 'The owner is overseas and is not due back yet.'

'I know he isn't due back. He is back. I came home early.' It was difficult but he managed to drag a skerrick of logic from his dulled brain and came to a few conclusions. 'So, you knew when I was due back but in the meantime you were squatting in my house. I suppose you were going to pack up the day before I came home and return when I left again. I am pretty certain breaking and entering, along with squatting, are criminal offences. Rape results in a jail term. I think you had better leave before I call Shaun. You have five minutes to be gone. Five minutes before I dial Shaun's number.'

'But I didn't...'

'Four minutes and fifty-five seconds.'

'I've got no…'

'Fifty seconds.'

'You can't throw me out.' With her feet glued to the ground, the woman stared at him.

He fought to keep his features still to show he meant business and wasn't going to relent. Her hands moved to her hips in a show of her own defiance, probably to test his intent. For a split second he wavered but this was his house, damn it. He straightened and determined his stance.

'Four minutes thirty.' He took one step towards her, a scowl on his face meant to frighten her. What is she going to do? Will she leave? Did he want her to leave? All he desired was peace and quiet. No way was he going to show weakness in front of her. She was a stranger who had taken up unsolicited residence in his home, his sanctuary. He needed the solitude to rid himself of the awfulness of the past couple of weeks. She was an unwanted interloper and had no rights and she had virtually raped him even though he enjoyed the experience. All of a sudden he felt an uncanny desire to find out how far he could push her.

'Four minutes.' There was a lengthy pause during which the woman stood her ground. 'For heaven's sake, woman, whoever you are, this is my home. You are the intruder and have no rights to be here. I need peace and quiet. Either you leave now or I call the police.' To show he meant what he said, he dialled random numbers. He had no idea what the station number was but figured his actions might show he was serious.

He saw the instant defeat registered. Her shoulders slumped and her mouth dropped its determined rigid line. Glancing at her eyes he noticed she was fighting back tears and a deep sense of discomfort settled in his gut. There was something about her which made him want to relent but before he could say anything the woman glanced at the window. He followed her train of sight and noticed salmon streaks lightening the sky, which meant he'd had more sleep than he realised. Her movement brought his attention back to the woman. With despair swamping her features she turned and headed towards the door. She stumbled and swayed from side-to-side before steadying herself. Even though she attempted to walk normally, her gait was awkward, confirming his suspicions about her being in a drugged stupor. This twig of knowledge made him even more determined to rid himself of the woman and not go after her.

As Paul watched her leave, his conscience pricked again. In fact it felt more like stabbing jabs. He thought about calling her back but decided to wait to see how far she would go. He saw her shoulders heave and heard her suck in a breath. It concerned him how her gait seemed so awkward but decided it was her problem if she wanted to destroy her life with drugs: a problem he didn't need right now. What concerned him even more was the way she was leaving without bothering to put on any clothes. Was she so out of it she didn't realise?

He stood in the doorway to his room while staring down the hall after her retreating body. It took her a concentrated effort to find the door handle and unlock the complicated security deadlock. A loud yawn escaped her mouth as she pulled the door open but she shivered at the blast of crisp morning air as she stepped over the threshold. In the height of summer, the night was warm but at this early hour it was cooler outside than in. She pulled the floor-length robe tighter around her body, turned and glanced back into the house. Paul stood in the open doorway of his bedroom with his arms folded over his naked chest and a fierce face. She shuddered, turned back and slammed the door shut behind her.

The very moment the door closed with a resounding bang, Paul flew along the passage and into the front room. At first he couldn't see the woman until she moved away from the front door, stumbled a few steps and lost her balance. She sank to the wooden slats of the veranda like a slowly folding concertina. His heart went to his mouth as he watched her push her body upright. Guilt surged inside his gut. This was so against his grain to treat a woman, any woman so callously. It took a while for her to negotiate her way across the veranda. She stopped at the top of the steps. After a lengthy pause she grabbed a hold of the post. One foot wavered in the air before she swapped to the other as though she were trying to figure out which one should make the step down.

His conscience finally got the better of him, Paul decided to end this charade and moved away from the window to bring her back inside. Not looking where he was going, he tripped over the suitcases he had left in the hallway and swore profusely as he slumped to the floor, hitting his head against the door with an almighty thud as he fell.

* * *

Hearing a heavy thud, absolute terror surged through Abby. The man must be coming to attack her. She panicked, screamed and stepped off the veranda with her left leg. When her foot landed on the first step, her weak muscles gave way and she tumbled down both steps, landing in a crumpled heap on the crazy paving. A resounding crack cut the still morning air as her head hit a concrete paving stone. With her head spinning and no strength left to pull her body upright, she gave up the fight. Her eyelids closed and oblivion took over.

Four

An ear-splitting scream tore through the air. Paul scrambled upright and staggered towards the front door. He jerked it open and swore when the bottom of the door caught his little toe and bent it in the opposite direction from where it should be. A round of expletives echoed through the stillness of the morning as he hopped around on one foot while rubbing the injury.

Another scream: he remembered the woman, took one step onto the veranda, expecting to see her on the top step but she had completely disappeared from sight. Shirtless and shoeless, he shot across the veranda while attempting to draw up the zipper on his pants which began slipping from his hips. He was moving so fast as he leapt over the two steps, he almost trod on the woman curled up in the foetal position on the footpath.

To prevent imminent crushing, he grabbed a hold of the veranda post and swung his body around but came to a grinding and painful halt when he crashed into the railing along the edge of the veranda. His grazed fingers slipped from their grip and he slithered into the rockery along the front of the garden bed.

More four-letter words spewed from his mouth as he extricated his battered body from crushed plants and damned hard and very sharp-edged stones. Blood dripped from a raft of cuts and grazes when he made a cursory sweep of stinging bare flesh. A stifled snort of laughter slipped from his lips at the irony of the situation. He had escaped physical injury from a bomb in Afghanistan which had blown twenty people to smithereens only to come home to what was supposed to be a safe environment and wreck his body on a door and a flaming garden bed.

A soft moan brought his full attention back to the woman. His eyes lifted from his smarting bare flesh to settle on the comatose woman. His breath hitched in his throat. In the early light of day she was even more beautiful than she had appeared in the dull light of the bedside lamp. Sun's rays poking through the heavy cloud of an imminent summer storm turned short hair feathering around her face into spun gold. She looked like what he imagined an angel would.

He leant over for a closer scrutiny. A smatter of pale freckles dusted her cheeks and nose. Dark bronze lashes lying against her ivory skin curled up at the ends. Her face was so pale and her lips... damn, they had a tinge of blue. Was she dead?

As though to answer his thoughts, he heard her moan. Sweeping his eyes lower, he noticed her robe and recalled her searching for it, and him acting like a voyeur as he watched mesmerised while she wrapped it around her naked body and jerked the sash really tight. Another thought hit, her ungainly walk to the door. She could barely walk. He paused while he dragged the recesses of his mind for fuzzy recollections of a few minutes ago. She said she had taken drugs. With his brain feeling so confused, he wasn't sure what was fact or fiction. What had really happened and what had been a dream? He was certain she had made sweet love to him, especially since he was still wearing the sticky residue. He recalled becoming angry and demanding she leave, but for the life of him couldn't figure out why. Anger wasn't a normal state with him.

He was still staring at the woman when she moaned again and started threshing around. A high-pitched scream startled him at the same time he noticed fresh blood oozing from a graze on the side of her head when it turned towards him. He bent over, felt her limbs for injury and held the pads of two fingers against the pulse beating under her jaw. Her pulse was strong but her skin was frozen. What scared him the most were the unhealthy pallor and the definite, blue-tinged lips.

'What have I done?' The words were a hoarse whisper as he knelt beside her and gently wriggled his arms under her legs and shoulders. His powerful muscles lifted her thin body with ease. She felt so light but so cold against his bare chest. Spinning around on one foot, he strode up the two steps and continued on until he reached his bed. With her body held against his chest, he reached down with one hand and flung the covers back but reeled back in shock when he spied traces of blood on the sheet.

'You are injured.' His quiet words went unheard but his thoughts continued. What was he supposed to do now? Damn, what a mess. Warm – she needs to get warm first. Coming to his first logical conclusion of the night, Paul settled the stranger in the bed with her head on a pillow. Gently he pulled the covers up over her shoulders and tucked the edges around her body to ensure no cold air could sneak in. To warm her quicker, he pulled a spare wool blanket from the top shelf of his wardrobe and spread it over the top of the woman. Undecided as to what to do next he dragged a chair alongside the bed. Dropping into the chair, he sat and watched her while he thought about what he was supposed to do now.

A drop of blood dripped from a cut on his chest and landed on the denim stretched taut over his bent knee. After watching it spread through the fibres and weighing up the conclusions he was coming to he decided he needed a shower and get cleaned up first. Next, he needed to treat the woman's head injury, preferably while she still slept.

He opened the vast doors to the bank of wardrobes built in along one entire wall. His eyes widened at the sight of a small pile of feminine and very lacy underwear. Next to it were half a dozen neatly folded T-shirts – each a different vibrant colour. Two pairs of what looked to be almost new jeans sat on top of the shirts. The sight of two very sexy nightgowns had him pull his head out from the cupboard and stare at the still sleeping woman. If she possessed slinky nightwear, why was she naked last night? And still naked underneath the tightly belted towelling robe. The thought of her body made him remember the blood on the sheets. Somewhere on her body was another injury. He didn't dare look. Murphy's Law would have her waking up at the very second he undid the belt. She had been fit to kill earlier. Another gaffe and he figured he wouldn't survive her onslaught, despite the difference in their size.

He turned back to the shelf containing her clothes, counted six pairs of socks, two folded jumpers and a spied box of feminine hygienic products. Heat rose up his neck. Never before had such intimate feminine apparel graced his wardrobe. It was something he was well aware of but not something he had ever had to face head on. As he continued his study of the wardrobe, he discovered the clothes of his which he normally placed on the small shelf had been very carefully stacked on top of the clothes above. Compared to the quantity of clothes he possessed, including those still packed in the bags he had dumped inside the front door, she owned very few. He felt even more intrigued about the mystery of his unknown house-guest and now looked forward to her explanations.

After finding a clean set of clothes, Paul retreated to the bath-room where he wallowed under hot water. It felt so damn good to wash away Afghan dust, seeping blood and scrub his mouth with a large dollop of peppermint toothpaste he found on the vanity bench. Despite a quick search there was no new brush in the cupboard and with his still packed, he used a finger to scrub the insides of his mouth. While towelling dry he noticed a discarded nightdress tossed on top of the small pile of dirty clothes in the bamboo laundry basket. Lifting it out, he fingered the filmy fabric, noticing the dampness. He held it up to his face. Why was it wet? He was still rubbing water from his hair when the phone rang.

At first he ignored the ringing since nobody knew he was home. Everyone of importance in his life had his mobile number and thought he was still in Afghanistan. He snorted. His mobile phone had met a crushing death in the bomb blast, ending up in so many pieces the only thing he could retrieve was the sim card. After the sixth ring, he realised the call might be for his mystery guest so he shot down the passage and lifted the receiver to his ear.

'Sanders here.'

'Paul?'

'Mum?'

'What are you doing home?'

'Why are you ringing me at home?'

'I wasn't phoning you, where's Abby?'

'Who the hell is Abby?' The moment he asked the question he knew the answer and swore profusely under his breath.

'Paul!'

'Sorry, Mum. Who is Abby?'

'Abby is staying at your place. I rang you, left you messages to explain. You didn't ring me back.' There was a long pause. 'What are you doing home?'

'Long story, Mum. My phone was damaged in an incident and they sent me home to recuperate.' He bit down on his bottom lip. Damn it, he shouldn't have said anything. Now his mother will worry and want to know every last detail.

'What sort of incident? Are you hurt? Where's Abby?'

'I'm not injured. I'll give you all the details when I see you and I assume you are referring to the naked woman who was...' He paused. How was he supposed to explain this? 'Who was sleeping in my bed,' he added slowly. Dear, God, so awkward.

'She was naked?' There was another lengthy pause. 'How do you know she was naked?' The tone had altered to one he didn't appreciate.

'Hell, Mum, when you fall into your own bed in the early hours of the morning without turning lights on, you don't expect it to be occupied by some stranger. She was naked.' And still is, he added in his thoughts. 'Do you mind telling me why she is here?'

'She has been ill and is now recuperating. What happened?'

Now there's a leading question, Paul thought with a slight smile but before he could answer, his mother continued.

'I am coming over and Abby had better be sitting on your lounge when I get there.'

The loud slam of the receiver rattled around Paul's jangled head. Ill? He let loose with a string of obscene epithets as he replaced the receiver and headed towards his own bedroom. He was about to open the door when he realised he was still naked so he slung the towel he had tossed over his shoulder, around his waist and tucked the end in over one hip.

'You,' hissed at him from the direction of the bed as he opened the door.

Lifting his head, he stared at a pair of very irate but sexy hazel eyes. 'Abby, I presume.'

'What are you doing here?'

The tone was definitely frosty. How was he going to handle this? 'I live here. This is my house, or at least it was before I went away and I sure as hell have no recollection of signing any sale papers since I left – nor before.' Bemused, he watched as Abby dragged her body upright. Her lips, he noted with grateful thanks, had lost their bluish tinge but thinned into a tense line and her arms folded in definite defiance across her chest. Yes, she was still angry and not in the least amused by his attempt at humour.

There was an ominous silence during which Paul observed a range of emotions flit across Abby's face. Since she appeared confused he decided to explain as much as he could. 'I found you asleep at the bottom of the steps outside. You were frozen so I carried you inside and put you into my bed so you could get warm.'

'You touched me?'

Ouch. The venom in those three words. 'It was for your own welfare. Why didn't you explain things earlier?'

A furious blush rose up her face. 'You hardly gave me the opportunity.' A long pause ensued. 'You raped me.'

'Actually, I beg to differ. If I remember rightly, it was the other way around.'

'Excuse me?' Her chin rose and eyes widened.

'I am positive I already explained everything. I was so dog-tired my memory is a bit hazy but I am certain we discussed this already. You grazed your head on the path outside but you might want to check your body for other injuries.'

As she lifted her hand to the cut on her head her expression altered in an instant from anger to fear. She lifted the quilt. Paul found it hard to suppress a grin while he watched the quilt take on a life of its own as she wriggled to inspect her body. When her head emerged again, her hair looked like a scarcely put together bird's nest but she looked gorgeous.

'I'm not injured. Why did you think I was?'

Paul hesitated. Maybe it was the certain time of the month. If so, how was he supposed to broach such a delicate subject? Nothing like being direct. 'There's blood on the sheets.'

Her face paled in an instant as she dropped back onto the pillows and turned away from him, tugging the quilt around her ears. 'That's what happens on your first time.'

Despite her words being no more than a harsh whisper, and he felt sure they weren't meant for him, Paul heard every single one as though they were shouted. Stunned, he stepped closer. 'Please don't tell me you were a virgin.' His voice sounded more like a plea, even to him.

'Fine, I won't tell you.'

From where he stood at the side of the bed, Paul observed every action, every nuance of her body language. A tear trickled from the corner of her eye. She swiped at it then screwed her eyes shut as though daring anymore to leak out. He felt so bad even though it wasn't him who had started things.

'Abby, I am so sorry. If I could change things I would. I should have stopped you but I was so damn tired and didn't know what was going on until it was too late. When I woke... umm, I was too close to the edge - had no control. I'm sorry.' Reaching down he placed one hand on her shoulder but she jerked it off as though he was the grim reaper.

'Don't touch me. Don't ever touch me again.'

With his apology thrown back in his face, Paul pulled away with hands up in submission. 'Fine. I will leave you to shower and dress. Mum's on her way over.'

'Good. I'll leave with her.'

It was ridiculous to realise it wasn't what Paul wanted to hear. He didn't want her to leave. 'You don't have to, Abby, but we need to discuss things so I can understand what the hell's going on around here.' Not waiting for an answer, he left the room, drawing the door shut behind him. When he realised he still needed clothes, he dragged his suitcases into the office, unzipped both and found the cleanest clothes he could find. All needed a thorough wash since the past couple of weeks had been so frantic, getting laundry done had been down on the bottom of the list. Getting out of the country before all hell broke loose had been his only priority.

Five

The moment he spotted the maroon sedan sweep into his driveway, Paul sprang from the cane chair he had perched on and strode across the front of the house. He was waiting by the driver's door and had it open before his mother even had a chance to turn off the engine. 'Mum, how are you?' Bending at the waist, he brushed his lips against her cheek, straightened and held out a hand to assist her from the car.

'Paul, you look well.' Grace alighted and stretched her limbs. She paused a moment while her curious eyes searched Paul's face. 'What is the problem and where is Abby?'

'Abby is inside. She had a shower but seems to be hiding away.' After attempts to lure her from his bedroom had met with a stony silence he hadn't been game to force the closed door but instead retreated to the front veranda hoping to chat to his mother before she had a chance to speak with Abby. He grasped his mother's elbow and began walking towards the beach, forcing her to go with him. 'Can we talk a moment before we go inside? I need to know a few details about what the devil is going on around here.'

'Abby, is she all right?'

There was a lengthy pause before Paul figured out how to answer. 'Apart from a small graze on her head, she is uninjured but I need to sort out a few things.'

Grace had no choice but to follow since he refused to ease the tight hold he had on her elbow. 'Uninjured and a graze, and with you home early after an incident doesn't sound as though things are hunky dory around here. Can you enlighten me as to exactly what it does mean?' Grace jerked her arm free, rushed forwards and spun around, glaring at him so he couldn't advance any further. 'Spill it out, Paul.'

'I will. But first I need to know why this stranger is living in my house and why the heck I knew nothing about it. I wanted to ask her but she locked herself in my room and won't speak to me.' He also wanted to discuss fully the taking of her virginity but so far hadn't had the chance and it concerned him a great deal. 'You mentioned Abby was ill. How ill?'

Grace sighed. 'You remember the ghastly train derailment a couple of weeks before you left?'

'Mechanical failure. Thirty odd lives lost. What about it?'

'Abby is one of the survivors. The only one in her carriage.'

Paul drew in a deep hissing breath as a shudder swept across his shoulders. Newspaper photos and reports of the carnage flittered through his mind. It had been a shocking accident.

'They took twelve hours to cut Abby from the wreckage. Her pelvis was badly fractured, as were both legs. Her left leg was so severely damaged, the specialist hinted more than once, the possibility she would lose it completely. Along with lacerated muscles and ligaments there were compound fractures. They pieced her together using plates and enough screws to set off every single metal detector in the biggest of airports. She has been in hospital ever since, the last three months in rehabilitation. They released her only a week ago. To start with, they didn't think she would ever be able to walk again but she is a determined young lady and has fought hard to prove them wrong. She is so determined to regain her independence.'

Determined wasn't quite the word Paul would use to describe Abby. Testy? Definitely. Cute, sexy and gorgeous came to his mind, as did downright stubborn. 'So, how did you meet her?'

'My voluntary work at the hospital. I met her about two weeks after the accident and since she had no-one else who visited I took her under my wing and have spent umpteen hours with her since. I have virtually been her personal aide.'

'What about family and friends? Surely they would have helped.'

'Her parents died in the crash.'

A loud groan rumbled from Paul's mouth as he leant his out-stretched arms against the back fence and bent over with his eyes shut. He felt Abby's anguish along with lashings of self-disgust for the unwarranted treatment he had meted out. 'What about friends? What were they doing on the train?'

'Abby was taking her parents on a long weekend holiday. The train ride was a special treat for their anniversary. They died on the day of their thirtieth wedding anniversary. As to friends. A few came in the beginning but they soon petered out. A so-called male friend Abby had been dating walked out when told Abby might never walk again. He hasn't been back, hasn't called and when I rang him without Abby's knowledge, he was quite rude. Didn't want to be saddled with some cripple for the rest of his life. I think they were his words before he hung up on me.' Grace sounded bitter and Paul couldn't blame her.

'She must be better off without such a jerk. He obviously had no real feelings for her.' Paul released his tense grip from the top of the fence and turned to face his mother again. 'Abby seems to be doing fine from what I have seen. A bit unsteady on her feet but getting around okay.'

A movement caught his eye. He glanced up at the kitchen window, instinct telling him Abby was watching them.

'Abby has pushed her body until she was exhausted and in agony. Her determination has been unceasing to the extent she has stunned the doctors. When I brought her here a week ago, she barely made it from the front gate to the bottom of the steps without her crutches.'

Paul's glance at his mother was sharp and troubled. 'She uses crutches? I haven't seen them.' Inside, Paul was feeling about a centimetre tall. If Oscars were awarded for self-recrimination, he would have a bag full of the little statuettes. 'This doesn't explain why she is living in my house and why you never told me.'

'I left you several messages to call me back but you still haven't rung.'

'Sorry. Things were a bit - awkward.' He wondered how he could explain without going into detail about the bombing. 'Sorry, my mobile phone met an untimely death a few weeks ago.' Replacing it had been so low on his priority list it didn't register until the flight home. 'And you know I don't always get messages.' At the worried glance from his mother he thought about telling her but decided there were enough problems on his plate right now. 'I will explain later. Tell me more.'

'Abby has nowhere else to go. It was the only place I could think of to give her somewhere to stay. Otherwise the doctors wouldn't release her from hospital. She needs time to rebuild her muscle strength and from the daily reports she has been giving me, this place is doing wonders for her.'

'But why here? Surely she has her own place.' Paul dragged the cane lounge around into the shade and indicated for his mother to sit. Even this early in the morning the summer sun had quite a bite, the earlier clouds having passed over. His eyes lifted to glance at the kitchen again as he wondered how Abby had dragged the lounge this far since he had packed it away in the shed. Noting the dark outline still watching them, he dropped to the ground with his legs stretched out in front while he leant back on straight arms. Damp dew penetrated the seat of his jeans but he didn't move. It was far more important to hear Abby's story.

'Abby lost everything. It is quite an involved story but she was a Physical Education teacher in a private school. She had no choice but to resign after she had used up what sick leave she had. Unfortunately, she will never be able to return to the same job. Her legs will never be strong enough or have the freedom of movement to play sport. No job means no money. No money means she couldn't pay the rent on the house she shared with her parents. They lost their life savings in a shonky investment scheme and had to sell their house to pay off debts and survive. In a sense, Abby was supporting them. She sold almost all of her belongings to pay for their funerals. I organised the garage sale for her since she was too ill to leave the hospital. There are half a dozen boxes of her personal gear stored in my spare room. Until she can retrain for a new career Abby can't earn.'

'So what is she living on?'

'A temporary disability pension. We had to fight to get it and the government are making it difficult for her to keep it. The authorities are also fighting the findings of neglect of the train maintenance so they don't have to pay out. There were over a hundred passengers on the train, which means a huge compensation claim. Unfortunately, it could take years for Abby's claim to get to court.'

There was a long silence while Paul considered how he could broach the subject of the previous night's encounter. One thing he felt sure of, if he didn't tell his mother, Abby would. 'There's something I need to explain to you, Mum.' He stared at her while trying to find the right words. Nervous to the nth degree, he stood and began pacing, his eyes glancing towards the kitchen window every few seconds.

'Stop pacing. I get the feeling I'm not going to like this. You better spill the beans.'

'This is so hard.' He paced back towards Grace and perched on the end of the lounge. 'Last night - I didn't get here until the early hours. I've not had much sleep over the past week, none on the plane and was dog-tired when I arrived home. All I had the energy to do was to strip off my clothes and fall into my bed.

'Oh, I get the picture. Abby was sleeping in your bed. Oh, heavens, please don't tell me? You didn't.'

A loud groan spilled from Paul's lips. 'I didn't, but Abby did.'

'Pardon? Abby did what?'

'What the hell do you think? I dropped into bed... um... naked, didn't see her in the dark, was asleep before my head hit the pillow and woke up with her on top... doing... hell... what a mess.' He swept his hand across his face in frustration. 'I was too far gone when I woke up and... how is a man supposed to tell his mother things like this? To get to the crunch, we both climaxed at the same time.'

'Paul!'

At the shouted word, Paul glanced at the window and noticed Abby jerk before going still. There was no doubt in his mind she knew what the discussion was about. He flew upright and began pacing again. At this rate he would soon have a trench in the lawn. 'She said she was on drugs.'

'Medication, yes. She has strong painkillers to ease the constant pain and sedatives at night to prevent the nightmares.'

'Nightmares?' Paul spun around to stare at his mother. He stilled, stuffed his hands in the pockets of his jeans. The more he heard, the worse he felt.

'She has vivid recollections of the accident in her sleep. The sedatives were the only way the doctors could prevent them. They tried all sorts of things. During the nightmares she thrashed around so much she compromised her injuries. The trouble is she can't yet recall all the details of the accident. Her mind has blocked off the twelve hours she was awake while waiting for them to cut her out. I know what happened, the paramedics told me but her specialist doesn't want us to tell Abby. The medical gurus insist she needs to remember by herself. They are sure she will remember when the time is right.'

'It was so bad?'

'It was ghastly.'

'Which explains something I couldn't figure out. I feel sure Abby was so full of drugs she wasn't aware of what she was doing. Hell, I thought I was dreaming at the time. She probably did too because all of a sudden she became alert. I must have woken only seconds before she did. Trouble is, she blames me for what happened. The word rapist has been flung around so often I think it is still reverberating off the walls inside.' Squatting down in front of his mother he grasped both her hands in his. 'I swear I didn't rape her. I promise I didn't start things rolling. I don't treat women with such disrespect, even when I've had a few too many.'

'I know, dear.' Grace patted her son's hand.

'There's more.'

'More? What more can there be?'

'Afterwards... damn it... she had been a virgin. The evidence makes me believe her.'

'Oh, dear, the sheet, traces of blood?'

'Yes. Even though it wasn't my fault, I feel like an absolute heel and have no idea how to handle this.'

'It is awkward. Let's go inside and talk with Abby over breakfast.' Grace stood and waited while Paul unfolded from his squatting position.

Awkward wasn't the word Paul would use. He could think of a whole heap more – none of them with even a hint of pleasantness.

Six

'What do you think you are doing?' As he stepped through the back doorway, Paul caught a glimpse of Abby dragging a small suitcase into the entry hall. He sped after her and managed to settle his large outspread hand against the front door, barring her way.

'Leaving.' Since her head was hanging low, Abby's single meek word was so quiet he had trouble making it out but he heard.

'And exactly how were you planning to reach where-ever it was you were going?' He found it difficult to hold back his amusement as he spied her quick glance towards Grace, sending a silent plea.

'You have somewhere in mind Mum can drive you to? I understand, now someone has taken the time to explain things to me, you don't have a home.' He dared to reach out and cup her chin with the crook of a curled finger, forcing her head up but Abby refused to focus her eyes on him, instead slamming her eyelids shut.

The amusement escaped into a smile he had no hope of preventing. Abby looked chastened but cute. 'I didn't think so. You can stay here.'

This virtual order sparked Abby up. Her eyes flew open as she jerked her head from his touch. 'Not likely.'

'Why not?' Both Paul and Grace asked at the same time as Grace neared the pair.

She grasped Abby's hands. 'You have nowhere else to live and are doing so well here.'

'I can't, not after … I don't even know you.' An embarrassed pink blush rose up Abby's face as she glared at Paul but immediately dropped her chin to her chest again.

Paul grinned. 'On the contrary, if even half of what I thought I was dreaming last night really happened, I think you know me very well. Intimately, in fact.' He softened his voice as he bent his knees and stuck his face underneath Abby's hung head until they were eye-to-eye. 'Very intimately.'

Abby's hand shot out, punching Paul in the chest as her furious eyes sparked open. 'I didn't know what I was doing – nor did you. Now …'

A grunt of pain gushed from Paul's lips as he stepped back, his hand moving to his chest. 'Damn, that hurt.'

'Oh, my gosh.' Abby stared at the crimson mark spreading across Paul's shirt. 'You… you are bleeding. I didn't injure you. I couldn't have.'

There was a long pause while all eyes turned to the rapidly increasing streak of red. Grace stepped forward, grabbed the edge of Paul's shirt and yanked it up. 'You said there was an incident in Afghanistan but you told me you weren't injured.' She gasped when she saw the extent of the gouges and scrapes across Paul's chest and abdomen. 'Those marks don't look like uninjured to me.'

Paul brushed away her hands and yanked his shirt back down. 'I wasn't injured in Afghanistan. I… um… had an accident this morning.' Sheesh, how was he supposed to explain this one? Not game to admit to his mother how he had lost his temper and ordered Abby from the house, he struggled to find the words to change the focus. 'Leave me be. I will be fine.' He spun around and headed towards the bathroom but paused and swivelled the top of his torso around, pointing towards Abby. 'Make sure she stays here.'

While Abby bristled at another order, Grace raced after him. 'You are not fine. Those scrapes need attention.' To annoy him even more, she grabbed his elbow and stepped in front of him. 'Paul Sanders get in the kitchen right now and sit down. Those cuts need to be covered.'

'Heavens, Mum, I'm a grown man. I can look after myself.' Even though he sounded determined, he altered direction and headed for the kitchen, not having any choice with his mother shoving at his back. Embarrassment 101, flicked through his brain but to fight would be useless and only increase the already fire-cracker tension of the morning.

* * *

Uncertain as to what to do, Abby tagged along behind, concerned about the amount of blood. Somewhere in the dark recesses of her mind, a sinister sensation began tugging away. She couldn't see any visions or feel anything but something insidious swirled, trying to get out. At the same time she wanted whatever it was to surface, she tried to shove it back - instinct telling her it was really unpleasant. She came to a standstill in front of the seated Paul and watched in silence as his mother stripped off his shirt and gave his wounds a close inspection. While Grace searched a top shelf of the pantry for Paul's first-aid kit, Abby stared. A trail of crimson dribbled down Paul's chest from the worst cut. Mesmerised by the trail of red, she traced the bottom of a smooth, shiny globular ball as it flowed downwards, through the dark, coarse hairs, over the slight bumps of his muscles, down to the hollow of his waist.

'Abby, are you all right?'

She heard Paul but didn't acknowledge because her mind was in turmoil. It was as though she was stuck in the middle of an enormous marshmallow, not knowing which way was up or down, while she waded through the sticky morass desperate to find a way out. With one finger, she reached out. The tip of her finger moved ever so slow towards the globule. Her eyes were unblinking as she stared.

* * *

Paul heard his mother muttering under her breath as she pulled out the bits and pieces she needed. He raised one hand to prevent her from moving or saying anything and pointed with his other hand to Abby's ashen, statue-still face.

Abby's finger glided closer and closer, paused, and like a single blush of a butterfly wing, dabbed at the trail of blood. She lifted her hand away, smeared her thumb over the pad of her finger as her eyes made their first movement from his chest and stared at the sticky smudge on her hand. Her mouth was set with lips barely apart, her head cocked to one side as though puzzled. There was a worried frown across her forehead.

'There was blood. Lots and lots of blood,' Abby said to herself.

Grace's sucked in breath was audible. Paul glanced at his mother. She caught his eye. 'Abby is remembering,' Grace whispered.

Both Paul and Grace turned their eyes back to Abby who still rubbed the blood between her fingers, her eyes scrunched as though she was trying to drag the rest of the memory forward. Paul reached out with one hand and placed it over Abby's other hand in an automatic move to comfort her.

At the touch, her fingers curled around his larger hand in a tight grip. Ever so slowly, her staring eyes turned towards the grasped hands and she gasped. 'There was a warm hand. I can feel it holding mine. When it let go I felt afraid, panicky. When it held mine, I felt safe.'

'The paramedic stayed with you.' Grace said in a low, soft voice.

'I can hear a voice. Male. So soothing, so calm. Deep and melodious.' Abby turned to stare back at her right hand, twisting it over from side-to-side. 'This hand feels so cold.'

A strangled gasp came from Grace. Paul glanced at her, concerned at the shocked look on his mother's face. 'What...?'

'She's remembering,' Grace whispered as she lifted a hand to prevent him from saying any more.

As she tugged her hand free, Abby shook her head and glanced at Grace. 'It's gone. A couple of flashes: a voice, a feeling, a vision – nothing more than brief flashes. What does it mean?'

'Your memory is coming back.'

'Tell me what they mean.' She swung pleading eyes towards Grace.

'I can't. The counsellor made me promise. They want you to remember by yourself, in your own good time. I'm sorry, Abby.'

Really worried about the white face and body which had taken on a definite unsteady sway in front of him, Paul dragged a chair from under the table and gently guided Abby until she sat. 'Are you okay?' he asked as he laid a hand on her arm.

'Yes, I'm fine.' She didn't sound fine with her voice hesitant and shaky. 'I wish I could remember. I wish I didn't have this continuous dark energy swirling around in my brain. It keeps jabbing away to get out but pulls back and hides in a really sinister game of hide and seek. I want to remember it all. This not knowing, not understanding is so confusing. The nightmare last night was exactly the same as usual. I stop at the darkness but still can't recall any more yet deep down I know there is more - a lot more.'

'You had a nightmare? With the sedatives?' Alarm spread across Grace's face when she knelt in front of Abby.

'No. At first I didn't take any sedatives. I dropped them in the basin and lost them all. I had intended to do without them, to see if I could. But with the pills gone, I didn't have any choice and the same dream came back so to get some sleep I took...' Her hands flew to her shocked open mouth as her eyes widened.

'Took what, Abby?' Grace reached out and dragged Abby's hands away from her face.

'I found some ... umm, over the counter sedatives in the bathroom cabinet and took two instead of one because I figured they would be low dosage.' As Abby dropped her head the embarrassed whisper was muffled against her chest.

'Two? You didn't read the instructions? What about the side effects?' Grace turned to Paul. 'What were they? I recall a certain brand has been banned because they cause weird things to happen. If it is the type she took no wonder she had no idea what she was doing?'

Noticing the tremble in Abby's body, Paul knew she understood his mother's last statement and where her thoughts had gone. 'Look, ladies, let's get this all out in the open and clear the air. What happened - happened. I honestly don't think either of us can blame the other. Neither of us was coherent at the time. I was so exhausted I slept like the dead. Abby was, to say the least, sedated out of her brain. I presume they weren't the same as your regular tablets and you never took a double dose before.' He watched Abby slowly shake head from side-to-side. 'I know what they were and believe they were the ones which have now been banned because there were quite a few media reports about them doing weird things to your subconscious if you overdose. I should have thrown them out after Jasmine...' He couldn't continue when ugly memories stabbed and swirled around. Glancing at his mother's mystified face, he added, 'They were Jasmine's, not mine.'

A look of understanding passed between the two before Paul shut the memories from his mind. The last thing he wanted to think about was Jasmine and the number she had done on him. 'I feel wretched I didn't wake up in time to call things to a halt. I feel even worse about your first time not being as it should be.'

A choked whimper emanated from the direction of Abby's chest. Paul grasped her chin and forced her head up to look him in the eye. 'Abby, we can't deny what happened. At a guess I would say we both enjoyed the experience at the time and let me tell you, for a lady with no experience, you were quite spectacular.'

'Paul,' cried Grace.

'Come on, Mum. We are all mature adults. Having sex is a normal, human function. I can't see any point in sniggering behind raised hands and being all coy and secretive as though it is a taboo subject. We are both mortified about what happened last night. We both have the same regrets but no matter what we do or say, we can't undo it. There is no blame to be had even though as a man I feel I should accept responsibility.' Becoming aware of the sticky, cloying sensation on his chest, Paul glanced down at the congealing mess. 'Let's get this cleaned up first, after which, I think we could all do with a coffee and something to eat.'

His words caused a frenzy of activity. Grace fussed with his wounds while a pink-cheeked Abby gave the preparation of coffee avid attention. Paul guessed since human intimacy was a new experience for her, it was possible she felt mortified by his frankness. The rattling of a mug on the granite bench as it was placed by unsteady hands, had Paul settle his eyes on Abby's face. She looked completely unnerved. When he caught her eye and she quickly turned away with another rising redness to her cheeks, he knew what she was thinking.

He smiled, figuring she had enjoyed the experience as much as he. But he bet the entire payment for his project in Afghanistan, she would never admit it. Abby was an intriguing lady. She had some prickly barriers but he sensed underneath those barriers she was sweet, soft and innocent. Four weeks was not long to delve into the mysteries of a woman but he determined he was going to have a damn good try.

Seven

After two days of living together in the same house, Abby was totally confused. Paul Sanders was an enigma. It had taken a great deal of coercion for her to agree to remain in the house, her feelings of being an unwanted squatter overwhelming to the point she made up an extensive list in her mind on where else she could find somewhere to live. When she came up blank, she agreed when Paul had insisted she stay but she was certain it was only out of pity and not because he really wanted her here. To her, his behaviour in the past forty-eight hours confirmed her initial thoughts.

After a long argument about who would sleep in the master bedroom, with a large king-size made to accommodate Paul's huge frame, Abby had shoved her bag outside the front door, returned inside to pick up her crutches but spied Paul leant against the passage wall, watching her. Determined to ignore him, she managed to get outside the front door where she stood on the top step with her hands on her hips, insisting she was leaving if she wasn't allowed to sleep in one of the prettier, more feminine rooms.

With the picture clear in her mind, Abby smiled, stretched and took her time to turn over on the large beach towel she had sneaked from the closet. A giggle escaped at the memory of Paul stalking down the passage, onto the veranda, where he picked her up in his arms and carried her down the passage and gently deposited her on the bed in the spare bedroom opposite his. She couldn't help the grin which crept out when he turned around, stomped back outside and returned with bag and crutches, which he dumped on the floor with a great deal of noise. He slammed the door after he had left – all without saying a word. She hadn't seen him for the rest of the day but had heard him moan at various times from behind his shut bedroom door. At one stage he must have made himself a coffee because she found the messy remnants of his foray into the kitchen when she assembled a ham and salad sandwich to assuage her rumbling stomach early in the afternoon. Breakfast had been a non-event apart from the coffee she had made with such ill grace before Grace left to return home.

To carve out a more comfortable shape in the warm sand near the edge of the waves which crashed at regular melodic intervals onto the beach, Abby wriggled and thumped at a high wodge of sand until it flattened. It had been hours before she heard the shower after which there had been silence for the remainder of the afternoon. Abby assumed Paul had been catching up on lost sleep. The only words he spoke to her were, 'I'm going out,' after she knocked on his bedroom door to ask if he wanted to join her for the evening meal. She hadn't heard him return, her single sedative from a renewed prescription Grace had purchased before she returned home, ensured Abby slept long and deep without the troublesome interruption of a nightmare.

At a sharp nip, Abby jerked upright, slapped the side of her face, felt around with her fingertips and scraped off the flattened remains of a bug. She gave it an intimate inspection and guessed it had been a midge. Time to leave. With the sun beginning to drop low on the horizon, the pesky insects were on the hunt for supper and she didn't relish being the main course, or dessert. She rolled over onto her stomach, eased her body onto all fours and pushed with her hands, managing to raise her backside upwards as she bent her knees. Finally, she straightened upright. After practising different slants on figuring out how to stand after lying on the ground, she found this to be the easiest. She prayed no-one was watching because she had no doubt she looked ridiculous but with such little muscle tone in her left leg, it gave her little option. But at least she had passed another goal – she could stand without the crutches.

* * *

From his position standing at the bathroom window while he scraped off shaving cream and whiskers, Paul watched Abby in the distance. He held his breath when she wavered from side-to-side after taking ages to stand. When she found her balance he released his held breath in a whoosh. It was ridiculous the way his own nerves were on edge and he didn't dare move, his razor held in mid-air, while she bent over to lift the towel and one crutch from the sand. Her body imitated a bowl of wobbly jelly until she draped the towel around her neck and set the circular brackets of the crutch around her right arm. Still staring as Abby made her now familiar ungainly waddle across the sand, he didn't concentrate on what he was doing and nicked the flesh on one side of his chin.

Emitting an unpleasant curse, he tore a small corner from a tissue and glued it to the offending dribble of blood. 'Damn it,' he muttered as he shook his head in disgust and mentally added the injury to the other dozen healing scrapes he had incurred in the mere few days he had been home. War shattered Afghanistan suddenly looked like a very safe place to live. After wiping his freshly shaven face dry, he glanced back out the window at the approaching cause of all his injuries. She was one beautiful woman with stubborn independence as her middle name.

When the two met halfway across the vast family room, Abby stared at the clean jeans, dress shirt and leather jacket Paul wore. 'I'm going out for dinner,' said Paul as he passed Abby.

'Again?' The moment the word slipped from her mouth; Abby dropped her top teeth over her bottom lip. 'Sorry, it's none of my business what you do.'

'You have a problem with me eating out?' Paul paused in his passage towards the front door, twisting his upper body around to stare at Abby but grimaced when a flash of hurt swept across her eyes.

'No, of course not, I apologise for my comment.' Abby turned away.

Before continuing on his way, Paul watched her retreating back. His heart managed a small tumble-turn at her down-turned head after he caught the glimpse of the distressed look on her face before she managed to mask her features. He fought back the strong emotions Abby had stirred up. He couldn't allow her to creep into his heart. Experience had taught him women were fickle creatures who twisted the knife with unremitting pressure after you lost your heart to them. He could never trust a woman. Besides, he had another six-month stint away. Toughen up, Sanders, he thought as he hardened his emotions and continued on his way to a lonely dinner at the same pub in town.

* * *

When stupid tears threatened, Abby gritted her teeth and screwed her eyes shut until she was certain they weren't going to form. Why should she be upset because a man didn't want to give her the time of the day? Why should she feel sad he wouldn't share meals with her? What did it matter if her sense of loneliness had increased ten-fold since he came home? It had never bothered her living alone before so why should it bother her now? But Paul's presence changed things. Having another human being in the house was a constant reminder of the loving closeness of the parents she missed so badly, but with his aloofness and continual absence, for some reason she missed him. Which was ridiculous since he had only been home a couple of days. Determined to get over her bout of misery-guts she waddled into the kitchen, yanked the fridge door open and searched for something to eat.

A hollowness settled in her chest while she nibbled her small snack of cheese cubes, sliced apple and a handful of mixed nuts, in front of the television. It was as though the emptiness swallowed her up. She turned off the inane programme she hadn't been able to concentrate on and wandered around the house to find something to do. After a few minutes of mindless ambling, picking up small objects, inspecting them and putting them back down again, she was bored witless. Not yet tired enough to retire for the night, she grabbed a light jumper from her wardrobe, tied the sleeves around her waist and left the house via the front door, wincing when she noticed a different dish on the hall cupboard. She still felt bad about the breakage but Paul had dismissed it as of little consequence when she apologised. Even though he said it held no value to him, she was still determined to replace it when she was able to get to the city to search antique shops for an identical dish. Her hand reached out of its own accord, lifted the dish, held it up high so she could inspect the marks underneath. Good grief, another expensive antique. To ensure there would be no more accidents, she took utmost care to place the dish right at the back and in the middle of the table.

Since she had no intention of walking far, Abby left without her crutch, something she regretted the moment she reached the two steps. She thought about going back to get it but after pondering the pros and cons, decided to continue on. A slow hundred metres to fill in time was all she needed to appreciate the night air, listen to the creatures, absorb the peace and hopefully fill her mind with anything other than this painful vacuum. With both feet together on the edge of the veranda, she stared at the first step.

'I can do this,' she said under her breath. She closed her eyes, breathed in long and deep, opened them again and studied the step. Only about twelve centimetres down but her left leg wouldn't have enough strength to support her weight, so she wriggled her right toes over the edge while grasping onto the veranda post. She shuddered when her right foot dropped onto the step and a spear shot into her left hip. No way would she be able to repeat the process so instead, she eased down and sat on the edge of the veranda so she could wriggle her way down the last step using her hands, bottom and feet. Easy-peasy but unless she mastered descending steps before actually going to the city, she was going to look ridiculous.

Despite the elation at making it without a crutch, despair at being so useless swept over her but her determined pride came to the fore. 'One step at a time,' she said to the first odd-shaped paving stone. 'Another step,' she said to the second, and third until she reached the gate with a smile of triumph spreading across her face.

She rested at the gate before daring to go any further. The darkness made her wary of each careful step to the road. Step, hitch her left hip, balance. Right foot forwards, drag the left, balance. She couldn't help the little high-five to herself when she reached the welcome smoothness of the bitumen on the roadway. It was so much easier on a flat surface and pure pleasure to listen to the cicadas chirrup with their wings, and a single hidden mopoke who hooted from a nearby tree while she shuffled and crumped along the side of the road nearest the beach until physical exhaustion set in from the effort.

When she turned around for the return journey, she glanced up to measure the distance back to the gate and winced. Stupid, stupid woman. She had gone too far. There was no way she was going to be able to make it back without a rest. Even the neighbour's house was not an option since she had been stupid enough to go in the opposite direction. Lesson learned: one of hundreds since the accident.

Disgusted with herself, she searched the darkness, scanning along the side of the road for a rock or log she could perch on long enough to catch her breath and ease the agony. All she could make out in the dim light from the half-moon were gravel edges running down into a shallow drainage ditch filled with knee-high weeds, probably home to millions of creepy-crawlies she really, really, really didn't want to meet or deal with. Even though snakes and goannas usually curled up in the cold, there was no way she was going to tempt fate, especially since she had managed to wreck Paul's house from a simple bump against a door. The log she wanted and had used on a previous foray, was in the opposite direction close to the neighbour's gate. A long growl rumbled out at her stupidity. She added another groan for her aching muscles and pronounced limp. 'One slow step at a time,' she whispered at each tortoise-speed step to close the long distance, pausing after each step to find another ounce of energy.

By the time headlights from a car came sweeping up behind and lit her up like a flash of lightning, Abby was certain she wasn't going to make it. Fear slammed into her when brakes screeched and tyres skidded behind. Sweet mercy, but she was stupid coming out in the dark alone, she thought as she tried to figure out how she could defend herself or get out of the way. There was no way she would be able to run. Unbidden tears welled as she folded to the ground in utter defeat and swept her hands over her head, ready to defend her body from physical assault.

'What the devil do you think you are doing?' The harsh voice came from the darkness. Even though the voice sounded angry, Abby dissolved at its familiarity.

'Paul?' It was the only word she could manage before relieved, exhausted sobs replaced her ability to reason or speak.

'Abby, what happened?' Paul squatted in front of her and lifted her hands away from her sodden eyes. 'What the hell happened? What drove you from the house so late at night? Abby, please talk to me?'

Incapable of speech Abby kept sobbing in relief while she gripped his hands tight. She heard him drop to the ground, felt him lift her into his lap. Next he wrapped his arms around her shaking shoulders and held her tight. One hand cradled her head to his chest while the other ran calming circular motions around her back. She couldn't control the amount of moisture she knew was soaking into his shirt and jacket. Why was she such a wimp? Oh, God, get over yourself Abigail Sharpe, she thought as she fought the tears and swept the stupid moisture away with a clenched fist.

Once her distress eased a bit, Paul released his hold, squatted on his haunches and lifted her from the ground with a grunt. As he carried her back to his car, she squinted at the blare from the still burning headlights. After depositing her into the passenger seat, he rounded the bonnet, sat next to her and held out a clean handkerchief he had withdrawn from the pocket of his jeans. 'Do you want to tell me what this is all about?'

'I was so relieved - it was you - and not some crank.' She sniffed an unladylike snuffle in the middle of her response, wincing at the embarrassing snort.

'I'm not sure whether that is a compliment or not,' said Paul. 'What I was really asking is why are you out here in the middle of the night to start with? What happened? You looked as though you were about to collapse and you have no crutches. We're at least half a kilometre from the house. Care to explain?'

To hide the guilt she felt sure was obvious, Abby swiped the sodden handkerchief across her face, taking time to remove all remnants of tears. 'I felt restless so came for a walk. I hadn't intended coming so far. I guess I overdid things a little.'

'Only a little?' His sarcastic voice rose. 'You could have been killed walking along this road in the pitch dark, especially with the traffic coming from behind you.' As he spoke he turned the key in the ignition and eased his foot down on the accelerator. 'What possessed you to do something so stupid?'

'I'm sorry,' he added more quietly at her gasp. 'You scared the living daylights out of me.'

How was she supposed to answer? I'm lonely. I don't understand why you hate me so much? Why you can't bear to be around me? Sure thing. Unable to think of a logical answer, Abby said nothing, but kept her eyes turned away, staring out of the side window into the darkness for the brief journey back to the house.

As soon as Paul parked the car, Abby lifted the catch to open the door but as fast as she tried to be in extricating her exhausted, unco-operative limbs from the car, Paul was faster. He wriggled one arm under her knees and the other around her back. Even though embarrassment hit at her weakness, she was relieved when he lifted her from the seat and carried her to the front door.

'Key.' The one word from Paul was a question as well as a demand.

Too afraid to comment, Abby wriggled so she could slip her fingers into the pocket of her jeans and withdrew the single key. Paul angled his body so she could reach the lock. He waited while she jiggled the brass key into the tiny slot and twisted it around. Once the door was open, he shoved it ajar with one shoulder and strode inside as though he wasn't carrying a dead weight in his arms.

He plonked her onto the leather lounge. In an instant, arms went either side of her head as Paul spread his hands out on the back of the sofa, trapping her in place.

'You ready to tell me what happened?'

She bristled at his terse, demand. 'I already told you, even though it's none of your business what I do.'

'When I have to scrape the remains of the woman who is living in my house, off the road, it is definitely my business. Now why were you walking in the middle of an unlit country road in the middle of the night, wearing dark clothes? Don't you have any road sense?'

Abby shut her eyes against the intense, irate stare. 'I'm sorry,' she murmured. She could tell he was angry but didn't know how to explain.

'Good grief, she's sorry.' Paul straightened, brushed one hand against his closed eyes in frustration. When he bent down again, he replaced his hands, trapping her once again. 'Do you have any idea how much you scared me when I almost ran into you? The fear level shot off the charts when I saw your body fall to the ground. Strewth, woman, I thought I had hit you. I should put you over my knee and spank your cute little backside.' Paul wheeled away and stormed into the kitchen where he clattered and banged filling the kettle and taking out the makings for something, probably coffee, she thought.

Mortified, Abby struggled her way out from the cushioned seat. After getting upright it took a moment to gain her balance before she began a painful retreat towards her bedroom. Every single move-ment caused a shaft of pain to shoot from her pelvis through her body and down her legs. She was almost at the doorway when both of her arms were grasped in a gentle but firm hold.

'Abby, I'm sorry I lost my cool. Please come back so we can talk. I know I shouldn't be angry with you but you scared the hell out of me.' With gentle force, he turned her around, and thank goodness, he supported her weight as he guided her back to the sofa. After she settled, he reached over to the side table and retrieved two mugs of hot chocolate. Handing her one, he perched beside her, but didn't quite touch.

Before taking a sip, Abby eyed the chocolate. There was a chance it would keep her awake if she drank it all but Paul had actually made it for her and for the first time was sharing a meal with her – even if it was only a hot drink. So she took a tiny sip. 'I'm sorry if I scared you. I didn't mean to. I couldn't sleep so decided to take a short stroll. I truly didn't mean to go so far. I was looking for some-where to sit and rest but couldn't find anything to sit on. I'm sorry.' She glanced up to see Paul staring at her.

'I will accept your apology if you make me a promise,' he said as he settled the mug into his lap with both hands wrapped around it.

'Am I going to like this?'

'Probably not since you seem to bristle at anything I have to say but I want you to promise you won't ever go for a walk along the road at night again. You have miles and miles of beach you can wander up and down where there are no cars. But please, not on the road.' One hand released its death grip on the mug and snaked over to settle on Abby's lower arm. 'Please?'

His gentle touch sent her blood thrumming. The breath hitched in her throat so hard she had to force herself to breathe. 'I promise. I was scared. Not knowing who you were, I thought you were going to attack me. I was too darn exhausted to fight back and had no hope of being able to run. Believe me, it won't happen again.' There was a wry grin on her face when she glanced up at Paul.

'You have no idea how relieved I am. Thank you.'

'Can I go to bed now? I ache so much I have to lie down.'

Paul placed his mug on the table and stood. 'Are you okay? Is there anything I can do?' Without giving her time to answer, he scooped one hand under her arms, removed the mug from her hands, wriggled his other hand under her legs and eased her from the seat. One heft and she was in his arms where she relaxed while he carried her to her room, taking utmost care in depositing her onto her bed.

* * *

After returning to the lounge, Paul sat contemplating while he listened to Abby prepare for bed. He heard the cistern flush, the shower turn on, run, turn off again, followed by a lengthy silence while he assumed she dressed. He didn't ease up until he heard the silence after she had retired to bed and he figured she was asleep. All the time he listened he thought about the deep emotions this woman had stirred up. Maybe it was because he hadn't been with a woman for so long – since Jasmine. He knew he was in trouble as he made his own preparations for bed. With memories of his disastrous relationship with Jasmine surfacing, Paul fought back all thoughts of pursuing Abby. Jasmine had taught him a harsh lesson in trusting women.

Eight

Confused, Abby lay in bed staring at the ceiling. The truce between them was tense at the very least. There was far more conversation but it was nothing more than a polite repartee despite her attempts at friendly openings. If Abby was up first, Paul seemed to wait until she was out of the kitchen before he made an appearance for his own breakfast. If he was the first to rise, he vanished the moment Abby walked in. The morning after their confrontation, she made him a mug of mid-morning coffee and he seemed taken aback when she carried it out to the back veranda to hand it to him. He accepted it with grace and appreciation but Abby thought he had been over-effusive with his thanks like a person was when they opened a gift they hated but good manners dictated they accept with grace, so she didn't have the courage to attempt the same courtesy again.

Paul still left the house for lunch and dinner. Not once did he tell her he was going or say when he would be back, but since it was his house and they had no ties she couldn't figure out why it upset her. He went for long walks along the beach and swam in the ocean but never invited Abby to join him. Twice, when Abby made one of her regular fitness walks to the beach, he left the moment he spied her. There was no reason she should feel hurt by his actions and the way he withdrew from her presence but there was no way to prevent the pain in the region of her heart.

Her determination to wean herself from sleeping tablets had resulted in enduring the same nightmare tormenting her night twice in a row and both times she had awoken with the sensation of Paul by the side of her bed. Why she feigned sleep, she couldn't fathom but she had, by forcing her breaths to calm and keep her eyes closed until she heard him leave.

The nightmares were a problem but after a great deal of in-decision she decided not to take any more sedatives. She couldn't recall the exact moment she realised the drugs inhibited her ability to recover her mental state. Being zonked out in a drug induced coma-like state was never going to allow mother nature to repair Abby's memory. After two nights without the sedatives, she knew her decision had been correct for the pictures, sounds and smells had become less vivid, less graphic and the recurring images didn't distress her anywhere near as much. But she was certain she still moaned or called out during the dreams. It was the only reason she could think off why Paul would come into her room. Last night, she was certain his warm hand brushed the hair from her face. His touch ceased the very second he sensed she had calmed.

As she turned onto her side, Abby wondered how she could approach Paul and get him to remain in her presence long enough for her to have a chat. She needed to purchase supplies, visit the bank and had three important letters to post. Even though the distance into town wasn't much more than a mile, it was out of the question her legs would make the distance, even with both crutches. Determined to catch him, she waited until he was rattling around in the kitchen before she eased from the bed and tugged on the pink robe over her nightie. Not bothering with slippers, she crept along the passage to the kitchen so he wouldn't hear her approach and have time to escape.

The moment Paul saw her he picked up his plate of cereal and headed for the veranda door.

'Paul, please, I need to ask you something.'

He paused at the open door. 'What do you want to know?'

'Are you going into town today?'

'Yes, why?'

'I need a few things.'

There was a lengthy pause while Paul appeared to mull things around his brain. 'Write a list and I will purchase them for you. I will be visiting someone first and will be out most of the day.'

This isn't what she expected or wanted. Paul couldn't do her banking for her. By the way he had thought so long and hard about how to answer, Abby was certain he plain didn't want her with him. And what was wrong with simply wanting to spend time away from being cooped up in the same place? What was wrong with her desperate need to be with other people, to socialise, have a coffee? He sure wasn't sociable company. Devastated, she turned away. 'Don't bother.'

'It's no bother, all I need is a list.'

'Forget it, Paul. It's not important. I'm sorry I asked.' The hurt was impossible to suppress. Her emotions bubbled to the surface with moisture desperate to leak from her eyes. Determined to not let the tears fall, she fought them back, turned and retreated back to her room as fast as she could, only managing to get the door closed before she heard Paul knock.

'Go away,' she yelled. It wasn't difficult to ignore all his further knocks and calls since waves of anger and disappointment along with something else she couldn't name, swept over her. Maybe it was sheer loneliness. All she wanted was a two-minute ride into town. Why would a simple ride be so difficult? He could have dropped her off before visiting whoever was more important than her. It wasn't far out of his way. Her angry frustration built until she heard him drive away an hour later. I'll show him, she thought as she headed for his office where she knew he kept a local town phone book.

It took a bit of time to search through the pages, but she found the number of a local taxi company and booked a taxi to take her into town. It wasn't until after she had replaced the receiver she remembered she was short of cash, hence her need to visit the bank, so she counted the money she still had while waiting for the cab to arrive. After mentally calculating how much her list of supplies would cost, she had no doubt she was going to be short so prayed her disability pension was in her bank account. Yes, she had a debit card but one needed to be able to actually get to a shop to use the darn thing. When she heard the horn blast from the taxi, she waddled to the bedroom to grab both crutches because it would be too tiring to walk around town without them.

After alighting outside the supermarket, Abby spent longer than normal selecting the items on her list, mentally calculating the costs as she went. To her the taxi fare had been exorbitant for such a short distance, taking a larger chunk from her limited resources than she had anticipated. It didn't take genius status to figure she wouldn't have enough money so she replaced the slightly more luxurious wants, limiting her purchases to desperate needs. Toothpaste – definite for she'd scraped the last skerrick out this morning. Shampoo – hmm, if she diluted what was left, she could make it last another week. Put it back. Bread - a must, along with butter. She could do without jam and there was enough vegemite left in her jar. Fruit – absolutely but keep it to two pieces a day. She counted out the bananas, apples, oranges and pears; put back four oranges and two apples because they were the heaviest and would lighten her load. She could do without steak but keep the sausages. If she had only one sausage each meal it would be enough protein. Cabbage – yes she could eat it raw in a salad or cook it as a green vegetable. Same with carrots. Happy, she went to the checkout, paid and shoved her purchases into two plastic bags. When they were heavier than she had anticipated she figured there was a reason she couldn't buy any more. Karma worked in mysterious ways,

It was awkward shuffling along the footpath with plastic bags swinging from the crutch handles but she managed to reach the post office without any major dramas. After posting three letters in the red box standing guard duty in front of the building, the lengthy trek across the other side of town to her bank was difficult. By the time she reached the swing door the shopping was a darn nuisance, swishing, splatting and tangling between legs and aluminium. Maybe if she tied a knot in the plastic handles it would shorten them enough they wouldn't swing so far.

Frustration simmered as did mounting aches while she negotiated a way in through the heavy glass doors of the bank. They certainly weren't built for people with limited mobility or strength. The constant thrumming ache in her hips didn't help one little bit. The wait in the long queue meant the creaking twinges in her pelvis turned into dull throbs. The myriad of stainless steel screws were making their presence felt. The throbs turned into agony when she finally reached the teller who told her there was no money in her account for her to make a withdrawal.

Damn it, why? A couple of tears managed to escape from the corners of her eyes and trickled down her hot cheeks before she was able to rein them in. By the time she plodded her way out the door of the bank, helplessness and despair had turned her innards into a leaden vacuum. What the hell was she supposed to do now? Without money, she couldn't catch a taxi home and with every single healing injury already aching to a level her endurance couldn't manage, walking home would kill her, if she could even make the distance.

With a numb brain she clicked blindly down the street in the direction of home but stopped at the window of a café. Desperate to rest, she paused, thought about the remaining coins residing in the bottom of her purse and figured there might be enough money to manage a light snack. Coffee would be good, black tea at a push if it were cheaper but the milk would do her good. She managed to shove the door open with her backside but struggled to swing around and enter the café with a plastic bag slapping against each knee while she manoeuvred the flipping crutches. Scared her jellified legs would give way, she headed for the nearest vacant table and flopped into a seat, the clatter raising eyes at the noisy interruption to their various conversations. It hurt but she managed to ease the crutches from her aching arms, settle her belongings by her side and reach for the menu. A server arrived with a glass tumbler and welcome bottle of water. Eager to fill the glass, her hand shook so much she spilt some, and groaned at the mess. It took two paper serviettes to sop up the spilt water, but it left her with the problem of not knowing what to do with two wads of soaking wet tissues. She dropped them in her bag of shopping, lifted the glass and drank down the entire contents without a pause.

* * *

Across the room, Paul stopped listening to the incessant chatter of the woman next to him. He didn't mean to be rude but the sight of Abby had flummoxed him. How the hell did she get here? He watched as Abby read the menu but couldn't figure out why it took her so long, apart from the fact she swallowed down three full glasses of water while she read. He was even more mystified when she removed a small coin purse from the pocket of her jeans, tipped out the contents onto the table and meticulously piled up the coins into small heaps. The way her fingers worked, he presumed she was counting the money. When the server moved up to her, Abby spoke, pointed to the menu and the server walked away. Paul turned back to his companion and offered an answer to a question.

The next time Paul looked up it was to see Abby's backside vanish through the doorway. Puzzled, he caught the waitress's eye and summoned her over. 'The young lady who was seated over there.' He pointed to where Abby had been seated. 'She left less than a minute ago. Is she coming back?'

'I don't think so, sir.'

'But her meal – she gave you an order.'

'No, sir, the woman was short of money. She asked if she could buy half of a sandwich. I went to the boss but he said no.'

'Thank you.' Paul turned to Dianne. 'Excuse me a minute, I need to check on something.'

'Who is she?'

'A friend of Mum's. The woman I mentioned. I'm worried about her. I won't be a minute.' After he shoved his chair back and wove a path through the crowded tables he pushed the door open and searched one way down the street but saw no sign of a golden-headed waif. The other way yielded the same result. 'Where could she have got to so quickly?' he muttered as he stepped further out onto the path. Despite walking down both sides of the busy main street, Paul saw no evidence of a woman on crutches so figured she had organised a ride back. Since there was nothing he could do about Abby, he returned to his lunch companion and waiting coffee.

* * *

From the park bench hidden behind a dense bush bearing long, feathery, red bottlebrush blooms, Abby followed Paul's tall body up and down the street. She knew he was searching for her but there was no way she was going to give him the satisfaction of finding her. The hurt from his lies dug much deeper than they had a right to. It had shocked her when she rose from the table in the café, to see Paul seated across the room next to a gorgeous brunette. While she fixed the crutches to her arms, searing anger soared. She wasn't angry at him being with a woman, he had every right to visit whoever he damn well liked but he told her he would be visiting someone. Yet here he was sitting in a café right slap bang in the middle of town: the town she only wanted a lift to and by the looks of the empty plates sitting in front of them, the cosy couple had been here long enough to order, wait and eat which would have taken the entire time since Paul had left home. His lie hurt far more than the stab of jealousy. There was no way he had visited anyone except to pick this floozy up and drive her here. The least he could have done was to be honest with Abby. When a surge of bitter disappointment swamped her, Abby fled the premises and turned down the first street corner she came to.

It wasn't the only thing which hurt. The fact he completely ignored her most of the time yet was able to give his undivided attention to another woman, stabbed deep, further confirming her thoughts Paul couldn't abide her. He wouldn't even take the time to talk to Abby. Even after she saw him return to the café, she waited. When she figured it was safe to move without him spying her, she pushed her body from the seat by pressing down on the crutches and levering her body up onto hip bones which really, really didn't want to carry her torso another centimetre.

With a huge heft of her shoulders, Abby sucked in a deep breath. Not sure she wasn't a complete idiot; she paused before daring to take the first step towards home. She had watched the speedometer turn over during her taxi-ride into town. 'Two kilometres – two thousand metres,' she mumbled to thin air. To her it was going to be like climbing Mount Everest. The most she had managed so far was a quarter of the distance with one crutch. This time she had the benefit of both crutches, which would make the journey a little easier but she also had two heavy plastic bags of shopping.

'One step at a time,' she whispered under her breath, relating her mantra since the first step she took after the accident. 'All it takes is one step at a time.'

As she walked, she counted. It helped keep her mind off the distance as well as the increasing level of pain. At one hundred she forced a smile and increased her determination. At two hundred paces, her smile was nothing but a grim line, the overwhelming ache in her limbs taking the shine away from the achievement. After one thousand, Abby reckoned she had completed the five hundred-metre mark of her last record but deep down, knew she wasn't going to make the distance home. There were blisters forming on the palms of her hands, her fingers ached from holding the plastic handles of the shopping bags which had stretched and tightened and now felt like thin strands of barbed wire cutting into her flesh. Weak muscles had jellified, giving her the sensation of the footpath now being a deep soft sponge each time she put a foot down and the ache deep in her pelvis was abominable.

There was no choice but to pause for a rest. Why, oh, why did healed bones have to ache so darn much for so darn long? She had seen the x-rays showing all the plates and screws the surgeon had put in to patch together her shattered bones. Right now she could feel every one of those screws grinding against bones.

Certain she was unable to continue, she searched around for something – anything, to rest on. There was still a footpath but the fence was too high to sit on. She could sit on the ground but would have get up again. Not going to happen. Up ahead, the property she was passing ended but she noticed the fence along the next garden was lower. At a guess, it was only about twenty metres to go. So near, yet so darn far away, she thought as she took the first step. It was a struggle and took forever to stagger the distance, swearing under her breath at each step. Three more steps to go – two – one - at last. A long, low groan rumbled out.

The fence indeed was low but fate had a row of upturned sharp-edged stones embedded in cement along the top row of bricks. Fabulous, exactly what she needed. Abby could do nothing but stare at them. Despite the pain, she needed to rest so unclipped the crutches from her arms, plonked the shopping on the footpath and wiggled her bottom onto the top of the fence. There was a space where a couple of stones had been dislodged. The sun-warmed hard cement was a relief against the throbbing inside her pelvis but was damned uncomfortable. She wriggled two or three centimetres one way only to find a sharp protrusion jabbing into the back of her thigh so she wriggled the other way until she found relative comfort. It was almost impossible but she forced her body to relax into the pain with the controlled breathing she learnt how to do in rehab. Eyes closed. Breathe slow. Long breaths - in and out, she chanted in her mind but didn't dare move a muscle.

* * *

As he planted his foot the moment the restricted speed zone changed after he left the confines of town, Paul didn't take any notice of the blurred flash as he passed something leaning on a fence. At least until it registered the something leaning so still looked remarkably like a golden-headed angel called Abby. Shifting his foot, he jammed on the brakes, jerking the two occupants of the car forwards then ricocheting them backwards and thumping against the seat.

'Paul, are you crazy?' Dianne turned to him with a fierce frown as she planted one hand on the glove box and the other pressed against the console.

'Sorry,' he muttered as he stabbed the gear into reverse. Twisting his head around, he reversed to the statue leant so still against the fence. 'Stupid woman,' he mumbled under his breath as he jammed on the brakes again to bring the car to a jerking halt.

'I beg your pardon?' Dianne's eyes flashed at him in anger.

'Not you – her.' He reached across his companion and pointed to Abby who was so still, she appeared to be a gnome cemented to the wall.

Furious, he shoved his door open with undue force and stalked like a man possessed.

'What the hell do you think you are doing?' he yelled as he strode up to Abby.

Her eyes flew open with a look of alarm which immediately changed to anger. 'What the hell does it like?' she yelled back.

'It looks a lot like you have lost your mind.' Without waiting for a response, he grabbed her crutches and stomped back to the car where he flung them into the boot after jabbing the key in the lock and hoisting the lid so hard it shook the car. He returned to Abby, hefted the two plastic bags from the ground at her feet and stowed them on top of the crutches. Opening the rear door, he turned to Abby. 'Get in.'

'Since when did you have the right to order me around?'

'Since you took leave of your senses.'

'I,' she pointed to her chest, 'am perfectly sane. You,' she stabbed her finger in his direction, 'go back to your little floozy there. I am sure she won't appreciate me playing gooseberry.' Abby's hands moved to her hips as she tried to dismount from the fence and straighten her body. Her attempt came to an unceremonious end when the back of her top snagged on the sharp stones, preventing her from moving. She looked like a marionette hanging in the air, an embarrassed puppet for everything reddened from the neck up.

While he watched every action, Paul noticed the slight grimace before Abby's face turned to a still mask. When he realised her predicament, he reached out as his face twitched in amusement.

'Don't you dare touch me, Paul Sanders.'

For the briefest of seconds he hesitated but shook his head before he forced his hands under her armpits and lifted her from the fence. 'Stubborn little minx,' he muttered as he hoisted her into his arms, turned, took four determined steps and plonked her into the rear seat.

She gasped as she landed: a gasp she wasn't able to suppress. Still in a crouch position, Paul studied the face mere inches from his own. Blood drained from her cheeks as her top teeth bit into her bottom lip. 'You are in a lot of pain. Why didn't you tell me?' Paul said with a stab of guilt.

Her raised eyes were not in the least friendly. 'Congratulations, you win first prize for deductive skills.' The sarcasm dripped from Abby's tongue before her eyes closed and her hands flew up to hide her face from his scrutiny. After closing the door with a lot less force, Paul moved around to the other side of the car where the door was still standing ajar. As he folded into the seat he heard Abby speaking to his companion.

'Hi, I'm Abby. If you didn't already know, I am unfortunately staying with this brute but I guess he didn't want you to know about me either but don't worry, he barely speaks to me, let alone spending a second of his time in my presence.'

'Abby, enough.' He turned around in time to see the sugary sweet and obviously supercilious smile Abby bestowed on Dianne.

He turned to face his companion. 'Dianne, allow me to introduce Abigail Sharpe. She is the friend of Mum's who is living in my house while she recuperates from an accident. While I was away the arrangements were made without my knowledge. Abby, please meet my cousin, Dianne Rogers.' The emphasis on the word cousin, was deliberate.

Abby's shocked eyes shot across to Paul. 'Your cousin?'

He hoped she interpreted the look he returned as an insidious gloat.

Abby dropped her eyes as she sank back against the seat. Even though she screwed her eyes shut, she couldn't hide white cheeks and drawn features. Abby was not in a good place. Why she was even here, he would suss out later. In between keeping an eye on the road as he drove, Paul kept glancing at Abby's face in the rear vision mirror. Pain etched her ashen face with lips set in a tense thin line. 'Why don't you lie down, Abby?'

'I'm fine.' The whispered words came through the thin line of white lips without opening her eyes.

'Don't lie. You are far from fine.'

Her eyes flew open, meeting his in the mirror in an unblinking stare. 'All right, I am not fine. I ache like billyo but I don't dare move because it will hurt a damn sight more. Happy?'

'Not really, I will be far happier when I get you home and shove a couple of painkillers down your neck and have you lying stretched out on your bed.'

The sharp glance from both women at the intimated meaning of his words caused an unbidden heat to rush up his face.

'Alone.' He emphasised the word but forced his concentration on driving to avoid any more blunders, even though he knew the addition of the single word had only made his comment even more suggestive. He also knew when to quit.

'Where are we going?' asked Abby.

'I need to take Dianne home first.' He didn't say any more and the car remained silent with an ominous atmosphere so thick with tension it felt as though it was about to splinter apart. Being the gentleman he was brought up to be, Paul saw Dianne to her front door, bestowed a brief peck on her cheek and returned to the car but said nothing during the journey back to his house. Once he parked the car, he removed crutches and shopping from the boot and carried them inside before returning to assist Abby. He had to bite down on his tongue to prevent another caustic comment slipping out when he saw the way she had to struggle to alight.

'You are one stubborn woman, Abigail.' Before she had a chance to retort, she was in his arms. He carried her through the house to her bedroom. Not content to ease her to the floor, he lay her down on the bed. 'Now stay there while I get you a glass of water for those painkillers.' Before he left he lifted both packets of prescription pills from the bedside table, read the labels and handed the required packet to Abby before tossing the other back onto the wood cabinet.

'Thank you but can I ask a favour?'

'Ask away.'

'Would it be possible for me to have a soak in the spa? The warm water eases the ache.'

His whole demeanour altered in an instant. He smiled as he brushed a finger across her brow. 'I'll start filling it for you. I'll be back in a minute with water. Don't move.' Abby eyed Paul for a moment before he turned away and strode across the carpet.

After returning, Paul hovered over her while she swallowed a single tablet. 'Are you sure one is enough? It says two on the label.'

'They are pretty strong. One will be enough but I need a few minutes for it to take effect.'

Unsure as to whether or not he should pursue the subject, Paul hesitated for a moment but his curiosity got the better of him and the bath needed time to fill. 'How did you get into town?'

'None of your business.'

'Please, Abby, let's not go down the path of stubborn pride. I don't feel up to arguing every point with you and I figure you don't feel so crash hot either. How did you get there?'

'Taxi.'

'Why didn't you catch a taxi back? You must have known you wouldn't have been able to walk the distance.' The moment he asked the question, the answer came to him. She didn't have enough money to buy a sandwich so there was no way she could have afforded a taxi. Her embarrassed blush and closed eyes made him feel like something gross stuck to the bottom of his shoe. 'Never mind but I told you I would buy whatever you needed.'

'Some errands require a body to actually be there in person. How were you going to discuss my personal affairs with... umm... institutions?' Her eyes had opened but looked anywhere but at him which made him wonder if it was because she felt embarrassed about her personal financial crisis. But he realised she didn't know about his discussion with the server.

'Why didn't you explain this to me this morning instead of telling me it wasn't important?'

'Because it was the truth. To you, my need to go to town was not important whereas your need to socialise held precedence. Although I can't figure why it was so difficult for you to take a two-minute detour since you did nothing more than pick your cousin up and drive straight into town.'

'How did you know?'

'Your plates were empty in the café so you must have been there quite some time and I hadn't been in town long.'

'You saw me there? Why didn't you come over?'

'What and be party to *ménage au trois?* No thank you.'

'She's only my cousin.'

'And I was supposed to know this – how? I'm not into breaking up cosy little dinners for two.'

It was too difficult to broach the subject of Abby's lack of money, so Paul turned away. 'I'll check on the water level in the bath.'

When he returned Abby was lying on her bed with her eyes shuttered. She was so still he thought she had fallen asleep. 'Abby?'

Instantly her eyes opened wide but there were definite lines of strain and fatigue around her mouth. Her cheeks had taken on a hollow look with her face a sickly grey. Something inside him shifted but he couldn't name what it was. Guilt was high on the list but also admiration for her independent pluck. At the same time he cursed at the way his heart felt so tight. The last thing he needed was to become emotionally involved with this gorgeous scrap of a woman.

'The level is deep enough. You can leave the water running a bit longer until it covers the jets if you want to use the spa.' He watched as she attempted to lever her body up. One grimace of pain was all he could handle. He stepped closer, bent over and scooped her into his arms even though he knew it was against his better judgement to hold her so close to his body.

'You don't have to carry me.'

'I beg to differ. You want straight into the bath or for me to remove your clothes first?' He smiled at her rising blush.

'I think I can manage on my own, thank you.'

'Pity,' he shot at her as he closed the door behind him after leaving her standing on the bathmat. Visions of him denuding her beautiful body of each item of clothing teased his brain as he made a rapid escape to the kitchen.

* * *

Abby stared after him, shocked at his daring words. While she stripped the clothes from her body, folded them and piled them on the vanity, she wondered about the sudden change in his attitude towards her. Giving the matter thought while she soaked in the fragrant bubbles Paul had generously poured into the water, she figured he must be feeling guilty about not driving her into town. Well, good, let his guilt eat away at his conscience. No, gnaw would be a better word, with humungous crunching bites.

When she finally emerged from the bathroom after soaking so long the water had cooled and her skin replicated dry prunes, she began to feel human again. The painkillers had kicked in which gave her more freedom of movement without the dull but intense ache. It was a pleasant surprise when she entered her bedroom to find in the middle of her bed, a tray set out with two thick salad filled sandwiches, a tall glass of chilled orange juice, an apple and a banana. Next to the tray was a note with a single pink rose lying across it. A raft of emotions piled onto one another as she reached out and lifted the paper. *You missed lunch. Enjoy. Spend the day relaxing. Dinner is on me. Meet me on the back veranda at seven. Dress is casual.* The letter was not signed; there was no need.

Nine

She still couldn't believe it. Not game to aggravate overused and still sore muscles by repeating yesterday's stupidity, Abby took her time to dress for the day. While brushing her hair in front of the mirror, she noticed the smile she had on her face as she went to sleep, still hovered around her lips.

Last night. Dinner had been amazing. At precisely seven o'clock she stepped out onto the back veranda into darkness after she had been barred from the vicinity for the hour before. At a tiny click from her right she turned around to see the flickers from a match as it flared and moved to one side. The glow strengthened when it caught on the wick of a candle. In the soft hazy light, the outline of Paul moved along the veranda as he set the flame to candle after candle until there was a whole row of different coloured lights shimmering along the entire veranda rail. Next, he moved back towards her and set alight the five candles of an elegant silver candelabrum set in the middle of a round table.

She could do nothing other than stare at the formally set table, with a white linen tablecloth, polished crystal glasses, sparkling silverware and plates from a formal setting she knew resided in a glass-fronted cupboard along the wall of the kitchen. The smile on Paul's face had been enigmatic but his eyes had held hers in a sultry gaze. She still couldn't believe how her body had reacted to his held gaze. Everything inside her had gone all shivery and hot to the extent she hadn't been able to move.

Even now, while she stood by the side of her bed after pulling a T-shirt over her head, Abby felt the same strange warmth spread outwards from her clenching womb as she continued her reverie.

Chilled champagne was ensconced in a silver bucket filled with ice-cubes. Before Abby had a chance to lift her amazed jaw from the ground, she heard the cork pop and the sudden fizz of the wine as it shot up and over the neck of the icy bottle. Seconds later she was handed a flute of tiny bursting bubbles. 'Non-alcoholic since you are on medication,' Paul had told her with a cheeky wink sent in her direction as they chinked glasses.

The amusing irony of the whole setting was how they had eaten a vast array of Chinese take-away which had arrived moments after they had taken their first few sips of sparkly. Paul had ordered a dozen different half-serves, because, he said, he didn't know her preferences. To Abby it was the best meal she had ever eaten. The food had been delicious, the setting idyllic and the company perfect. Conversation had been light-hearted and witty for the entire three hours they sat there enjoying the warm ambience of the summer's evening accompanied by the local mopoke, chirping cicadas, two distinct croaks of frogs and occasional other grunts, snorts and cheeps from other night creatures on the scavenge for food. And in the background had been the calm rhythm of waves as they rushed shore-wards before beating against the sand.

While she made her way towards the kitchen, Abby wondered which Paul she would encounter this morning. Would it be the romantic, friendly, easy to talk to Paul, or the standoffish un-communicative Paul? She paused in the doorway when she spied Paul standing at the bench with his back to her. He must have heard her for he turned around. She studied his face for clues to his demeanour. He looked hesitant, almost afraid – the same as she felt.

'Good morning, are you feeling better?' He handed over a mug a black tea, which surprised her. How did he know it was her preferred early morning beverage? Not once had he been in the kitchen the same time as her.

'Much better and, Paul, can I say thank you for last night. I can't think of an evening I have enjoyed more.'

'You are very welcome. I also enjoyed the night. I have already eaten so the kitchen is all yours.'

When he lifted his own mug and stepped towards the back door, his usual morning practice to escape her presence, a wave of bitter disappointment washed over her. After last night, she thought things had changed for the better. Deep sadness enveloped her. Things were back to normal. 'Before you go can I ask a favour.'

Paul paused for a second before turning back. 'Certainly.'

'Would you mind if I used your phone in the office this morning? I need to sort out a problem.'

'Go for it and you don't have to ask. Let me know if you need any help with your problem.'

'Yes I do have to ask. I would never take advantage of you. I already feel indebted to you for allowing me to stay here. A debt I can never repay, which makes me feel mighty uncomfortable.' Too scared to say more she turned away and plodded with an ungainly hitch from the room, carrying the mug of tea, pushing her legs to move faster than she thought they were capable of because all of a sudden a wave of self-consciousness settled into her gut, shoving her hunger away. Why was she so unsure of herself?

* * *

Paul watched after her, unable to believe her words. He had yet to meet a woman who didn't take advantage of a man in some form or another. Hell, he had been suckered in, masticated into mush, rolled into a hard ball and spat out again – twice now although the second time was much worse than the first. And if he wasn't careful, it was going to happen again. He was waiting to see the results of last night's foolishness even though, he had to admit, he had enjoyed the evening, too much.

The look on Abby's face had been worth the effort of setting up the scene and the entire shebang had given him a great deal of plea-sure. They had chatted without the usual distrust and angry tirades. There had been no animosity, no sarcastic rejoinders, no sad faces and no defiance. Abby looked so damn beautiful when she smiled and it had tugged at his heart to see the happy glow which had radiated from her face the entire time. He figured there hadn't been many occasions over the past seven months when she had smiled like she had last night. But this morning she looked wary. Hell, he felt more than wary. Would she see last night as the beginnings of something more, something he could never give. He had given his heart before and it had been wrenched apart and torn to shreds. He couldn't afford to let a similar thing happen again.

With a regretful sigh, he continued on his way outside and settled into the cushioned cane lounge he had moved from the back lawn and set at an angle across the corner of the veranda where he could enjoy the sounds and sights of the ocean as well as the surrounding bushland without being burned to a crisp. In the background he could hear Abby's muffled voice talking to an unknown person who he hoped could solve whatever problem it was she had. She was too far away for him to be able to make out any words so he didn't bother to move further down the veranda. He wasn't into eavesdropping.

As he settled back in the lounge he allowed his eyelids to cover eyeballs while his brain fought with his heart over the dilemma of Abby who still reminded him of an angel every time he caught sight of her. At the moment, his heart was winning the argument but his brain fought back to find hundreds of reasons why it should win.

He was in the process of convincing himself any kind of a relationship was not on the cards because he had to return to his rebuilding project when clear, angry words broke his reverie. Startled, he glanced around in search of Abby but realised she was still on the phone, which meant she had opened the office window.

'How do you expect me to get to your office? I sure as hell can't walk to the city. I can't even manage to get as far as the local town two kilometres away.' There was a pause while he assumed the other party spoke. 'Oh, sure, with the grand total of three dollars and forty-five cents to my name, how do you propose I pay for this taxi or public transport? They won't even let me on the bus if I can't pay for the ticket.'

After another long pause Paul heard a distinct sniffle. Abby was crying. Damn to whoever she was talking. For the first time he had seen her happy and now she was in the depths of despair. He hated himself for having listened in but he had to do something to help. He rose from the lounge and snuck towards the office window where he knew the phone usually sat on the desk under the window.

A quick glance in the open window caused his heart to tumble-turn. Abby sat in the office chair with her back to him. One hand held a scrunched-up tissue against the side of her face while the other had the receiver held against her ear. After watching her scrub at her eyes with the shredded remnants of the tissue he saw her toss the ball into the bin. In an instant she yanked a clean one from the box on the end of his desk. She rubbed at her face and blew her nose, rendering the tissue as useless as its predecessor.

He reached into the window, grabbed the receiver and held it against his ear. 'This is Paul Sanders, to whom am I speaking?'

'John Simpson.'

'And how do you know Abby?'

'I deal with invalid pensions. This has nothing to do with you, where is Miss Sharpe.'

Paul stared at the wretched but sad face of Miss Sharpe. She stood facing him with her hands on her hips, staring at him with her mouth agape and a flood of tears pouring down her face. It alarmed him to see the pallid colour of her cheeks and the deep lines of tension between her eyes. The exact opposite to what she looked like less than fifteen minutes ago. Barbed wire wrapped around his heart, which sent a message to his brain to get lost.

'Right at this very instant, Abigail Sharpe is in no fit state to be taking bullshit from you or anyone else. I have no idea what you want from her but from the little I overheard and the little snippets I know about Abby, I presume you have cut off her pension. Am I correct in my assumption?'

'Yes, but I am not at liberty to discuss this case with anyone other than Miss Sharpe.'

'Well you had better find the liberty because Miss Sharpe is in a state of total distress and I fear for her wellbeing right now. She looks as though she is about to collapse, is quite ill and in a great deal of physical pain. So either you tell me what it is you want or I will contact my lawyer.'

'There's no need for such behaviour Mr... err ...'

'Sanders. And there is every need. So exactly what do you want?'

'Miss Sharpe is supposed to come to this office for her monthly review. She failed to show so we assumed she had no further need of financial assistance.'

'And you cut off her only means of financial support without notification or without giving her an opportunity to explain her difficulties.'

'She knew the terms of her pension.'

'So exactly what do you want Miss Sharpe to do?'

'Come to our office for an interview.'

'How do you expect her to get there? She has no car and is physically incapable of driving one. You have cut off her only source of income, which means she is broke to the extent she couldn't even buy a simple sandwich or cup of coffee for her lunch. This in turn means, as she has already pointed out to you, she can't afford any kind of fare for transport and sure as hell can't walk more than a hundred metres without becoming a physical wreck. She tried the walking trick yesterday and it almost killed her. I had to rescue her when she turned into an immobile statue stuck on a fence, incapable of taking another step.'

'So you can bring her into the city.'

'Excuse me? Abby is not my responsibility. She happens to be living in my house at the moment because you have refused her a pension, which means she has no-where to live since she has no financial means to pay rent. It's the flaming government negligence which put her into this position to start with and now you are deny-ing her assistance because of a bureaucratic stuff-up. Give me a time next week when I can have her in your office.'

During the long pause, Paul stared back at the fuming Abby and held his other hand over the phone, which Abby was doing her best to wrestle away so, he presumed, she could hang up.

'Thursday at nine-thirty,' came the angry voice in his ear.

'We will be there. By the way, Abby will have a lawyer with her. Good day.' Paul slammed down the receiver, glanced up and grinned at Abby.

'How dare you?' she spluttered.

'Very easy. He was taking you for a ride, taking advantage of your weakened state.'

'I can fight my own battles.' Abby turned around and stormed from the office, even though her ability to storm consisted of nothing more than a slow waddle and crump.

Paul sped around the veranda, through the house and managed to catch Abby before she could hide away in her room. 'I will drive you to the city on Thursday and together will get this mess sorted out. I trust you know the address since I was too angry with the little upstart to think of asking him for it.'

A weak smile turned up the corner of her mouth. 'I know the address. Grace and I have spent numerous hours sitting in his waiting room. By the way, I don't have a lawyer and couldn't afford one in any case and shouldn't you be going to work during the week?'

'I'm on leave and I can get you a lawyer who does pro bono work for people in financial difficulty. He works in the city and is a good friend. Or at least he was until you insulted his wife yesterday.' He smiled at Abby's indrawn breath and reddening cheeks. 'I will explain the whole situation to him today so he can study the relevant legislation.'

'Why are you doing this?'

'Because, little Miss Independence, even though you are going to deny it until kingdom come and hell forgets it is supposed to be burning, you need help. None of this is of your doing. I am almost certain this is what the disability pension is for – to assist people who are incapacitated and are unable to earn. In the meantime, I can give you any money you need to get you by.'

'No way, I will never accept your money.'

Paul sighed but confusion reigned at her statement since he was unable to believe the verity of her statement. Experience told him women had no compunction in using his money. Being free with his wallet or more like his credit card, was the usual standard and when he hinted at tightening those purse strings he had been well and truly screwed. 'Would you accept a loan to tide you over? You can't survive on less than four dollars for another five days.'

'How long were you eavesdropping?'

'I didn't eavesdrop. You opened the window, your voice travelled. I couldn't help but overhear, especially since you were virtually yelling at the jerk, something he deserved. Now about the loan.'

There was a long pause during which the flitting facial expressions told Paul she was mulling things over in her mind. Fascinated, Paul watched the changing expressions wash over her face. Her eyes closed on a deep sigh, opened again, skittered over his shoulder as though she was afraid to look at him. 'Okay, but I will only ask if I am desperate for something and I want it written down as a formal I.O.U. with us both signing the paper.'

'You don't have to be so formal. I trust you.'

'No paper, no loan.' There was a pause accompanied by a mystified look on her face. 'Why are you doing this all of a sudden?'

To answer, Paul grasped her shoulders, turned her into the bedroom and led her to stand in front of the floor length mirror set into one of the wardrobe doors. 'Take a good look. Your face is pale, tense and quite frankly you look ghastly. A far cry from the woman I dined with last night when you looked carefree, happy and beautiful. You laughed all night. There was no anger and the continual frown of worry had disappeared. I believe I saw the real Abigail Sharpe for the first-time last night. You were so happy you slept all night without the torment of terrible memories.' He stopped at the look of wonderment on Abby's face.

'I did, didn't I? I can't believe it. The first time I have been able to sleep through without sedatives.' She turned to Paul, her brilliant smile causing his heart to make another tumble-turn in his chest.

'I'm getting better.' She was so excited she flung her arms around his neck and gave him a hug.

Paul groaned as he hugged her back. This was not such a good idea. He had avoided physical contact as much as he could because he knew he would feel exactly as her touch made him feel. He wanted her again. Wanted her as she was the first night – in his bed with both of them naked. He wanted to feel her hands explore the contours of his body, wanted to do the same to her. It took a monumental effort to force his brain to reason. He pulled from the embrace and hurried towards the door, desperate to get away. As he dared to pause in the doorway, he twisted his head. 'We can sign an I.O.U. if you insist and I will be out for lunch. There are plenty of leftovers. Feel free to use them up.'

* * *

Stunned at the sudden change, Abby stared after him and still stood in the same spot when she heard Paul's car drive away less than five minutes later. Why the sudden about turn? What had she done or said?

Ten

At the *brnng* of the phone, Abby glanced at the kitchen clock and settled her mug on the sink. It was eight-thirty which meant it would be Grace for her daily up-date on Abby's wellbeing. Abby smiled as she took utmost care to turn around so she wouldn't stumble. Today, her hip hurt so she could do nothing more than limp to the phone. Grace was the highlight of each day. The only person in the world who actually cared about Abby's well-being. Her one and only friend. Without her support, Abby was certain she would have given up months ago even though sometimes she had been so despondent and angry, she had hurled harsh words at Grace – more times than she wanted to recall. Grace had never said a word in retaliation but had always smiled her sweet smile and encouraged Abby to keep on going – one step at a time.

After a brief conversation, Abby stuck her head around the back door but had to stretch the curled cord to its full length. 'Paul?'

Settled back in the cane lounge with his head stuck in a newspaper, he mumbled something, which Abby couldn't quite make out but took it as an acknowledgement. It was the first time she had seen Paul since he had walked out of the house yesterday morning. 'Your mother has asked us to dinner tonight. Are you free?'

'What time?' The reply was muffled by the open pages without any movement of his head.

Abby asked Grace the details and turned back to Paul with the receiver held in the air. 'Six-thirty. Can I tell her we'll be there?'

'Sure thing. I'll leave an hour before.' He folded the paper in half, dropped it on the couch, stepped from the veranda and headed towards the beach.

A long sigh of regret hissed from Abby's throat as she watched his back disappear and her old feelings of Paul not liking her, re-surfaced. A distant yell brought her back to reality. She replaced the receiver against her ear to complete her conversation with Grace.

'How are you getting on with Paul?' asked Grace.

Abby thought about how to answer. 'Fine, Grace. He keeps him-self busy. I think he catches up with all of his friends for he's hardly ever here.' What else could she say. She didn't have a clue. 'You have no idea how much I am looking forward to dinner tonight. It feels like forever since I have been out for a meal. See you tonight.' As she hung up she recalled the candlelight dinner and wondered where the wonderful caring Paul had gone to. What did she do wrong for him to retreat back into ignoring her presence?

After another day of keeping herself company during her daily walks to the beach and back, interspersed with lengthy rest periods, Abby showered early so she had adequate time to dress. After apply-ing a blush of highlighter to her cheeks and a careful layer of coral lipstick to match the top she wore, Abby picked up her brush in an attempt to mould her flyaway gold waves into something which looked like a decent hairdo – an impossible task. Since her long locks were lopped off during the rescue, her unruly curls had a bad habit of always looking unkempt. 'No amount of conditioner controls this flipping hair,' she groused before sending a prayer skywards, begging for the day her hair was long enough to tie back.

The sound of footsteps passed her closed door. She needed to hurry but the word was no longer in her vocabulary and it would still be a long time before she could actually do anything in any form of haste. When the footsteps continued on to the front entryway and she heard the front door open, Abby grabbed her small bag and hobbled to the corner to pick up her crutches but hesitated and left them there when she figured the steps she would need to take tonight would be miniscule. Not tonight. She would manage without them.

She was only halfway across the lounge when she heard Paul's car engine rev. Assuming he would wait for her outside the garage door, she detoured from her route towards the back door and headed for the front door, cursing under her breath at the thought of having to negotiate the front steps. At the crunch of tyres running over the fine gravel stones of the driveway, Abby hurried the only way she could – with an increase in her waddle and crump. It took too long to undo the wretched deadlock, pull the door open and step onto the veranda only to see Paul pull away after having reversed onto the road.

Stunned, Abby limped to the top of the steps, her eyes glued to the rapidly diminishing dark blue metallic boot. 'What the devil is going on?' Abby muttered. 'Paul?' she yelled as she waved one hand in the air to catch his attention but he kept driving. Maybe he's gone to town to purchase some wine, she thought. But there were three chilled bottles in the refrigerator and dozens in the long wine rack next to the sound system. Besides town was on the way to Grace's place. Surely he wasn't playing a practical joke.

Unable to believe what had happened, Abby plonked into a white painted cane chair set against the wall of the veranda with tears of disappointment washing across her eyes but she forced them back. She didn't do tears any longer. 'No tears, no tears, no tears,' she chanted under her breath, while thoughts pummelled through her mind. What sort of game was he playing? He knew the invitation was for them both. Thinking hard, she recalled the conversation earlier in the morning. She definitely said *us*. She remembered asking if she could tell Grace if *we* would be there, recalled saying they were *both* invited. He hadn't said otherwise. He must be coming back to get her.

After thirty minutes of waiting with frustration levels on par with a boiling kettle, it didn't take genius status to know Paul wasn't coming back. The pain in her heart at his deliberate snub, stabbed like shards of razor-sharp glass. How could he be so mean? If he didn't want her to go with him, he could have at least had the decency to tell her instead of letting her build up the excitement of actually going out somewhere for the first time since forever before he drove off without her. For heaven's sake, he heard the shower running, he acknowledged when she said the bathroom was free.

Deep disappointment turned to utter devastation, followed by angry frustration when she went to open the door only to find it wouldn't budge. Damn it, no key. Since she assumed Paul would use the key on his key ring to let them in on their return she had left her key on the hall table which was set against the wall less than a metre inside the damn door. She kicked it and almost tumbled over. A grab at the door-knob saved an ignominious tumble. Not that she damn well cared if she fell and undid months of surgery. It would serve Paul right to find her dying on his front doorstep.

Her sucked in breath hissed through gnashed teeth before she began to negotiate the steps. Too frustrated to take the time she resorted to her backside shuffle to reach the bottom without losing her balance. She checked each window along the front and one end of the house as she made her way around to the back veranda. No amount of tugging or jiggling moved the door from its frame. The back door was as secure as a bank vault. She muttered a four-letter oath in Paul's direction for having the sense to lock the damn thing on his way out. All of the windows were locked, because knowing they would be away for several hours, she was the bunny who had gone around the house to check every single damn one, except for the large window in Paul's room. No way had she ever been game to step foot in his room again.

A huge wodge of something really uncomfortable stuck in her throat as she swung her body around and waddled along the veranda. After joggling the frame around the pane of glass she hit it with a closed fist when it didn't move. 'Damn you to hell and back,' she yelled at the top of her voice. 'I hate you, Paul Sanders!'

She pressed her fingers to her eyes to prevent a severe leakage. 'I will not cry. You, Paul Sanders, are not worth the effort. You don't deserve my tears.' It was a struggle but Abby managed to reclaim control over tear ducts which threatened to renew the forty-day flood. To add to her misery the thick lump of disappointment lodged in her throat made it painful to swallow while a vice-like clamp around her heart squeezed the life out of her at the hurt as she hitched and swayed back to the cane chair where she slumped down into the cushioned seat. She dropped her head into spread out fingers and rested her elbows on her knees.

* * *

After listening to his favourite jazz CD while he drove, Paul felt more relaxed than he had since arriving home. Apart from the entire day's catch up sleep he had over the first twenty-four hours it had been almost impossible to relax enough to maintain the deep sleep he needed to rest. His nerves were always on edge with his subconscious on alert for the next bomb to explode. Even the slightest moan from Abby in the room opposite and he was wide awake, listening, waiting in silence before creeping to her side to watch her. He often ran his fingers across her brow or down the side of her face to calm her in her sleep but left her side when he felt sure her nightmare was over and she settled back to a restive slumber.

He pulled into his mother's drive and alighted, clicking the remote control to lock the car as he headed towards the front door. He knocked. While waiting, he turned to absorb the familiarity of his childhood neighbourhood. Even though he was an only child there had been plenty of friends and a happy upbringing. The brick house next door had been occupied by an elderly couple who kept to themselves but were always friendly and kind to him. Across the road had been a houseful of girls, who he avoided as a youngster for girls were taboo. His attitude changed when teenage hormones kicked in but the family moved away about the same time. Two houses down to the left had been a home he practically lived in with his best friend, Brett. If he wasn't staying over with Brett, it was the other way around. Boy, they had got up to mischief, most of it harmless but there had been more than one incident which had overstepped the boundary. Thank goodness his parents never found out.

At the click of the key in the lock, he spun back around and leant forwards to place a kiss on his mother's cheek. 'Hi, Mum. It's good to see you.' He stepped past her, held the door open and waited for her to move into the room but instead, she stepped outside and searched the front yard with her eyes.

'What have you done with Abby?' she asked with her back to him.

'Pardon?'

She turned to face him. 'I said, where is Abby?'

'Abby?'

'Yes, Abby.' Grace's finger jabbed him in the chest, the same way it had when he had stepped over the boundary as a kid. 'You know - the woman living in your house: the one who you were supposed to bring to dinner tonight. Where is she?'

'Oh, hell.' Paul's hand went to his head where his fingers grubbed through his hair in tense frustration. 'She didn't say anything.'

'Oh, yes she did. I heard her ask you. She mentioned you were both invited. I distinctly remember her saying, "Can I tell her *we* will be there?" I cannot, for the life of me, believe you would come without her. Surely she showered and dressed. She would have rung me if she changed her mind.'

Nausea rose as Paul paced into the front room. He hadn't really been giving Abby his full attention when she mentioned the phone call. Abby had showered before him. He had waited until he heard her go to her room. He didn't even think about what she was doing or why she had showered earlier than normal. How could he be so obtuse? Hell, she was going to be angry. No, angry was certainly not the right word.

'I'd better ring her. Damn, damn, damn. It would take me over two hours to go back to get her. Your dinner will be ruined and I doubt Abby will agree to come now, if she speaks to me at all. Which I doubt.' His pacing ceased as he turned to face his mother. 'Help me out here, what can I do?'

'Not my mistake, Paul. I can't believe my son would even think of leaving a woman behind, especially Abby.' He shuddered when she reached up on her tiptoes so she could glare into his face. Grace looked fierce. 'Ever heard of humble pie? I know from experience how strong-willed Abby can be. You,' she stabbed again, 'are going to need a giant-sized piece. You had better phone her and start apologising now.' As Paul headed towards the phone, she called after him. 'If I were her, I would hang up on you with a definite slamming down of the receiver.'

'If I were her, I would do the same. The thought doesn't make me feel any better.' He dialled, waited, jerked to attention when he heard a click. He didn't wait but began speaking until he heard his own voice on the recorded message. With lips drawn in a tight line, he waited until the message ended. 'Abby, pick up please. I'm sorry. I didn't realise you were coming.' He paused but with still no answer, he hissed in a long breath through clenched teeth. The excuse he spouted was so lame. 'Abby, I'm really sorry. I messed up big time. Please forgive me.' The beeps told him he had run out of tape. When he dialled again he begged Abby to pick up the phone. She had to be there. After the fourth message he replaced the receiver with a wodge of lead settled in his gut.

'She won't pick up.' Disgusted with himself, he spun around to face his mother who didn't look in the least bit pleased. Sanderson, you are in big trouble.

'I would refuse to pick up too. Can you blame her?'

'No. Hell, how am I going to apologise?'

'Could I suggest you take her out somewhere really glamorous? Buy her flowers, a really nice dinner out. The poor girl has no social life at all. She has been stuck in a hospital bed for over seven months. No meals out, no dates, no outings, no friends to bring cheer to her life, nothing but hospital wards, surgery after surgery, emotional turmoil and pain. And there has been a great deal of agonising pain. This is why I invited the pair of you. To give her a pleasant night out. I never thought I would say this to you, Paul, but for the first time ever I am disappointed in you.'

A long groan rumbled from deep in Paul's chest. 'You know how to rub it in, don't you? Maybe I should return home.'

'I figure we should eat first, even though I doubt I'm going to enjoy this meal.' Grace stalked into the kitchen and began serving up with the abnormal clatter of dishes and pans telling Paul of her displeasure in her son.

* * *

Abby heard the phone ring. The muffled but clear messages unleashed a storm of verbal abuse towards Paul, which, in turn, caused her long held-back misery to pour out in a deluge of hot salty tears. By the time she had retreated back to the cane lounge on the back veranda, a sense of devastation had set in, with a hollow empty ache inside her chest. Overwhelming loneliness invaded every pore of her body. In the ensuing hours, she cried for her dead parents, cried for the pain she had endured, cried for the train accident, cried for everything she had lost, cried for the so-called friends who had drifted away, cried for the man who treated her with such cold disdain, cried to release all the anger, frustration and despair she had bottled up since she had woken up in the critical ward of the hospital two days after the accident.

After she ran out of tears, she curled up in the foetal position on the lounge, not giving a damn about the gnawing night insects and increasing cold.

* * *

The meal he ate, Paul didn't enjoy. Too anxious to get home, he barely tasted the hurriedly swallowed mouthfuls of casseroled lamb with vegetables. 'Thanks for the meal, Mum, but I should get home.' One hand brushed through his hair on a long sigh. 'I'm not looking forward to this. Abby is going to be more than angry.'

'At a guess, knowing her as well as I do, I would use the word hurt, rather than angry.' Grace accompanied him to the door and held it open with a wry grin.

'Rub it in, why don't you?' Paul said. He didn't appreciate her laugh but he sure as hell deserved it.

As Paul drove home, he tested the speed limits to the extreme. Tension tightened everything inside him when he turned off the engine in the garage of the darkened house. He raced to the front door, shoved it open and ran to Abby's room without bothering to close the door behind him. The knots in his stomach tweaked to a painful level as he skidded to a halt outside her door. He sucked in a deep breath of courage before lifting his clenched fist to knock. When his knock went unanswered he turned the handle and dared to ease the door open, half expecting a hard object to come flying across the room, aimed for his head.

'Abby?' he called.

With still no response, he crept across the carpet and stood beside the bed. Even in the dim moonlight, he could see the bed had not been slept in and there was no Abby.

'Abby, where the hell are you?' Fear rose in his chest which further increased the tightness in his innards. What if she had been so angry, she left? Maybe she had gone into town. No, she wouldn't have made the distance and there had been no sign of her along the road. But it had been almost three hours since he left. He swore under his breath, spun around and strode towards the door, where he reached out to flick on the light switch. As his eyes focussed from the sudden bright light, he sensed the room was empty, but he searched every cupboard and corner. All her clothes were still in the wardrobe and the aluminium crutches stood against the wall in the corner. They glared at him. 'Damn it, Abby, where are you?'

A hot sting of adrenalin surged and kept on spurting while he searched the rest of the house, which was as empty and untouched as her room. In the kitchen he flung the refrigerator door open. It looked exactly the same as when he had replaced the carton of milk after making a cup of coffee before having his shower. The take-away remnants looked at the same levels, which meant Abby had eaten nothing. So far she hadn't asked him for the loan they had agreed on, therefore, logic told him she didn't have enough money for a taxi, plus she wouldn't have eaten in town for the same reason. She could have searched the house for any cash but all he had was in his wallet which sat, as always, in his jacket pocket. To make sure, he patted the leather of his jacket to feel the bulge. Besides, Abby would rather die than steal from him, he was now certain. She wouldn't even eat the food he had paid for when he filled the fridge but only ate from her own stash kept on a separate shelf.

With confusion and wild ideas of what ifs running on a roller coaster ride through his mind, he zipped up his jacket and raced out the still open front door, headed for the beach. If she had gone for a walk, he felt sure she wouldn't attempt the road in the dark again. Not after the really bad scare she had received last time. Abby knew her limits but drat the woman, she had a habit of testing those limits and when she was as angry as he figured she would be - well, there was no doubt she would push herself well over those limits.

Something more than fear ate away at his insides as he tore towards the beach with his eyes skittering sideways to search the darkness for the slightest unusual shadow or movement. She had to be here. He scrambled through low dunes covered in native coastal plants, searched behind clumps of bush and low trees before running back in the opposite direction along the beach. All the while, he sniffed the air for any trace of the soft floral fragrance of the perfume she always wore but could only make out salt from the spray and the distinctive aroma of pigface. With no sight, smell or a single sign of her he went the opposite way, searching every possible hiding place and those places she couldn't possibly fit to hide. Worry turned to panic as he made his way back towards the rear of the house, bending to look under bushes, twisting behind trees, even scouring the branches above which was ridiculous. Abby could barely walk let alone climb a tree.

Instead of opening the gate at the back fence, he vaulted over the low gate and headed for the back veranda, his eyes still flicking over and under every item whether it was animal, vegetable or mineral.

His breath hitched in his throat and his heart ceased beating when he spied the curled-up body on the lounge. 'Abby?' There was an unusual sensation of prickling eyelids and glaze of moisture across his eyeballs as he knelt on the dew dampened wood by the side of the lounge.

'Sweetheart,' he whispered as he reached out and laid his outstretched fingers on her arm. 'Oh, Abby, you're like an icicle.' Pulling his hand back, he dragged the jacket from his arms and wrapped it around her, covering as much of her body as he could. It alarmed him even more when she didn't stir. With the pads of two fingers he felt for the pulse in the hollow of her neck under her jaw. His held breath whooshed from his mouth when he felt the even rhythm. Horrified at himself, he eased his arms under her back and curled legs and lifted her against his chest. 'God, I'm so sorry, Abby.'

The words whispered against her ear as he carried her around the house to the front door, must have stirred her. She moaned, wriggled and snuggled against his chest, automatically seeking out the warmth from his body. His heart almost leapt from his chest at the feel of one arm snaking around his neck. Deep down, he knew he was sunk. No amount of arguing in his brain was going to convince his heart he hadn't fallen for her, but hell, he didn't need the complications of a relationship when he had another six months away. It was an iron-clad contract, unable to be broken.

Paul didn't stop until her reached her bedroom where the still blazing light stirred Abby from her sleep. He felt her agitation but didn't release his hold until he had settled her in the middle of the bed. When he looked at her face, pure hatred lasered from her hazel eyes. 'Abby, please forgive me. I am really sorry about tonight. I have no excuses apart from admitting I didn't give you my full attention this morning. I'll make it up to you.'

'Like hell you will. I hate you, Paul Sanders. You are nothing but a mean-spirited, selfish, cold-hearted pig. I really thought we were making headway the other night. I thought you were actually beginning to like me. But the next morning you treated me with the same cold disdain, ignoring me as though you can't stand the sight of me. What you did to me tonight has confirmed my feelings.'

'Abby, I don't blame you for feeling this way, what I did tonight was reprehensible and I would love to make it up to you. Can I take you out for a nice meal tomorrow night? Somewhere really special.'

Abby jerked upright. 'You have to be joking. Do you honestly think I would go out with a man who can't stand the sight of me, who only invites me out to assuage his guilty conscience? A pity date? Really? Do you think I am so stupid? Give me a break. I only accept invitations from people who actually care about me as a person, people who like me. Please leave.' To make a point, she tore his jacket from around her body and flung it at him. To highlight the point even more, she yanked her nightie from under the pillow and stumbled to the bathroom.

Unable to move, he stared after her, smarting from her words even though he deserved every single one of them and a whole heap more. By the puffy redness around her eyes and the dark half-moon bruises which had taken residence underneath, he figured there had been a long bout of tears and she hadn't been asleep long. Even though he felt like the scum of the earth for the deep hurt he had inflicted, her distress gave him hope. Tears meant she hurt inside. Hurt meant she cared which in turn had to mean she had feelings of some description. He could only pray those feelings slanted towards him in a positive sense. He snorted. Maybe they weren't right now. But he could prepare a meal for her even though there was every chance it would be hurled back at him, with no hesitation about a breakable plate being part of the missile. Instead he made two mugs of hot chocolate and left one on her bedside table before taking cover in his own bedroom since he wasn't game to face her again tonight. Yeah, he was the biggest coward to ever exist – and the biggest fool. The last thing she would want was to see him hovering around the house. Abby would do one of three things; tip the drink down the drain, drink it or leave it to go cold. Or maybe there was a fourth, more likely option. She would hunt him down and chuck the lot in his face, mug and all. He clicked the lock of his own door in position. The first time it had ever been used.

* * *

Abby left the hot chocolate she found, to go cold, tipping it down the kitchen sink when hunger pangs drove her from her bed in the early hours of the morning. There were leftovers but no way would she eat anything bought with tainted money. Instead she made a couple of slices of toast with a thick lather of honey and a mug of hot black tea, which she took back to the warmth of her bed, slamming her door when she heard Paul turn the handle of his door.

Eleven

As with most mornings, unable to sleep, Paul rose before the sky had even thought about turning pink. Trepidation was a major factor while he dragged on a pair of baggy shorts, T-shirt and running shoes over white socks. With no sign of Abby, he left the house for his usual morning run of five kilometres along the beach. The air was brisk with a sheen of moisture still kissing the blades of grass and dune plants. The air had a crisp salty tang, so much better than Afghani dust with an ever-present atmosphere of fear.

Running was the fitness regime he preferred, managing to fit in time each day but since he had returned home, the distances had been far greater than normal in an attempt to physically tire his body so he would sleep better. Great in theory but it hadn't worked so far in practise, he thought as he pushed harder and faster, desperate for physical pain to over-ride emotional angst caused by his own stupidity and an image of an ethereal angel which had a habit of invading his every thought: an angel who was always mad at him.

His golden-haired angel was nothing like any other woman he had either dated or met. She made no demands of him, was adamant in refusing any assistance and was almost apologetic whenever she spoke to him as though she was being intrusive by uttering a few simple words. Determined and feisty, along with gorgeous and kind-hearted were more names he added between Abigail and Sharpe. She had a temper – usually aimed at him but her soft-spoken anger had far more impact than someone who yelled. In fact, one look from those beautiful, expressive hazel eyes and Paul knew exactly what Abby was thinking.

Pulling his T-shirt over his head as he slowed near the rear gate, Paul used it to wipe the dripping sweat from his face, neck and chest. He flung the sweaty shirt over his shoulder as he stepped onto the back veranda but came to a grinding halt when he almost bumped into Abby, who was coming through the doorway with a mug of what he presumed was black tea, the steam rising in white wispy curls.

'Good morning, you are up early.' Unsure as to how Abby was going to react, he stilled, studied her dropped eyelids. She looked drawn with a definite sad tilt to her mouth. The sight twisted his heart. 'Abby, I barely slept last night, trying to figure out how I can eat enough humble pie to apologise to you. You were right to throw my invitation back at me. I admit I was grovelling for forgiveness. I wish I could take back last night and start all over again but I can't. All I can do is tell you how sorry I am and pray you can at least begin to forgive me.'

He took one step backwards when Abby lifted her eyes and glared at him, glinting golden green ice shards. She said nothing but stepped past him and headed for the cane lounge. The hurt in those hazel depths had his innards clench so hard he couldn't breathe.

Anguished at her obvious sadness, he strode after her and squatted on his haunches at her side. It was sheer idiocy but he reached out with one hand and laid it on her arm. A shudder wove its way across his shoulders at her wince. 'It cuts me to the core to know I hurt you so much. I don't mean to, but somehow I always manage to cause you more pain. What can I do to make things better between us?'

Her shoulders rose high on a sucked in breath but sank again as she blew out her cheeks. Ever so slowly she swept her eyelids apart, revealing a depth of sadness, which did a great job of shredding his innards into a trillion pieces.

'I don't understand you. You are a complete mystery. One minute I feel as though you care about me. The candlelight dinner was brilliant. You went out of your way to make it so special. You treated me with such kindness but in an instant it all changed so dramatically. The next morning was completely the opposite. I feel as though you can't bear to have me around. You stay away all day. If you see me, you turn away and head in the opposite direction. I feel like I am something disgusting you want to squash under the heel of your shoe. But when I have a nightmare you calm me with such tender caresses yet as a complete paradox you treat me with obvious disdain when I am awake.'

Paul jerked. 'You know I come into your room? You never said anything. I thought you were still asleep.'

'The nightmare always wakes me. I think I wake up because I might be too afraid to keep dreaming.'

'You didn't have a nightmare last night which makes it two nights in a row.' The wondrous smile which lit up her face, blew him away.

'I didn't, did I? Two nights, I can't believe it.' Her smile altered to a frown. 'How did you know I didn't have a nightmare?'

With his haunches beginning to ache, Paul hefted upwards and settled on the end of the couch next to Abby, making sure he didn't touch her. 'I don't sleep so well. I guess I suffer from the same type of flashbacks you have. It's almost impossible to get ugly visions from my subconscious.'

'Is this about the reason you came back early? You said there was some kind of incident.' As if afraid to look at him, she took regular sips from the mug held clasped in both hands while she kept her eyes focussed on the ground.

'Yes. There was a bomb blast outside a shop in Kabul. It happened only moments after I walked out through the shop doorway. I had only gone about ten metres along the footpath when there was an almighty explosion.' He paused at the sound of Abby's indrawn gasp. 'The concussion wave from the blast of a suicide bomber threw me across the other side of the road. How I wasn't injured from shrapnel is something I am still trying to figure out. It was a blooming miracle. Unfortunately, although it was fortunate for me, there was someone directly behind me who took the brunt of the blast. The young woman had no chance and died instantly from her massive injuries. Twenty people died from the blast. I received wave concussion. The sound waves ruptured an ear-drum and gave me a pounding headache for several days.'

'Oh, sounds so ghastly. Are you a soldier?'

'No, an engineer. I'm overseeing a rebuilding project: a new hospital and school. I helped design them and am on-site to ensure structural specifications are met. It's not an easy job for decent materials are hard to get and experienced labourers who know what they are doing are scarce. So many young men have become soldiers, so many have been killed or maimed. War is not pretty.' He paused, wondering if he should tell her the rest of the story. Her story was far more gruesome and it worried him in case relating his details would bring back bad memories for her. 'Do you know what pink mist is?'

Abby squirmed in the lounge next to him as a mewling sound escaped her lips. 'Yes, I recall reading about it. Isn't it what they call the blown apart flesh, bones and blood of a human?'

'Yes, I was covered in it from the suicide bomber and those around him. No matter how much I scrub and clean my body, I can't get rid of the crawling sensation. It's one of the reasons I take off by myself. I go for long drives, swims in the ocean or run until the sweat washes the creepy itch from my pores. There is another reason.' He twisted his head to glance at her, wrapped the crook of one finger around her chin to force her hidden face around until their eyes met. 'It isn't that I don't like you. In fact it's quite the opposite, I like you too much.' At the stunned look on Abby's face, Paul stood before hurtling along the veranda to drown his hot, desiring flesh under a long cold shower. He was in so much trouble.

* * *

With her cheeks an inferno, Abby stared at the empty doorway Paul had fled through. An incredible sensation of tingling warmth radiated out from her clenched womb to the end of her extremities. It took a while before her brain cells aligned and began to function with a whole heap of questions beginning to formulate. Something didn't make sense and she needed explanations. Determined to get answers now Paul was actually talking to her, she rose from the lounge and moved to a position outside his bedroom door. There was no way she was going to allow Paul to escape this time.

When the bathroom door opened and Paul saw her, he hesitated. His shoulders rose but sank on a long sucked in breath. 'You need the bathroom?'

It was obvious his words were an attempt to divert her from saying what as on her mind but she was determined to have it out. She straightened. 'No, I need an explanation.'

Another sigh escaped Paul's lips. 'An explanation for what?' His attempt to step past her was met with her moving her body to stand in front of him with her arms reached out sideways and a hand pressed on each wall.

'I'm trying to figure out why you have such a desire to escape from my presence if you... um... like me. And how can you like someone too much? You either like them or you don't.'

A loud groan rumbled from Paul's chest. 'Do we have to talk about this now?' His step to one side was mirrored by Abby, but at the same time she moved closer. So close, she felt the warmth emanate from his body but she didn't touch him. There was no need to touch him.

'Yes, now. I am a little tired of this cat and mouse game, of monosyllabic answers and innuendos without adequate explanations. This is your house and if my presence upsets you so much, I will leave. I know I shouldn't be here. I understand I am an unwelcome intruder.'

Alarm spread across his face. 'I don't want you to leave.'

'Then talk to me. It was you who insisted we didn't beat around the bush after... well you know... the first disastrous night. So why can't we be upfront about things now? As you pointed out, we are both adults.'

Amusement hovered around Paul's mouth. 'Disastrous is not the word I would use. Sensual or erotic would be more apt.' The smile on his face widened at Abby's quick glance and rising heat turning her neck and cheeks into an inferno. 'I love the way you blush with such ease.' This comment instigated a poke to his ribs before Abby spun around, wavered to find her balance and headed towards the family room.

When she heard Paul's footsteps follow, a smile crept from the corners of her mouth. She wasn't sure he would follow. Normally he would have locked himself away in his bedroom or taken off in his car. When she reached the middle of the room, she paused for a second before spinning around to face him with her hands on her hips. It was hard to make out the look on his face apart from hesitant as he also stopped.

'You want my last ounce of blood don't you?' Paul asked.

'No, all I want is to understand you and your actions.'

Paul began pacing around the room, over to the window, spin around, back towards her where he caught her eye. 'Okay. I accepted the job in Afghanistan to escape a rather unpleasant relationship with a woman who... well... took me for a ride. I was foolish enough to think she wanted me for the person I am, to think she loved me the same as I felt about her. Right up until the time I asked her to marry me, she was gentle, loving, caring, fun. In fact she was everything I wanted in a wife. The minute she had a ring on her finger, she changed. I guess you could say she showed her true colours. I am fairly well off financially. Dad left me a substantial inheritance when he died a year ago; money which I invested. It took me a while to realise Jasmine only agreed to my proposal so she could make use of my money. When we met, she inferred she was from wealthy stock but I've since discovered her claims to be baseless. It was a ploy to make me think she wasn't a cheap gold-digger. After we became engaged I started to receive substantial bills for over-the-top expensive clothes, shoes, knick-knacks and a wide variety of goods. When I confronted her she insisted she needed these things to keep up appearances as befitting my status as a senior engineer within my company. Surely, as my wife she was entitled to these things. When I pointed out we were not yet married and refused to pay her bills after suggesting she should use her own money, she wasn't impressed. A strew of unpleasant and very unladylike words were tossed at me amongst other things. It was a battle but I managed to get her to admit to lying to me about her background. Essentially, she was broke and saw me as a source of income. I ended the engagement and sent her packing along with a pile of unpaid bills.'

'And you think I am like Jasmine?' The accusing tone of Abby's voice had Paul cease his pacing. 'You think I came to stay here to take advantage of you?' Her voice rose. 'Well, thank you very much. You don't know the first thing about me yet you jump to conclusions and assume every woman is exactly the same as Jasmine.' Abby turned around and headed for her bedroom. 'I would appreciate it if you could drive me into town. I'm leaving.'

'Abby, no!' He raced after her, grasped her arm and stepped in front of her. 'I don't think you are the same. It's... hell... I guess I'm too afraid to allow another woman into my heart. This is what I meant when I said I liked you too much. You keep tugging at my heartstrings and I try my hardest to not let it happen. I have another six-month stint away. My head keeps telling me it would be foolish to allow my heart free rein.'

A funny quivering sensation had Abby rooted to the spot as she tried to make sense of what Paul was saying. 'You like me so much?'

He chucked her under the chin and tugged her face up so he could look her in the eyes. 'Yes, I do but I'm fighting it.'

'Why?'

'I've got two and a half weeks before I have to leave again. I have a contract – an iron-clad contract, which I can't break. A great deal can happen in six months while I am away, especially in a place like Afghanistan. Despite hostilities now nowhere near as bad as they were during the height of the war, things are still unstable. I came this close to being blown to smithereens by an insurgent.' He lifted two touching fingers in the air. 'Life is usually fairly safe where I work but there are no guarantees: especially now ISIS is a problem and the Taliban may be less of a problem but they haven't gone away. They have only gone underground, emerging when you least expect it. How the suicide bomber managed to get through the lines of security is a mystery but it happened and can happen again. I would like nothing better than to get to know more about you, see if we can build a relationship but the timing as well as circumstances are all wrong. The progress you have made in the short time you have been here has been amazing. In six months' time you will have a new life, new friends maybe even a relationship with some lucky man.'

A snort of derision escaped Abby's lips. 'Fat chance of that ever happening.'

'What do you mean?'

'Take a good look, Paul. I am virtually a cripple. I walk funny and always will. I have ugly scars up my legs and across my lower body. No man is ever going to appreciate my body or accept my crazy waddle. I can no longer play sport, can't dance; I can barely walk and certainly not any distance. I don't have a career or even a job until I get strong enough to train for a new career. To top it all off and make myself even more of a bad choice, I am flat broke and have nowhere to live. I've got a big fat nothing to offer to any man. So who would be stupid enough to want me?' To escape, Abby waddled across the room, into the kitchen where she busied herself with filling the kettle and pulling out coffee, milk and mugs, the clatter, rattles, bangs and thumps indicating her angst.

'I would want you.' The whisper came from close behind her; so close she felt the warmth of his breath fan against her hair.

Not game to turn around, Abby kept fiddling with things on the bench. 'Which would put me in the same category as Jasmine. Taking advantage of you, something I could never do. I have to regain my independence. At the moment I don't have clue how I can go about it, but I will manage it somehow but only when I have enough physical strength to actually do anything.' She paused. 'Until I can gain better mobility I can't even think of having a relationship with anyone. So you are safe from me becoming too involved with you.' Her voice dropped. 'All I want is a civilised friendship for the time you are here. Do you have any idea how lonely my life is now and has been since the accident? I have no friends, no family, no-one other than Grace to talk to and she is going on an extended vacation with friends soon. I can't even get into town to go to the library, or chat on a park bench with a complete stranger. Even the homeless guy in a back alley would be welcome in my world right now.'

She heard his laboured breathing and could sense him cogitating but she was too afraid to move. With his body still right behind her, she was trapped. The kettle boiled so she poured water into the two mugs. 'Can you please pass me the milk?'

'What? Oh, sure.' He stepped across the room and pulled the fridge door open. After handing her the milk, he waited until she finished stirring both mugs. He replaced the milk and lifted the mugs from the bench. 'Come and sit at the table.' When she hesitated, he placed both mugs on the table, returned to Abby and grasped her hand before leading her to a chair he pulled out. He waited until she sat before dropping into the chair next to her. 'Can I make a suggestion?'

'I guess so.' For something to do, she wrapped her hands around the mug but kept her eyes averted from Paul's face, too afraid of what she would see. Pity would devastate her. All she wanted was a friend and someone to ease this soul-sapping loneliness.

'Why don't we see if we can maintain a friendship for the remainder of my time here. Keep things as they are.'

'Shouldn't be too hard since you are never here and when you are, you keep your distance.' A wry grin broke out on her face as she raised her eyes to peek at him.

He smiled back. 'This will change. Let me help you out a bit more; do things together, have meals with you. It has been pretty damn lonely eating out at various eateries by myself. Maybe we could start by taking a small picnic down to the beach.'

'Sounds good.' Everything inside her sparkled to life at the suggestion.

Twelve

The continuous loud scream woke Paul in an instant. He shot upright, shook his head to clear away the cobwebs of the deep sleep from which he had woken. On alert, he swung his legs over the side onto the floor. 'Abby?' he called as he dragged on a pair of shorts.

'No, no, Daddy, no!' There was nothing silent about the distressing scream coming from the direction of Abby's room.

While still straightening his shorts, Paul flew across the carpet and swung around the doorframe before pounding across the polished floorboards of the hallway. Still skidding, he grabbed the doorframe of Abby's door to halt his slide and shoved the door open with one hand. The piercing screams hurt his healing eardrum as he fled across the carpet. 'Abby.'

As an answer, Abby continued to emit a high-pitched squeal.

Even in the darkness Paul could make out wild thrashing arms swinging in every direction. He jammed his finger on the tiny switch of the bedside light and flung his body onto the bed next to her, wrapped his arms around the flailing body as he drew her against his chest and murmured what he hoped were calming words into her ear.

'Daddy, no-o-o-o!' The mournful cry wrung his heart into a tight squeeze.

'Abby, wake up.' He released one hand to shake Abby by her shoulder. 'Wake up, Angel.' This time he yelled the words in an attempt to break her nightmare.

Her eyes flew open but she looked dazed. It took at least ten seconds before it was obvious Abby had become aware of her surroundings. Hot tears poured down flushed cheeks to blend with the bath of perspiration on her heated face.

At the look of fear which swept across her face, Paul released his hold and dropped onto his knees by the bedside, afraid she would see his presence on her bed as a threat. 'Abby, you were in the midst of another nightmare. Your screams scared the living daylights out of me.' While he spoke, the fingers of one hand brushed tendrils of damp curls away from her face.

'Oh, God, Paul, I remembered.' Her voice hitched in her throat. Wild eyes flashed around in fear.

'Remembered what?' he asked while attempting to keep his voice calm, but his still pounding heart made it difficult.

'The accident.' The two words whooshed out in a harsh whisper. 'Please hold me, I can't bear it.' The fingers which grabbed him around his neck in a vice-like grip trembled but managed to pull him so off-balance he landed across her body.

'Abby, easy, Angel.' He reached up, levered her gripped fingers apart to release their tight hold on his neck.

A whimper of terror muffled against his chest. 'Please don't leave me?'

'I won't leave you. I promise but we need to get a little more comfortable.' All of his senses felt tight as they pulled his organs out of place. He eased his body from where he was half on his knees and half-draped across the bed, with Abby anchoring him down. It took a monumental effort to free himself but at last he managed to clamber to his feet but still bent over with her arms still gripped like a vice around his neck. He managed to wriggle his arms under her knees and shoulders and hoisted her into the air. She wasn't heavy but he had difficulty negotiating the pair of them through the house to the sitting-room with her spasms of fear taking on a life of their own. For a moment he stood in the middle of the room, wondering which seat would be most appropriate; the single recliner-rocker or the sofa. At the sight of a folded blanket on the armrest of the sofa, he moved towards it. It was almost impossible to ease his body down with the distraught woman in his arms but he collapsed in the middle of the long seat and somehow managed to keep Abby in his arms and not hurt her injuries. Well, he didn't think he hurt her for there was no grunt of pain but maybe she was too distraught for it to register. She had never been this upset before.

Once he had wriggled to get comfortable he reached out with one arm and dragged the rug towards them, unfolding it with one hand bit by bit before he draped it over Abby's shivering body. There was no doubt she was terrified. 'Shh, Abby, you are safe. It was only a dream.'

A deluge of hot, salty tears dripped down his naked chest before he was able to calm her. When he felt the tense grip ease from his neck, he loosened his tight hold from her upper body and positioned his head so he could see her face. 'Tell me what you remembered.'

'I can't, it was too horrible.'

The fear in her eyes worried him. He had to do something, anything to ease her fear. He dared to lift one hand to sweep his fingers down both sides of her face to wipe the worst of the moisture away and try to calm her. 'As ghastly as it was, it is always better to talk these things out of your system instead of bottling them up. I felt the same way after the bomb blast until I was forced to chat to a counsellor before they would allow me to come home. Talking does help, believe me. Even me relating events to you, has helped me sleep better and the crawling sensation of filth has eased. Apart from the counsellor, you are the only other person I have so far said those things to. I haven't even told Mum about what I experienced but telling you has helped a great deal.'

'I don't know if I can. It was so awful.'

An indelicate snort from Abby caused Paul to smile as he lifted the corner of the cotton throw rug and dabbed the moisture from her face before holding it to her nose. 'Blow.'

'I can't, it's your rug.'

'Which can be tossed in the washing machine, now blow.' After wiping the remnants of distress from her face, Paul scrunched up the corner of the rug and tucked it under his thigh. 'Now tell me what you remembered.'

Her body quivered in his arms before she sucked in a couple of deep breaths and slowly blew out the air each time. 'The nightmare started the same as every other time. Each time I could only ever recall everything that happened during the actual accident. I always woke up when I lost consciousness.'

'And this time?' Knowing how important it was for her to get the whole scene out in the open, Paul forced his voice to remain low and soothing but his innards were not being so co-operative.

'This time I remembered waking up in the wreckage. The pain was – excruciating; so intense I knew my injuries were really serious. I tried to move but was pinned down and everything looked really weird. It took me a while to realise the carriage was upside down and I was lying on the roof. I could see the outside through shredded metal, like one of those old fashioned can openers had torn it apart. There were seats on top of me and when I tried to wriggle free, I couldn't. The undercarriage was hanging above me and part of the side had caved in and was holding everything on top of me. I could see two wheels still spinning in the air. They had torn through the floor. The smell...' Her eyes screwed tight as she sniffed again. 'The smell was awful. Smoke, melted metal, sparks and a sickly, sweet, metallic odour. I think it must have been blood. Lots of people must have lost control of their... you know... their bodily functions.'

By her actions it was obvious to Paul she felt embarrassed about giving him the details.

'It's a normal thing when people are terrified and also when they die. All their muscles relax. It happened to quite a few people in the bomb blast. It's not something people talk about but it is normal. What else could you see?'

'Mostly wreckage. My head was trapped and I couldn't move it more than a few centimetres. My hair was waist length and my pony tail got caught around pieces of metal. They had to cut it off to free me.'

'Pity, your hair is beautiful, like spun honey, but it will grow again.' As he spoke, he ran the fingers of one hand through her gold curls, loving the sensation of the silken threads. 'Go on.'

'The silence was eerie, scary. Even though I could hear the continuous hiss of water as it hit hot metal and the whirr of the wheels as they spun, there were no human sounds around me. It was really weird. I called to Mum and Dad.'

The catch in her breath as she paused, echoed his.

'There was no answer but I became aware of Mum still holding my right hand.' There was a long pause but Paul could feel Abby flex and stretch her right fingers, over and over again against his neck. Her voice was nothing more than a frightened whisper.

'Over the hours I was trapped, her hand grew colder and colder and colder; her fingers grew stiff and I couldn't release the hold. I wanted to because I knew she was dead but at the same time I didn't want to because I couldn't face losing her and I needed to hold on to the contact. Oh, Paul, she didn't deserve to die such a horrible death.'

Fresh tears flowed from her eyes as Paul tightened his hold. He pulled the already damp corner of the rug from under his leg and dabbed the tears away. 'Nobody deserves to die in such awful circumstances. But if your mum was dead right from the moment you woke up, she wouldn't have had any pain. She didn't suffer the same way you have. You need to remember she was happy at the time, happy to be on a holiday with you and your dad. She died happy, holding your hand and probably never felt any pain. Mum told me your parents were celebrating their wedding anniversary so you have to believe they were on top of the world when the accident happened. You were a close-knit family weren't you?' He couldn't see, but felt her mouth against his chest, move into a smile.

'Yes, we were extremely close. Mum and Dad loved each other very much.'

'And I imagine you want the same sort of marriage: a man who loves you deeply and who you love as much. Am I right?'

'How did you know?' Her head moved so she could see his face.

Paul smiled back at her. 'Because it's what I want as well, only I am looking for a special woman, not a man.' His attempt at humour paid off and he was on the receiving end of one her gorgeous, brilliant smiles, causing his pulse to hammer.

'What about your Dad?' The minute he asked, he regretted his words. Her smile vanished in an instant, replaced by a mournful wail. Her body tensed so much he felt for a moment she would snap apart.

'Oh, Paul, it was the worst moment of my life.'

There was a long silence during which Paul was too afraid to utter a single sound. What scared him the most was the way Abby didn't release any tears. Her eyes simply stared ahead as though she was in a trance but there was wave after wave of tiny tremors weaving down the entire length of her body.

'I called his name over and over again. I couldn't see or feel him until... until... the carriage moved with a ghastly groaning wrench and I thought the whole thing was going to collapse on me. When it moved, Dad's head... oh, God... it rolled right in front of my eyes. Only his head. His eyes stared right into mine. There was so much blood - but no body - only his head.'

Paul's arms clenched tight. His stomach lurched; his heart felt as though a vice had squeezed every millilitre of blood from the chambers. 'Sweetheart, I am so sorry. Nobody should have to see something so ghastly. No wonder your mind blanked this out. God, I'm sorry, Abby.'

One outstretched hand cradled her head against his shoulder as he planted a soft lingering kiss on her brow. Nothing he ever said or did would erase the gruesome sight from her memory. All of a sudden his own trauma seemed so insignificant and deep down he knew he had been released from his own torment, but at what a cost.

They sat clasped together, Abby unable to speak while Paul held her close to give her the human contact he felt sure she so desperately needed, to give her the time to absorb and grieve. He figured the worst of her nightmare was out but knew there was more. She had been trapped for twelve hours. It felt interminable before Abby moved again, but knowing she needed to get everything out, he waited until she began talking again and let her ramble.

'Time seemed to take forever but at the same time, it stood still. I have no idea how long it was before I heard someone call out. It could have been five minutes; it could have been three hours. I couldn't bear to open my eyes and am not sure if I slept. The pain in my body was unbearable but at the same time I felt numb.

The numbness was as excruciating as the pain. I know it doesn't make sense.'

'Yes it does. You were in shock; probably severe shock.'

'When I heard someone call, people from other carriages called back. Some yelled, some were panicked and some moaned or cried. I didn't hear anyone from my carriage respond – only me.'

'Mum told me you were the only survivor in your particular carriage.'

'Yes, but at the time I didn't know. They told me later. There was a man, a paramedic. He was so brave, so amazing. He crawled through the wreckage and stayed with me the whole time it took for them to cut me free despite the danger to his own life. They had to get cranes in to lift the undercarriage away in case it fell in on me. It seemed to take forever.' She dragged her left hand from Paul's neck and flexed it in front of her face. 'Whenever he wasn't treating me, he held my hand. You don't have any idea how wonderful such a simple touch felt.'

Paul eased the hand which had been running circles around her back, and grasped her left hand, allowing his thumb to run the same circles inside her warm palm. Their eyes held. Abby released a weak smile. 'He talked to me, put a catheter into my arm to give me fluids. He treated what injuries he could reach and was able to stop the bleeding by squeezing his hand into crevices to apply pressure pads to my wounds. He covered Dad's head with a blanket until they could move him away so I didn't have to look at his staring glassy eyes and all the while he talked to me about anything and everything. His family, his job, his pastimes. We talked about films we had seen and books we had read, about my job, about everything. He never let up. Even when it became life or death dangerous for him when the jaws-of-life cut through the metal, he stayed, he talked, he calmed me, he held my hand. He was a saint.' Abby paused.

'I think I would like to meet him again, to thank him. He came to the hospital and brought me flowers but at the time I had no memory of him or what he did. Do you think it is possible to track him down?'

'I'm sure of it. Would you like me to start looking?'

'Please, I would appreciate it so much and I want to buy him a thank you present. What would you suggest?'

A whole range of ideas went through his head while Paul thought. 'Well, if it were me, I guess the best gift would be to see you recovered. So why don't we get a photo done of you standing without the crutches. I think a photo would have more meaning than some expensive trinket.'

'You think so?'

The feel of her hand holding the side of his face as she stared at him, caused his breath to hitch in his throat. He had a desperate urge to kiss her until her pain went away. Instead he pulled his head back a fraction. 'It would mean the most to me if I had been in the same position. To know my efforts in comforting you had paid off would be more than adequate thanks.'

'You really are a nice person aren't you?'

Unable to respond to the unexpected compliment, Paul felt the heat of a blush. 'I try to be, but I guess I haven't behaved myself with you up until now. How about you give me another chance? Let me start by making us both a mug of hot chocolate. Are you feeling better or do you want to talk some more?'

'I feel heaps better, thank you. You have no idea how glad I am that you are here because I don't think I would have coped so well if I had been alone when the memories came back.'

Before he eased her up from his lap, Paul brushed his lips across her mouth in what he hoped she would know to be a purely friendly kiss. Deep down, he wanted it to be so much more and had to fight to drag his mouth away.

Thirteen

They were no more than ten metres down the road on their way to the city for Abby's interview with Mr John Simpson, before Paul pulled over onto the gravel verge and turned off the engine.

'Why are we stopping?' Abby asked as she turned to Paul with a frown between her eyes.

'Do you have a driver's licence?'

'Sure, why?'

Without answering, Paul clicked open the driver's door and strode around to the other side of the car.

She jolted when he pulled her door open. 'Hop out.' He smiled at her screwed-up face, held out his hand and eased her from the car. 'You drive,' he added as he ushered her around to the other side.

In front of the hood, Abby stalled, planting her feet in refusal. 'I can't drive, I haven't got the strength.'

'It's only your left leg without the strength isn't it?' Paul moved in front of Abby with an enigmatic smile.

'Yes.'

'My car is automatic. You don't need to use your left leg. You should be able to manage the brake and accelerator with only your right foot. Why don't you give it a go while we have little traffic?' Without waiting for any argument, which he felt sure Abby was going to spout, he grasped her elbow and shoved her forwards. After he managed to settle her into the driver's seat, Paul slammed the door shut, strode back around the car and sat next to her, his body half turned to face her. 'Well, come on, start her up.'

'I'm not sure about this, what if I have an accident?'

'You have as much chance of having an accident as I do. Besides the car is insured. You do know how to drive an automatic?'

'Of course I do, it's...'

'Start her up or we will be late for your appointment.' As he straightened in his seat, Paul turned his head towards the side window in an effort to hide his grin. Tension radiated from Abby's body as she played with the gear stick, searched for the indicator switch and practised swinging her right foot from pedal to pedal before setting the car into neutral and turning the key. He heard her deep sigh as she hesitated before slipping the gear into drive. It was painful how slow she eased her foot onto the accelerator. There was a small kangaroo hop accompanied by a groan of discomfort from Abby before she pulled onto the roadway and made tentative progress.

'It's been a long time.'

Paul wasn't sure if the almost inaudible words were meant for him or if it was self-talk.

'Are you sure about this?' There was no doubt these words were meant for him.

'I'm sure, you are doing really well but if we keep going at ten kilometres per hour it's going to take us all day. Your appointment is for nine-thirty this morning. I am certain Mr Simpson isn't going to appreciate you keeping him until nine-thirty tonight.'

His sarcasm had the desired effect, although the jolt as Abby planted her foot all of a sudden had him wonder for a moment whether or not this was such a great idea. It took all of his willpower to not comment on the sudden burst of speed, praying Abby would ease down to the speed limit before she was either caught by a hidden radar gun or he heard a police siren. He dared a glance at Abby once the car slowed. His heart flip-flopped in his chest at the brilliant look of awe spread across her face.

She glanced at him. 'I can't believe I'm driving. I thought this would never happen.'

'There isn't a single thing you can't do now that you could do before. It will take time but you need to let go of your fear. Let me know if you want me to take over once we near the city but drive as far as you can.'

The drive towards the city was pleasant but as Abby negotiated traffic lights and heavy traffic, the tension in the car was palpable. Paul sensed her hesitancy on more than one occasion. Twice Abby muttered how she couldn't keep going but he encouraged her to continue for another block as there was nowhere for her to pull over. By the time they reached a multi-storey car park near the building they needed, Abby's face glistened with a thin layer of perspiration. It wasn't until she had pulled into an empty bay and turned off the engine, he heard her heaved out breath of tension and felt her relax. She sat for at least thirty seconds with her brow leaning on the top edge of the steering wheel while she forced deep breaths in and out of her lungs.

Paul smiled as he laid one hand on her shoulder and gave it a gentle squeeze. 'Congratulations. A few more runs to gain confidence and I will be happy for you to use my car to run into town for shopping when I go away.'

Abby shot upright, turned and stared at him with stunned wide eyes. 'I would never take your car out.'

'You will. It needs to be driven every week to keep it in good running order. Dianne has been taking it for short runs up till now. If you use the car it will save Dianne the hassle. She will appreciate it and so will I. Let's go.' He could see Abby was about to fire up with a spate of arguments so eased his long body from the car and removed her crutches from the back seat where he had stowed them earlier.

'I don't need both crutches,' said Abby as she glanced across the roof of the car.

Paul hesitated. 'I know but if you want every chance to restore your pension it might be a wise idea to make out you do. Let Mr Simpson see you struggle.'

'But it's not ethical, I don't believe in dishonesty.'

Paul slammed the rear door shut before striding around to assist Abby from the car. 'What isn't ethical is what your friend Mr Simpson has done to you. You are nowhere near fit enough to spend eight hours a day on your feet while you work. All we are doing is showing how things are. Bill suggested you use your crutches.' Paul held out the topic of their discussion to her.

'Who is Bill?' The question was followed by a sigh of resignation as Abby wrapped the circular bands around her arms and gripped the handles.

'Bill Rogers, Dianne's husband. He said he will meet us outside the main door.'

Abby stopped in her tracks. 'Now wait a minute, Paul Sanders, I told you I can't afford a lawyer.'

Paul grinned as he planted his spread fingers in the small of her back and gave a gentle shove. 'And I told you he's doing this pro-bono.' He didn't dare mention he had already paid for Bill's services because he knew there would be one hell of an argument and Abby wouldn't take one more step. Now he thought about it, he regretted he hadn't thought to mention it to Bill and prayed the man wouldn't let the true facts slip.

'I am so not happy about this,' she muttered under her breath as they made their way down the length of the concrete drive of the car park towards an elevator.

Ignoring her words of disdain as well as her sharp, angry glances, Paul pressed the button and stood back to wait for the arrival of the elevator. No elevator arrived so they wove through the parked cars, outside the building and headed towards a set of steps. It wasn't until they reached the bottom of the steps outside the towering office block which housed the Social Security Department, Abby eased the scowl from her face and Paul ceased grinning at her.

'Paul.'

At the sound of his name, Paul glanced in the direction the voice came from. 'Hi, good morning, Bill, Dianne,' he called to the couple on the other side of the busy street.

Abby's eyes shot up at the mention of Dianne's name. Her look said far more than any words. Paul grinned back 'Did I forget to mention Dianne is a journalist? When she heard the details of what happened to you, her nose began twitching for a story. She insisted on coming to observe.'

'Paul, did I mention I wasn't happy about all this?' Abby planted her hands on her hips as she stared at him.

'Only about fifty times so far.'

They watched in silence as Dianne and Bill ran through lanes of traffic stalled at the lights. Once across the road, they hurried towards them.

'Morning, Paul.' Bill greeted his friend with a handshake and turned to Abby. 'And you must be Abigail Sharpe. I've heard a lot about you.' His grasped her fingers in a second handshake.

'Call me Abby. I'm not sure if I should be pleased to meet you or not. Paul has been keeping things from me.' She turned to Dianne. 'I owe you an apology for my behaviour the other day. I wasn't quite feeling myself. Please accept my humble apology.'

'No need to apologise, Paul explained about the pain you were in.' She leant forwards and whispered towards Abby's ear, but loud enough for all to hear. 'You were jealous of me, weren't you?'

Abby's eyes flew open, followed by her jaw dropping. It took a moment before she could formulate an answer. 'I was not.'

'Was not what?' Paul asked as he glanced at the two women, pretending he hadn't heard but he sure enjoyed the look of mortification on Abby's face. A little voice in his head begged it was true.

'None of your business.' Both women chorused at the same time, paused for a second before they both burst out in laughter.

With a glance at his watch, Bill commented it was time to go. They surged forwards and were almost at the top of the steps before Paul stopped and turned around. Abby hadn't moved. He swore under his breath before running back down, glancing around in search of a ramp or elevator. He was still searching when Abby settled both crutches on the bottom step and hoisted her body upwards.

'Isn't there a lift?' Bill asked as he joined them.

A snort of derision slipped from Abby's mouth. 'They will only operate it if you are in a wheelchair.'

'Excuse me?' Paul's question was louder than Bill's, 'What did you say?'

'You have to be kidding.' Dianne pulled out a camera, focussed and snapped a shot of Abby balanced on the first step.

Abby pointed to the far-left hand corner of the building. 'There is a small elevator over there but they will only operate it if you are sitting in a wheelchair. Believe me, I know. This is the fifth time I've had to climb these stairs.'

'Well you are not climbing them today.' Without warning, Paul grasped one arm around Abby's back and the other behind her knees, swept her up into his arms and carried her upwards, not settling her back on her feet until they were inside the main glass door, which Bill held open for them while Dianne hovered around snapping photo after photo.

'Stay here.' Paul knew by the quick glance that Abby didn't appreciate his actions or his orders but ignored her and headed towards the reception desk.

'Miss Abigail Sharpe is here for her appointment with Mr John Simpson.' The woman glanced at a computer screen, fingered the mouse with pursed lips giving the impression she was sucking on something acidic. Her glance went over Paul's shoulder where her eyes swung from woman to woman.

'Miss Sharpe is the one on crutches who wasn't able to climb the steps outside. Why can't disabled people use the lift?'

The woman huffed up at the imperious tone of Paul's voice. 'Policy dictates the lift is for people in wheelchairs only,' she said.

'Policy made up by some bureaucrat who had the use of all his limbs, no doubt. I would love to see you negotiate those steps outside with a pair of crutches.' His sarcasm did nothing to soften the rigid face of the woman in front of him.

'I don't make up the policy. Mr Simpson is waiting for you in room 204. Second floor, fourth door on the right. Good day.'

It was obvious by the clipped tone of her voice, Paul had been dismissed. When he turned to go back to the others, he found Abby leading the way to the elevator.

'Room 204,' she stated. 'I've been here before.'

Her sudden stillness had Paul concerned. As he neared the elevator, he swore aloud when he read the sign Abby stared at.

'The lift is out of order?' Dianne joined them. 'How do we get upstairs?'

Abby turned and pointed the bottom of one crutch to a stairwell on the opposite corner before she huffed out a breath with shoulders drooping. She hoisted her body across the polished stone floor, swinging her hips between the planted crutches as fast as the others walked. At the bottom, she stilled and stared upwards. 'There is no way I will be able to climb so many steps.'

As she stared, Paul counted. There were twelve narrow steps before they reached a halfway landing and disappeared around a corner. Adding up in his head, he figured she had forty-eight steps to negotiate. Somehow he knew she had no hope of even reaching the first level. He turned around to find she had plonked her backside on the fourth step, removed her crutches from her arms, making a clatter as she flung them down onto the smooth tiled floor.

'Don't even think about carrying me up there.' She glared at both Bill and Paul while Dianne snapped photographs, her lips drawn into a thin line.

As Paul stood at the bottom of the steps, wondering what to do, he could feel tension radiating outwards. A supercilious smile escaped when he came up with an idea. 'Come with me, Bill.' Without giving the poor man a chance to say a thing, he grasped Bill's forearm, dragged him up the steps, not stopping until he reached the fourth door on the right at the second floor. Not bothering to knock, he shoved the door open and entered, dragging Bill in after him.

A thin, balding man glanced up from the file he had been reading, his face turning from shock to a glare. The desk was what Paul would call as prissy-neat with everything stacked in precise lines.

'Who are you?' the man asked as he stood. He didn't look too enamoured by Paul's unannounced presence.

Paul spied the man's hand moving to what he presumed to be an alarm button under his desk. 'Paul Sanders, I have Miss Abigail Sharpe waiting downstairs for her appointment.' He indicated Bill. 'This is her lawyer, Bill Rogers.'

'Bring Miss Sharpe up.'

'I would if she could manage it but it seems your elevator is out of order.'

'Use the stairs.'

As Paul bristled at the terse order, he pulled his body up to its full height. 'I did, but as you are well aware, Abby can barely walk so it would be impossible for her to manage fifty steps.' His words were deliberately clipped. 'She couldn't even get up the few steps out the front. So I suggest you move your butt out of your comfortable chair, use the limbs you have full use of, and come downstairs.' The moment he saw John Simpson redden in anger as he stood, Paul leant forwards until they were almost nose-to-nose. 'I guess I should inform you there is a journalist waiting with Abby. This lady is more than interested in the way you treat disabled clients and is in the process of taking photographs along with notes so she can write up an honest and interesting expose.'

'There is no need for such actions.' The man blustered, huffing and puffing as though he was unable to formulate words. His nose stuck in the air as he attempted to make himself look important but he led the way along the short passage, only to stop in front of the elevator where he jabbed his finger on the elevator button. His face reddened even further when Bill tapped him on the shoulder and pointed to the stairwell.

Bill and Paul grinned at each other behind the pompous man's back as they followed him down the stairs. Abby still sat where they had left her, with Dianne perched next to her.

Both women looked over their shoulder when they heard the men's footfalls behind them.

Paul was beginning to feel sorry for John Simpson by the time Bill had quoted sections of relevant legislation during the ensuing conversation held on the stairwell. Employees and members of the public gawked with curiosity as they sidled past. The poor man's ego had deflated so much his shoulders sagged and his face was ashen. The fact Dianne scribbled down the entire conversation in shorthand and snapped a whole heap more photographs hadn't helped the man maintain his haughty demeanour. By the time they left, Abby was assured all back payments to her pension would be in her account by the following day and she wouldn't have to present herself for another interview. Her regular doctor's reports would be sufficient evidence of her progress – as per the legislation, Bill had emphasised more than once.

While they still stood at the top of the steps outside the building, Bill shook hands with Abby and turned to Paul. 'Dianne and I are hosting a small pre-Christmas pool party tomorrow night for a few friends and work colleagues, why don't you two join us?'

'How about it?' Paul turned to face Abby with his question.

'What does one wear? I don't have any glamorous clothes.' With dropped eyelids hiding her eyes, Abby appeared embarrassed.

Since he knew the contents of Abby's wardrobe far better than Abby realised, Paul turned to Dianne, when an idea formulated in his head. 'Are you free for a couple of hours?'

'Certainly, why?' She looked mystified over Abby's still downcast head but must have read his message for she smiled. 'Sure, leave us alone and I will find the perfect outfit.'

Abby's head shot up as she stepped back with her hand waving through the air in denial. 'No way, Paul, I'm sorry but you go without me.' She turned and clomped away, coming to a grinding halt at the topmost step. She used the crutches as a lever to lower her body onto the top step. While the three of them stared in disbelief she shuffled her bottom down the steps one at a time.

'What are you doing?' Paul jogged down the six steps, reached over and put his hands under Abby's armpits and hoisted her upright.

She brushed the back of her denim jeans with her fingers. 'Walking down the steps, what does it look like? I've done it before. It is the only way I can get down more than a couple of steps without overbalancing.'

'No it's not. You have two men here who are quite capable of giving you a hand.' With his hand brushing through his hair in frustration, he muttered a few phrases under his breath. He saw Abby stiffen at 'stubborn little fool,' before she immediately began clomping away.

With thoughts of their earlier conversation about loans, money and Abby refusing his financial help, Paul wasn't concentrating and didn't notice what Abby was up to. Dianne nudged him in his ribs with her elbow. When he glanced up it was to see Dianne pointing at the diminishing form of Abby heading towards the crosswalk. He muttered an uncouth epithet as he raced after her. Damn woman wasn't even going towards his car and a jab of a message told him he was going to have his work cut out for him before she would accept his offer to buy her an outfit. After closing the distance he reached out and grabbed her arm. 'Hang on a minute, I am pretty sure I know what you are thinking but I was going to buy you a Christmas present in any case so let this be your gift from me. Please? The night will be fun and you haven't had an evening out for so long. Come on, as a favour to me? Come as my partner so I don't have to spend another night alone?'

'I can't, Paul. It smacks of... you know... Jasmine and I refuse to be seen in the same vein.'

'Sweetheart, you don't have it in you to be anything like Jasmine. Believe me. I would really like to go and would like it even more if you accept my gift to you without any argument. This is the complete opposite to what Jasmine did. She spent my money without even a hint at what she was up to. She never asked but went on a spending spree with the bills I knew nothing about sent to my address in the post. I'm not talking about a mere few hundred dollars. In a matter of weeks I received unpaid and unsolicited bills for close to a hundred thousand before I could put a stop to it.'

Instead of stopping at Abby's indrawn breath of shock, he batted his eyelids in such a ridiculous fashion Abby couldn't help but smile.

'Okay.'

'Wonderful, thank you,' Paul said before turning around so she couldn't see him withdraw his wallet and remove a wad of notes. With a grin, he handed the money to his cousin with strict instructions to spend the lot and ensure Abby looked like a million dollars. He leant towards Dianne's ear. 'Please don't let Abby see any prices and don't let her know how much you spend. Whatever you think she needs, buy it,' he whispered.

A quick glance at the pile of hundred-dollar bills had Dianne send a curious glance at Paul. 'Sure thing, how about you leave us in the city for a couple of hours and I will bring Abby home.' A smile lit up her face. 'I'm going to enjoy this.' After she slipped the notes in her handbag, Dianne grasped Abby's hand. 'Come on, girl, we are going to paint this city so many shades of red the people will need sunglasses to get around and you are going to knock this man's socks off tomorrow night.'

Abby wasn't given a chance to give her appreciation to Bill before Dianne had linked arms with her and she was almost dragged down the road in what looked like an ungainly muddle of legs and aluminium poles with swinging hips. He and Bill headed in the opposite direction.

Fourteen

Fear had a hold while Abby hovered in the open doorway which led onto the patio. It wasn't because she watched Dianne bustle around tweaking the odd cutlery item until each was perfectly aligned. Nor was it because Dianne shifted a pile of plates so the table had a more balanced look. Abby rubbed two fingers across the creases on her brow in an attempt to ease her concern for she felt utterly useless. To thank Dianne for a fabulous four hours in the city, Abby had suggested she spend this afternoon assisting her new-found friend with preparations for the pool party. Paul had driven her over in time for a shared lunch but he returned home when he was shoved out of the door, the two women giggling as they insisted he leave. But with the party catered for by professionals, there was little Abby could do and it was beginning to unravel her newfound self-confidence. How useless her legs were, had settled to the fore-front of her mind despite chastising herself for her negativity. This was a huge mistake. To think she would fit in was ridiculous.

All Abby had been able to manage was to lay out bits and pieces like paper serviettes and condiments after Dianne arranged outdoor furniture and carried out armloads of plates, cutlery, glasses and a host of other paraphernalia. While she watched Dianne undertake the bulk of the work, Abby had too much time to dwell on the use-lessness of her legs since Dianne hadn't trusted her to carry anything heavier than paper napkins further than ten measly metres. Dianne never said anything, there was no need but Abby knew she was virtually useless and always would be to a certain extent. With her eyes closed, she jumped when Diane slung an arm around her waist.

'Are you okay, Abby? We have enough time for afternoon tea before we need to get ready.'

Abby glanced at the cheap watch on her wrist, the sight of it always a reminder of how she lost in the accident, the gold one her parents had given to her for her twenty-first birthday. Along with her leather handbag, mobile phone and laptop computer, items she still couldn't afford to replace. 'It's a bit early to dress isn't it? I only need ten minutes to shower and change.'

'Not tonight.' Dianne urged Abby forwards by putting pressure in the small of her back. 'Tonight you are going to be the shining star. Come on, coffee first before I enjoy tarting you up.'

An hour later Abby had the distinct impressions she was in a mystical dream. After a brief shower to shampoo her flyaway curls, Dianne settled her into a chair in front of a mirror. Abby tried to protest but her protest was ignored so here she sat while Dianne coaxed Abby's hair into a neat style using a blow drier and circular brush. Satisfied, Dianne grinned, picked up a can of spray and covered Abby's puffed up hair with a mist of spray. It miffed her when Dianne turned Abby away from the mirror and used an array of different potions on her face. Never had she used anything more than mascara, a hint of blusher and pale lip-gloss, so the number of bottles, jars, tubes and brushes Dianne used was a worry.

After an hour on ministrations, Dianne spun Abby around in the swivel chair. Stunned, Abby stared at her reflection in the mirror above the dressing table of the frilly guest bedroom allotted to her. She didn't recognise her own image. 'I can't believe this is me,' she said as she swished her head from side-to-side so she could study all the angles.

'You look fabulous. I'm dying to see Paul's face when he sees you.' Dianne gave Abby's hair a final tweak, stood to one side with her head cocked and smiled as she dropped the comb on the painted tabletop.

'I'm sure he will hardly notice. It's not as though I am important to him.'

'Oh, he will certainly notice. Come on, it's time to dress. The first guests will be here in a few minutes.' Dianne turned away and pulled a hanger from the doorknob of the wardrobe. 'I'll leave you to dress in privacy but will be back in ten minutes,' she said with a wicked grin as she handed over the outfit. Abby wasn't sure she liked the strange smile which snuck across Dianne's face before she left and pulled the door closed.

Nervous anticipation caused her fingers to tremble as Abby undid the belt of the borrowed bathrobe and dropped it to the floor. It took a bit of effort but she managed to step into a one-piece bathing suit of deep blues, greens and purples, and worm it up her body. Peacock colours, she called them. Continuous peeks in the mirror told her the rich colours enhanced the gold of her hair and gave her healthier complexion a special glow, but deep apprehension still gripped her innards into a tight ball of tension. Feeling naked, she wrapped the angle-cut skirt around her waist, clipped the hooks at the waistband, pulled the skirt around until it covered the still vivid scars on her left thigh. The matching skirt went from ankle length on her left leg to nothing more than a waistband on her right waist, revealing the entire side along the length of her right leg. When she first tried the outfit on, she had argued over its suitability but Dianne assured her it was perfect. It was a struggle to slip on the new pair of flat silver sandals Dianne had forced her to buy, and even harder to bend over to do up the buckles on the slender straps at her ankles. She hated how she couldn't wear heels but the sandals were at least elegant despite the straps she needed to keep the sandals snug so she could walk. Upright again, she stared at her reflection in the mirror. Good grief, she looked as though she should be arrested for indecent exposure. Mortified, she grabbed the see-through, loose, flowing jacket made from fine cotton with the same design as the skirt and bathers and slipped her arms into the sleeves.

She gasped at her reflection in the mirror. Although she was wearing more, in her eyes she felt even more naked and was about to strip the lot off, dress back into the safe covering denim of the jeans she had worn all day and flee when there was a tap at the door and Dianne entered.

'Wow, you look amazing,' Dianne said as she glided across the room. 'I knew this was the perfect outfit for you.'

'So do you.' Abby's eyes moved up and down, taking in every detail of what Dianne wore, glad she was also clad in bathers but under a low-cut and revealing shift type cover which looked like fine gauze and outlined every curve of Dianne's model-like body. The tall genes must run in the family, Abby thought as she recalled how tall Paul was. The thought made her feel so insignificant. 'I feel much better now you are dressed in a similar type outfit but I still feel as though I am virtually naked.'

'Well it is a pool party and all the women will have similar outfits while the men will be wearing shorts over skimpy bathers or lairy baggy things I wouldn't be caught dead in. It amuses me to see some of these men in such loud outfits when I'm used to seeing them in their stiff legal suits.'

Both women turned when a knock interrupted their conversation. 'Paul's driven up,' Bill called through the closed door.

At the mere mention of Paul's name, Abby's nerves tingled with apprehension. The nerves tightened even more when Dianne grabbed her hand and yanked, giving her no choice but to follow Dianne through the doorway, along a passage and finally into a large family room where she was surprised to find a cluster of guests already milling around with filled glasses clutched in their hands. Dianne didn't stop as she murmured greetings to various people while they continued to cut a path through the house, taking it slow to allow for Abby's uncoordinated walk. When they reached the sliding glass door which opened out to a large undercover patio running the entire length of the house, Dianne paused, stepped behind Abby and planted her hand in the small of Abby's back, giving her a gentle nudge.

* * *

Paul stood in front of the large backyard pool, talking to Bill and another couple. His eyes lifted at the movement from the doorway and could do nothing but stare at the apparition. His breath hitched in his throat, rendering him unable to breathe for a moment. Coming to his senses, he stepped forwards and crossed the tiled concrete. 'You take my breath away; you look so exquisite.' His innards were doing wild, crazy things, clenching tight before somersaulting at random and his brain felt as useless as his jellified legs.

While his roving eye took in every detail, he noticed how Abby appeared shy and unsure of herself. Her top teeth gnawed at the corner of her bottom lip while she stared at a vague spot on the floor. Her first foray back into a social life and all her self-confidence had taken a nose-dive. Sensing her inner struggle, Paul placed an arm around her waist. 'Come and talk to Bill for a moment.' He supported her, slowing when he realised Abby was fighting to walk as normally as she could so as not to highlight her disability.

After introducing the other couple, Paul remained at Abby's side until he felt sure she was a part of the conversation before he dared to leave her for a moment to seek out his cousin. 'Dianne, have you got your digital camera handy? I have to get a photograph of Abby.'

'Oh, yes?'

At the speculative gleam in Dianne's eyes, Paul immediately added, 'Abby wants to present a photo to the paramedic who stayed with her during her rescue and dressed like she is now would be perfect. But I guess you will need to be surreptitious. I sense Abby's confidence has taken a nose-dive.'

He turned his head back towards Abby and smiled. 'You spent wisely, thank you.'

'We had fun. Abby has no idea how beautiful she is, does she? I have never met anyone before who is so unaware of her looks. She was really nervous before we came out and is super-sensitive about her scars. I'll find my camera. If she sees me taking candid shots of everyone she won't feel as though I'm picking on her in particular. You like her quite a lot don't you?'

Paul's glance was sharp. 'You would think I would learn from my mistakes wouldn't you, but yes, I like her too damn much.'

Dianne laid a hand on his arm. 'She is nothing like Jasmine. Abby doesn't even have a hint of a nasty streak in her body.' When Dianne turned away to find her camera, Paul moved back to Abby's side, where he stayed while they moved amongst the gathering so he could introduce her to those people he knew. If Abby was left alone, he was certain she would seek out a quiet spot to hide if given half a chance.

As the party livened up, people stripped down to bathers and cavorted in the pool. Paul watched Dianne move among her guests, laughing as she shot photographs. He caught Dianne's eyes and gave a small nod when he noticed every time she caught Abby unawares.

To rest her legs, Abby sought out a chair for lengthy periods. Paul sat with her and ensured she had a steady supply of finger food or drinks of the non-alcoholic variety. The pool was emptying when he leant towards Abby. 'Come for a swim.'

Startled, her head jerked up. He noted the look of fear in her eyes. 'I can't,' she said.

'Can't swim?'

'I was a physical education teacher - I can swim but I can't... you know... my leg. It's so ugly.'

Paul leant towards Abby. 'Would you like to know something? The first night when we both stood across from each other in all our glory,' he smiled at her rising colour of embarrassment. 'I took in every inch of your beautiful curves but I swear I didn't see any scars. They must have been there but I didn't notice them so they can't be as bad as you imagine.'

Her eyes flashed in disbelief. 'You're only saying nice things to make me feel better.'

He placed his hand on her arm. 'I swear I didn't notice. It wasn't until Mum told me about the accident, I became aware you were injured in the crash. Look, there's hardly anyone left in the pool. How about we wander around to the dark side over there?' He indicated towards one end, which was in the shadows. He turned back, stood and drew her up next to him. 'Come on, nobody will notice you.'

After leading her around the concrete deck, he dropped her hand, divested his body of his casual cotton short-sleeved shirt and dropped his Bermuda shorts to the ground, revealing his torso covered only in a brief pair of trunks. 'Come on, Abby. Slip the skirt and top off and I'll lift you into the water. Nobody is watching and even if they were, they won't be able to make out any blemishes.'

He didn't miss her blush as she dragged her eyes away from his almost bare body. He noticed how hard she fought to keep her face from showing her feelings while she stood still and stared at the aqua blue, cool water. 'Come on, the water will cool you off.'

A sigh escaped her lips but she turned her back, took off the jacket and unhooked the skirt. She dropped both garments on a chair but seemed to find it difficult to bend so she could unbuckle the pretty sandals on her feet. Paul squatted in front of her but didn't miss her indrawn breath when his warm fingers brushed against her ankle. His own body was reacting in such an embarrassing manner he rued wearing the racing bathers he usually wore in the surf and wished he'd had the foresight to wear something less revealing. It took a great effort to force his brain to think of swimming in a hole in thick pack-ice before he was game to rise, close enough so Abby wouldn't be able to see his male reaction to her touch.

There was a nervous, almost frightened look on her face as Abby stood in front of him after she wobbled while wriggling her feet from the shoes. So she didn't have a chance to change her mind, Paul grasped her around the waist, lifted her feet from the ground and slowly dropped her into the water with her back to the people across the other side of the manicured backyard. As soon as he released her, he jumped in. Sinking to the bottom, he pushed off with his feet and broke through the surface shaking the water from his head. He laughed at Abby's squeal when the droplets of water hit her.

'See it wasn't so bad. Why don't you go swimming in the ocean at home? Surely swimming is a gentle way to build up your muscles again.' While she began to breast-stroke down the length of the pool, he swam beside her.

'I did a lot of swimming in the therapy pool but I can't swim alone in the ocean in case I get into trouble. I don't yet have the strength to fight against heavy waves or currents.'

'You should have told me. How about I swim with you every day until I go away?' Without waiting for a response, Paul pulled away, completed a couple of quick laps of the pool to give his body a chance to cool before he was game to return to her side.

After the heat of the hot summer's day, the water was refreshingly cool. The night was perfect, still warm with no breeze to cool the water on their damp skin. Regret reigned when a group of ten people joined them, which caused Abby to linger in the water until they were alone. Paul understood her obvious excuses each time he asked her if she was ready to get out and smiled when, after the last man vacated the pool, Abby neared him.

'Can you lift me out now?' she asked.

'Sure thing.' He grasped her around the waist, hefted her upwards, but didn't release his hold until she sat on the edge. With careful deliberation he cast his eyes over the scars, lifted a finger to run over them. He felt her body tense and imagined she was mortified by his close scrutiny but he didn't halt his exploration until he touched every scar he was able to see. When he dared to lift his eyes, he smiled. 'They are not as bad as you make out and you know they will fade with time. Given how bad your injuries were, I expected the scars to look worse. The surgeon has done a fantastic job. I understand how you are self-conscious about them but your scars don't bother me and don't define you. They don't alter the person you are inside. Any person who cares about you, won't notice them. It might be a good idea to think of the alternative. Mum said there was talk of you losing the leg altogether. I believe a few a scars on a leg which still functions well, is a small price to pay. Think of the positives rather than the negatives. Let me find you a towel.'

Not game to hear Abby's response, he used his arms to hoist his body from the water and strode across the paving to a table piled with folded towels for those who didn't remember to bring their own. After wrapping one around his waist, he unfolded another and dropped it around Abby's shoulders. To help her up he slipped his hands under her armpits and hoisted her upright, supporting her until she had found her balance and was steady on her feet. So she wouldn't feel uptight, he shielded her from prying eyes while she towelled the moisture from her body and hooked the skirt around her waist.

To give Abby a chance to rest her legs, Paul guided her to a table and assisted her to sit. He had barely wriggled next to her on the bench when he heard Bill call him. Paul glanced up to see Bill beckoning him towards the house. 'Excuse me a moment, Abby, Bill has summoned. Will you be all right by yourself for a few minutes?' At her smile and nod of her head he sauntered across the tiles, tugging his shirt on as he followed Bill into the inner sanctum of his office where he stepped into his shorts, drew them up and pressed the stud.

'I've got those photos up on the computer. I can print some off now if you like.'

Heads bent, the two men perused all the shots Dianne had taken, pausing to study at length, those of Abby. 'She's a beautiful woman, Paul.'

'She's certainly beautiful. Stop, print this one for me.' His finger lingered on the screen as Bill enlarged the picture of a full-length Abby caught with a pensive look on her face, while she stared at an imaginary person or object. There was a hint of a smile which gave her face an almost Mona Lisa look. 'Print a couple, and this one.' He pointed to another.

* * *

While Paul was away Abby's thoughts centred on how things had changed over the past couple of days. After the cold disdain and distance he had kept between them, Abby found it difficult to believe the infinite tenderness and consideration he now showed her. It was as though there were two different Pauls but deep down she understood why he suffered post-traumatic stress. So had she and still did in one sense. It was a hard concept to understand unless you were the one who had gone through the trauma but it sure made a difference when you understood why your mind played such awful tricks.

She was so deep in thought she didn't hear anyone approach until she felt and heard the scrape of someone joining her on the wooden bench. Since she hadn't seen Paul exit the doorway she was still staring at, she wondered if he had come out another door she didn't know about. She was about to speak when a large hand dropped onto her exposed right leg and skated upwards, only halting centimetres from her crotch. Since there was no way Paul would act with such provocation, every muscle in her body tensed as she turned her head a fraction to see who dared to take such liberties.

'Hi, gorgeous, how come thuch a thexy beauty like you ith here all alone?' The slurred words huffed out a strong smell of alcohol which wafted into Abby's nostrils. Whiskey, she thought. And a lot of it.

At the sudden onset of tumble-turns in her stomach, Abby darted a glance around, hoping to spot Paul, Bill or Dianne but most people were now inside dancing while those over the other side of the pool were caught up in private conversations and took no heed of the couple seated at the outdoor setting. With the table and bench butted against the wooden slats of a wall, Abby was trapped.

Frantic to escape, she said the first excuse she could think of. 'If you will excuse me, I need to find the restroom.'

Her ploy must have been obvious for instead of allowing her to move away, the interloper inched closer. 'There'th no need to be coy with me. How 'bout we find a vacant bedroom?' With his words, the man leant closer and attempted to kiss her. At the same time one arm snaked around her waist and drew her tight against his torso while the other hand ran up and down the inside of her thigh.

A shudder of disgust wove its way down her spine as Abby pulled away as far as she could but it wasn't far since she was pressed against the wood of the partitioning wall.

When his attempted kiss missed its mark, the man wriggled his body closer, while his hand crept higher up the inside of her leg.

'Leave me alone, I am not interested.' Her frightened plea came out as nothing more than a squeaky whisper, fear tightening up her vocal cords. She grabbed the wandering hand and shoved it away from her leg as hard as she could but his superior strength negated her attempts. His hand settled even higher with two fingers attempting a more intimate intrusion by creeping under the hem on the slither of fabric between her legs.

Terrified, Abby tried to peel his fingers from her waist at the same time she struggled to stand but with the bench pushed under the table and the weak fragility of her muscles, she wasn't able to straighten her legs and plopped down again.

'Leave me alone,' she shrieked as she grappled with the wandering hands. Unable to think of any other way to free herself, she yanked on one finger on the hand trying to explore her crotch. Thankful she managed to get a good grip, she bent the finger back as hard as she could, ignoring the man's grunt of displeasure and pain. Even though she had managed to make him release her leg, she kept one hand fighting off his attempts to restart his intrusion as her other hand peeled back the fingers which gripped really tight into her waist.

'Leave me alone,' she yelled again. Close to tears from fear, her choked words came out louder but still not loud enough to rouse the attention of anyone else. She shivered at the cold moistness of his slobbery lips pressing a kiss against her cheek. Almost gagging at the acidic stench, she recoiled in horror before she managed to press one hand against his chest and shoved as hard as he could.

When the man moved away much faster and further than she had anticipated, she was shocked, unable to believe she had enough strength to push him so far but the sound of a scuffle and groans told her why the odious pig rose so rapidly from his seat.

* * *

'The lady is with me and I definitely heard her beg you to leave her alone, which makes your obscene actions unwelcome.' Paul hauled the man from the seat into an upright position. While the bastard struggled to free his legs from between the table and bench to find his balance, Paul held him by his shirt front.

'She 'vited me over. No thane man would 'gnore such an invitation.' The slurred words were cut short when Paul yanked hard on the man's shirt and twisted it tight around his neck.

'Not from where I was standing she didn't. You are drunk. It's going to look really good with a picture of a drunken local member plastered all over the papers tomorrow under the headline *Sexual Harassment by Local Member*. But I guess cretins like you deserve to be publicly humiliated. It might be the only way you cease such odious behaviour. Didn't you know we have a journalist in our midst? Surely you noticed her snapping photographs all evening.'

Still with a firm hold on the shirt, Paul turned to Abby. 'I suggest we visit the police station so you can lay charges to ensure Dianne's write-up is all the more credible.'

In an instant, a sudden look of panic passed over the man's features. He jerked his body from Paul's grasp and staggered away. 'There'th no need to make thith public. No harm'th been done,' he slurred over his shoulder.

Paul immediately shuffled onto the seat beside Abby whose body had taken on the appearance of wobbly jelly. 'Are you okay?' When she didn't answer, Paul glanced at her ashen face, wrapped his arm around her shoulder and drew her close. 'I'm sorry, I was a bit longer than I anticipated. Would you like to see why?' Without waiting for her answer, he plopped a photograph in front of her stricken eyes. 'I had Bill print this off so you could give it to your paramedic saviour.'

After her eyes focussed on the coloured print, they goggled open and stared. A red blush rose up her neck before blooming out all over her face.

Twisting his head so he could see her reaction, Paul grinned. 'Is it any wonder every man here would like to take you to his bed? You are an extremely beautiful woman, Miss Abigail Sharpe. I think when he sees you looking so wonderful, your paramedic will be delighted.'

Her mouth opened and closed several times but no words came out. Instead Abby reached out to finger the image. 'I can't believe this photo is of me.'

'I can, now how about joining me inside on the dance floor?'

Abby pulled away, her demeanour instantly changing from wonder to a return of her anguished fear. 'I can't dance.'

'The same way you couldn't drive or swim? Sure you can. The music is slow, so come with me and I'll show you how it can be done.' He pocketed the photo, shoved the table forwards to enable Abby easy movement. By refusing to release his hold on her struggling hand, he led her inside. At the rear of the group of dancers, he dropped his hands to her hips. 'Put your arms around my neck or waist and lean on me. We don't have to do any magnificent movements but can take it easy by simply shuffling around in time to the music.'

It took about five minutes for Abby to relax but when she did, her hands released their death grip from Paul's neck and crept around his waist while he supported her hips with his hands and they moved around the floor in a slow languorous shuffle. The feel of her body leaning on him sent his hormones on a rampage to the extent he felt certain she would be able to feel his aroused state pressing against her stomach but neither said a word. Knowing of her lack of experience with men, Paul glanced at her face to see if she looked embarrassed. Her eyes were shut but with a wondrous tilt to her lips he figured her joy of actually dancing blocked out any other more intimate sensations. God, he hoped so. Instead he grinned and tightened his hold, determined they would both enjoy the experience to the fullest.

By the time the music stopped and changed to a more modern beat, Abby had her head against his shoulder and his arms had moved to her back. With her eyes closed she looked to be in a state of pure bliss. He was about to speak when he heard Abby murmur against his chest. 'Tonight I achieved another milestone and am actually dancing.'

'You certainly are.' It wasn't the most graceful or technical dance movements, but she was moving in time to the music. As they shuffled he felt a heady sensation but decided to wallow for as long as he could. It was sad but once the night was over, the magic would end. Neither of them wanted a relationship but she sure made it difficult to suppress his increasing sensual feelings for her with her soft curves pressed against his harder frame and her sweet, familiar perfume creating havoc with his nose.

Fifteen

Abby continued to hum in rhythm with the heavy rain pounding on the corrugated iron roof. A wide smile was ever present on her face. She was happy – happier than she could ever recall being. Paul was coming home. Two more weeks and he would be here after six long months in Afghanistan but she was worried about the news headlines which told about the rise of Taliban activity. Already residents were scrambling to get out of the country, especially those natives who had assisted the American, British and Australian forces. Would Paul be able to get out? What if he was trapped in Kabul? The latest news was how the Americans were going to pull out.

To keep bad thoughts at bay, Abby set her mind to continue the flurry of activity all through the house. Even though she had always been scrupulous in keeping the house clean, she was in the process of ensuring every room was dusted, vacuumed, wiped and tweaked, even those rooms she never ventured into. Outside, the garden was pristine. Lawns had been mowed, garden beds trimmed, weeded and planted, outdoor furniture washed and polished dry.

The five and a half months had been long but Abby had filled the hours with constant exercise and during the periods when she rested her limbs, her brain absorbed facts and figures. Via the internet at the local library, and correspondence, she was studying units to gain a degree in accounting. After searching the internet, reading article after article and course outlines, and talking amongst the few friends she had now made, she figured accounting was a career she would be able to manage with the disability she now accepted she would always have.

She moved with ease around the study with a duster and polishing rag in hand, still unable to believe how different she was a year ago when she thought she might lose a leg or never walk again. Now her movements were free, her muscles strong, her limbs supple and lithe. But there was a definite limp and awkward hitch of her left hip at every step. Deep down, she knew they would always be there but her anger and self-pity had now gone, replaced by acceptance. She was sure it was Paul's words about what the alternative could have been, which changed her attitude. She had two of her own legs on which she could stand. Two legs she could walk with. She no longer tired with such ease and her greatest achievement was how she could now walk the distance into town and back without a crutch. It was only two kilometres each way but when there had been a very real chance she would lose an entire leg, two kilometres was a pure miracle, one she would never take for granted.

As she stood in the open doorway of the study, she spied her image in a small decorative mirror. There was a confident smile spread across her lips as she gave the room a final, super-critical inspection. Her hazel eyes were bright with no more bruised half-moons taking residence under them. Hollow, sallow cheeks had filled out and were now glowing pink and had absorbed the colour of the smattering of golden freckles instead of them being hi-lighted against the white skin of illness. Her hair had grown and now swung on her shoulders most of the time. Every now and again, she managed to tie it back into two curly pigtails. Like today.

Happy, she shut the door and moved into the kitchen for a well-earned coffee break, taking the hot mug out onto the veranda where she settled into the cane lounge and pulled a rug up to her armpits to keep the chill of the moisture-laden winter's day at bay. A steady pound of turbulent waves crashing against the sand sent a shiver of joy through her. She loved to sit here watching and hearing the ravages of a winter storm. To her, the beach was more wonderful in winter with its wild remoteness and so few people gracing the shore, giving it a unique beauty. As she sipped, she wondered if it was why Paul had purchased the property.

Paul. She twisted her lips into a brilliant smile as her eyes stared at the curtain of heavy rain and recalled those last few days of his stay. They had been beyond wonderful. They shared meals and outings with Paul the most considerate and caring male companion she had ever experienced.

The most amazing outing had been an all-day event. Paul had made a raft of enquiries, not giving up until he finally tracked down the paramedic who she now regarded as her saviour. They met him in a restaurant for lunch. Abby could still feel the amazing sensation at the look on Michael Baker's face when he watched her walk up to him without the aid of crutches. His jaw snagged open as he slowly rose from his seat. She felt sure he had been incapable of moving until she reached him when his arms went around her in a hug so tight she was unable to breathe. There had been tears in both Michael's and her eyes when they drew apart. After the initial hesitation on her part, happy chat and even laughter ensued while they ate the delicious food. Abby sighed as she recalled how Michael had stared at the picture of her, which Paul handed over before they departed the restaurant.

'I will always treasure this photo,' Michael said. 'I will keep it on my desk to remind me my job is worthwhile when I have one of my down periods after losing a patient. Thank you. I could never express how much this means to me.'

Abby pulled the blanket tighter as other memories surfaced. There had always been a hesitancy, a holding back and she knew it was because Paul was hurt in the past. Jasmine's behaviour had done a great deal of damage to Paul's emotions. Deep down, she knew he had lost the ability to trust a woman on an emotional level. But the diffidence hadn't only been with Paul. Abby had kept her own emotional distance as well. Due to her injuries, she knew she had been overly cautious about any man finding her attractive but figured her caution was because of her loss of confidence in her ability to be the type of woman a man would want.

Until the kiss.

A long sigh escaped. She knew damn well when Paul had kissed her goodbye, it was only meant to be a chaste, friendly farewell peck and it had started off as nothing more. But it had grown into something deeper; a lot deeper and more meaningful. She knew it and was startled at the intensity. When they drew apart they stared into each other's eyes. Abby was certain they were both as stunned as each other. Before he released her, Paul said, 'Wait for me, Abby. Please stay in my home until I return. How I wish I didn't have to go back, but I must. I have an ironclad contract to finish this job. But please wait for me.' With a last lingering stare into her eyes where she was certain they had been able to read each other's thoughts, he turned and raced full pelt to the taxi, not glancing back until he was down the road. Abby had watched after him, her hand held in the air as the knowledge had sunk in.

She loved him. At the last minute, when Paul turned and waved farewell, her tears had fallen.

So she had waited and now he was at last, coming home. There had been letters but the mail service was unreliable at its best. She had lost her mobile phone and laptop in the accident. Even now, she couldn't see the point in replacing the phone for there was no-one to call and because she had to live on such a reduced income, the monthly fees for owning a mobile phone was an unnecessary expense she could do without. Paul had managed to phone on the landline a few times, usually when she was out and getting back to him to return the call was a hit and miss exercise. It was ridiculous how, in this time of modern technology, some places weren't as efficient as others, especially those countries recovering from years of war where basic services were still unreliable.

Her most difficult letter was sent two months ago where she finally divulged her deepest secret but a letter had come back in the return mail, thanking her for her missive. In it Paul said how much he looked forward to seeing her and how hard he was pushing the workers so he could come home sooner. It had been a surprise how the return letter was so quick when it usually took weeks for letters to arrive if they arrived at all. His response had brought immense relief and joy for she thought the contents of her letter would have been the death knell to any future relationship. But it hadn't and he was coming home. With a delighted squeal, Abby drank down the last dregs of her coffee and returned to her spring-cleaning spree.

* * *

Even though he was bone-weary tired, an air of suppressed excitement kept Paul awake as he sat back in the rear of the taxi with his eyes closed. He had worked long hours, pushing teams of workers until his task of overseeing the construction was completed. He wasn't needed for the fitting out of both the hospital and school so his contract was fulfilled. Which was a darn good thing with the withdrawal of foreign troops and threat of another Taliban uprising. He had been damn lucky to secure a flight to Dubai before all hell broke loose. If he'd waited for the flight of his original booking, there was every chance he would still be there – trapped, with every possibility he would have been a target for reprisal. From the news reports he had seen on television at the Dubai airport he now knew thousands of others were not so lucky.

Despite his best attempts, sleep had been elusive during the long flights home interspersed with interminable hours waiting for planes. Thoughts of seeing Abby were foremost in his mind. Even though he was physically exhausted and he closed his eyes, there was no way his brain was able to switch off enough for him to sleep.

In sharp contrast to the hot, dusty climate he was used to in Afghanistan, this torrential rain was more than welcome but it made the roads slippery and dangerous, causing major hold-ups in traffic flow, which went a long way to increasing his eager frustration. He eyed the town buildings as they passed, remembering the night in detail – the night he met Abby. A spurt of adrenalin coursed through his blood stream as they left the town behind and familiar landmarks came into view, his eyes looking ahead for the first sight of his home; the home where Abby was waiting – he hoped. Wanting to surprise her, he hadn't told her of his homecoming two weeks earlier than anticipated. But with chaos during his bid to escape there hadn't been a chance to contact a single person.

The taxi pulled into his driveway. One hand held the fare plus a generous tip while the other had the door open even before the car had come to a complete standstill. In one lithe movement he was out and strode towards the boot to retrieve his two suitcases. Cases in hand, he strode across the lawn and leapt onto the veranda before shaking the water of the still falling rain from his shoulders.

Certain the back door would be open, he left his bags on the front doorstep and hurried along the length of the veranda, around the corner and sped around the back. He flung the door open, strode inside and went in search of his prey. He came to a standstill. She was there, standing with her back to him doing something with the sideboard. A flick and he noticed the duster.

'Abby?' he called softly.

She stilled, paused and spun around. 'Paul!'

Keeping his eyes on her beautiful face he stepped forwards but paused as his eyes dropped lower. His jaw sagged. His eyes opened wide as shock froze his features. It took a moment before he was able to speak. 'You're pregnant?' A cold wave of dread swept through his body. She hadn't waited. She had met someone else and hadn't had the decency to tell him. How could she do this?

'Yes, of course, I wrote to you about it.' Her features stilled in a look of alarm.

'How could you do this to me?' He wasn't sure if he felt despair or disgust.

'Huh? What do you mean?' Abby stepped forwards but came to a grinding halt when Paul raised his hand to stop her.

'Don't come anywhere near me. God, but I have been so stupid. I thought you were different but you're not. All you women are tarred by the same brush aren't you? You are nothing more than a lying bitch exactly the same as Jasmine. I want you out of here – now.'

With a stunned look on her face, Abby cocked her head as though she was trying to make head or tail of what he said. 'What are you talking about? I wrote to you about it. You answered my letter saying how thrilled you were about receiving my missive. They were your words. I don't understand.'

'Don't understand?' The words roared from his lips. 'Take a look at yourself. How could you do this to me? And in my house? I received no letter about... about... his hand wavered in the direction of the protruding mound. 'And I sure as hell didn't answer it, now get out.' Spinning on his heel, Paul sped outside and raced full pelt towards the beach, too numb to care about the rain. Devastated by Abby's treachery he kept running along storm-strewn sand, not bothering to avoid clumps of black seaweed or flotsam but instead, he leapt over them or kicked them aside. Unbidden and unstoppable tears of despair mingled with the rainwater flowing from his head. He ran until he was so exhausted, he knew his legs wouldn't lift any longer from the cloying wet mud. Exhausted, he sank to the soaked sand and buried his head in his hands. A vacuum had sucked everything from his innards.

* * *

Shocked to the core and with the region of her heart tightening in acute pain as it squeezed the life from her, Abby stumbled blindly to the office where she fumbled around searching for the number of the taxi company. It took several swipes at her tear bleary eyes to be able to focus on the tiny numbers in the local phone book. She had to dial three times before she managed to press the correct buttons. Even after she heard the voice on the other end, she shuddered, gulped and sniffed before she was able to get her message across with any coherence. She grabbed a couple of tissues, swiped at her face and blew her nose. Too devastated to move, she plonked into the swivel chair and dropped her head into her hands on the desk, great wracking sobs heaving her chest.

When she knocked the phone with her elbow, she remembered the taxi. She managed to tug another couple of tissues from the box, scrubbed away as much moisture as she could, dropped them on the desk as she stood and stumbled her way across the room in a stunned stupor.

Back in her room, she pulled her small suitcase from the top shelf of the wardrobe, zipped it open and flung her scant belongings into the case, not caring about neatness or how some items missed their target entirely and ended up on the floor. She left them there, especially the bathing costume outfit Paul had bought for her. After flinging the lid down with a thwack, she wrenched the zipper around, dropped the case to the floor and dragged the case after her as she headed for the front door. Everything inside her tangled up in tight knots of turmoil. She had to gulp down another bout of nausea which was ever-present from the continual morning sickness she had battled with for the entire pregnancy.

When she realised there was no choice but to rush to the bathroom, she dropped the bag and hurried the final couple of steps, barely able to reach the ceramic bowl in time to empty the meagre contents of her stomach. Not being able to face breakfast, she only ate half a dozen salted crackers and weak black tea each morning and she'd only managed a cup of black de-caffeinated coffee since her meagre breakfast. Cooking was out of the question – the mere smell of food cooking resulted in her stomach broiling before ejecting. Apart from her regular morning fare, Abby lived on a diet of raw fruit and vegetables since the six-week mark of her pregnancy. The sudden onset of nausea and vomiting was the reason she had sought out a doctor. The result of the blood test had sent her into shock, the cessation of her monthly cycle not unusual for since her accident irregularity had become the norm.

The loud blast of a horn dragged Abby up from the tiled floor. Still not sure it was safe to leave the bathroom, she wiped her mouth on a wad of tissue paper and pressed the button of the cistern. As an afterthought, she grabbed another few sheets of tissue, in case she needed them and grappled for the handle of her bag. Despite trying to walk tall in defiance, her body wouldn't obey and she could do nothing but limp along the passage to the front door. She repeatedly scrubbed the continual flow of tears from her face during the journey into town. When the driver asked where she was going, she had no idea so said, 'into town.'

When they reached the centre of town the driver glanced at Abby through the rear vision mirror. 'Where do you want to be set down, lady?'

With her brain numb and confused, Abby glanced around through the windows and noticed the large Anglican church. 'There, at the church,' she said as she pointed. It took too long to search in the bottom of her small handbag to find the correct change for the fare, and after an ungainly run through the rain, Abby stood on the porch of the church with her bag beside her but didn't have a clue what to do next. She had no home and nowhere to go. She thought of Grace but she was on the cruise section of a long overseas holiday. Besides how would she get there with no car? She sure couldn't use Paul's again.

* * *

Even though he had yelled for her to leave, Paul was stunned to find Abby had taken him at his word, when he finally returned to the house,. The uncanny silence as he entered the back door told him Abby had gone. Dripping puddles of moisture as he went, Paul traipsed inside. The ache in his heart made him feel contrite for his hasty outburst but she had betrayed him, sleeping with another man – in his house. Despite knowing she wasn't there he searched through the rooms and came to a standstill by the side of her bed where items of her clothing were scattered on the floor. Amongst them was the outfit he bought her for the pool party. Hunching down, he lifted the three skimpy garments to his heart, clutching the fabric in a tight grip as a groan in despair rumbled upwards from deep down. 'Oh, God, Abby, why?'

Ignoring his saturated clothing, he crawled onto the bed with the outfit clutched against his chest and sank his head into the pillow, absorbing the sweet perfume of Abby. Numb with grief, he slept until a gnawing cold woke him late in the evening. After a hot shower to wash away clinging dry sand which itched abominably he returned to Abby's bed and fell into a stupor of sweet dreams interspersed with less pleasant nightmares, hovering between fidgety wakefulness and being virtually comatose.

* * *

After sitting on a cold stone bench in the entrance alcove of the church until the rain ceased, Abby hid her bag in a tiny niche inside the building before she was able to figure she needed the warmth of a nearby café and something to eat. Since she didn't dare spend much of her meagre supplies of cash, she asked only for a mug of the hottest chocolate they could make, hoping the milky drink would be enough to fill the void in her empty stomach. She lingered as long as she dared but made use of the facilities to freshen up before she left. With no idea what to do next, she returned to the church, thankful there was a lull in the downpour. This time she figured it would be much warmer inside where she could have the solitude to be able to think about what the heck she was going to do. It took a lot of soul searching to come to a decision to seek out Dianne for help. What other choice did she have? Yes, she had met a few people, had a couple of new friends but not of the deep friendship status where one could lob on their front doorstep and ask for a sofa to sleep on for a day or two or maybe even longer. How long would it take to find a place to live?

Decision made, she pulled her money purse from her bag, turned back and crept outside. At the door she halted and peered in all directions to ensure no-one was around before she straightened her back, planted a smile on her face and forced her legs to stride boldly. When she reached the only public phone-box still in existence, standing like a lonely sentinel in front of the post office, she studied the directions, miffed when it didn't take coins. She had to use a credit card. Good job she now had a debit card with enough funds to make a call. She slotted the card in, followed the instructions and dialled Dianne's number. Hope turned to despair when the phone rang out at the other end, telling her neither Dianne nor Bill were home.

Frustration gnawed while she stood in the phone-box with her head hung low and her mind numb. At a loud rap on the door of the box she jerked from her reverie and became aware of exactly where she was. Mumbling an apology, Abby stepped onto the pavement and returned to the warmth and relative safety of the church. With her emotions drained away and no-where to go, she curled up on the carpet which ran down the central aisle and nestled her head on her bag as a pillow, determined to phone Dianne every half hour.

'Wake up, Sleeping Beauty.' Abby fought to open her eyes but jerked upright at the sight of a stranger's smiling face peering at her.

'It's okay, you fell asleep in my church.'

Abby struggled to stand. Church? Oh, yes. She eyed the stranger and winced at the sight of a white collar. 'Oh, I am so sorry. I didn't mean to fall asleep. I was…' She glanced down at her watch. 'Oh my gosh.' Her hands went to her mouth. She had been asleep for hours. How embarrassing.

'Come and sit here.' The Reverend indicated a pew. 'You have a rather serious problem.'

'I'm all right. I…' Abby paced around in a circle but could do nothing but plop onto the pew. What else could she do?

'You are an unmarried pregnant woman with no place to stay if what I see is true.' He indicated towards her suitcase.

Far out, did he have to be so pointed? Abby hung her head. 'Yes, you have managed to sum things up pretty well.' Her breath hitched as she lifted one hand and held it to her eyes which were beginning to itch with the need to leak.

'Don't get yourself all upset.' The Reverend placed one hand on her shoulder and gave it a comforting squeeze. 'Tell me what happened and we'll see what we can do to help. How about you come over to the rectory where my lovely wife will make us both something to eat for supper? I take it you haven't eaten in a while.' He smiled but it in no way dissipated the rising heat in her cheeks as she shook her head.

Over the next half hour, Abby devoured a plate of freshly cut sandwiches and a milky hot chocolate drink after she spent too long in the bathroom. While she ate, the Reverend asked discreet questions until he had the entire story. Somehow his clever questions managed to elicit the name of someone he could call and thirty minutes later he opened the door to Dianne Rogers.

Dianne flew across the floor and dropped down at Abby's knees. 'Abby, what on earth happened?'

Seeing Dianne brought a fresh wave of tears Abby had no control over. Damn hormones had taken over her life, 'Paul hates me – told me to get out.'

'Paul? He's back? But I thought...'

'He came back this morning, took one look at me and began yelling. Told me I was nothing more than a lying bitch and ordered me from the house. He said... he said... I was the same as Jasmine. Why? What did I do? I have never taken anything from him - never used a single cent of his money. I paid as much rent as I could afford, paid all my bills, my phone calls. I don't understand. But he was - so angry.'

'Paul said those things? I don't believe it. He's not so vindictive.' Dianne's arms went around Abby and hugged her close. 'Do you want me to talk to him, to find out why he was so angry? Was it because of the baby?'

All Abby had the energy to do was to nod her head against Dianne's breast. Dianne eased her hold and leant away but only far enough so her hands still held each side of Abby's shoulders.

'But I thought you told him and he answered.'

'I did,' Abby wailed, 'but I'm not so sure now whether or not he received my package. I don't think he knew.' She stared at Dianne. 'He was so angry about the baby. He doesn't want it - or me. What am I going to do?'

'But it's his child, how could he not want it?' For a moment there was silence and Abby's confused mind tangled itself into knots along with everything inside her tummy and her nerves. Dianne stood and drew Abby up. 'We will sort things out but in the meantime, you are coming home with me. You can use our spare room for a couple of days while we figure out what to do.'

When a distant phone rang, it dragged Paul from an exhaustive sleep. It took a moment to realise where he was before he managed to get upright and stumble from Abby's bed. Still groggy, he reeled along across the passage to his room, dropped to the side of the mattress and lifted the cordless receiver to his ear.

'Sanders here,' he barked.

'Err, umm is this Abby's phone?'

The mention of Abby's name by a female voice he didn't recognise had Paul sit up straight but at a loss as to what to tell this stranger. 'Yes, how can I help you?'

'Are you Paul?'

Now he was mystified. Who knew about him and what did they know? 'Yes, I'm Paul. To whom am I speaking?'

'Oh, sorry, you won't know me yet but I am Abby's obstetrician, Doctor Kelly Carstairs. Abby must be delighted you are home. Can I speak to her please?'

For a moment he sat staring at the phone wondering what to say. The fuzziness of a sleepy brain cleared in an instant as he recalled the past twenty-four hours. 'Abby's not available at the moment. Can I ask what this is about?'

'I was concerned about her. She missed her antenatal class last night and didn't turn up for her check-up this morning. It's not like her. I hope she's not ill again.'

'Ill? I know nothing of this illness, she's not said anything.' He prayed he was carrying this conversation off right. The doctor wasn't obliged to tell him a damn thing and if she knew Abby wasn't living here any longer - well he would be left in the dark.

'Her morning sickness. Poor girl. She's one of those unfortunate ones who suffer all day, every day right through the pregnancy. I had to hospitalise her several times. Please tell me she's not ill again?'

How the hell was he supposed to know, he thought as he scrabbled through groggy brain cells to find a reasonable answer. 'She's fine.' And damn me to hell for lying, he added under his breath. Another thought edged forward, somehow he needed to find out how long after he left, Abby had waited before seeking the comfort of another man. He knew he should feel guilty for asking but she was the one who had lied to him all those months. 'Tell me, Doctor, how long has Abby had this morning sickness she hasn't told me about.'

'Well she came to me... let me see my notes.' There was a pause during which he heard the turning of pages. 'Five months ago.' Five months. Anger surged. It was only a couple of weeks after he had left. 'And she was already six weeks pregnant when she first came.'

Paul jerked. 'Excuse me, would you mind repeating what you said? Exactly how far along is she?'

'Around seven and a half months but surely you already know since you are the father.'

The phone dropped from nerveless fingers. By the time Paul roused from his stunned stupor and picked the phone from the floor, the doctor had given up waiting and had hung up. Shaking fingers replaced the receiver. Unable to believe what he'd heard, he remained seated on the side of his bed staring into space as two words spun around his head non-stop. 'My baby?'

Too stunned to think, he sat while trying to sort things in a still fuggy brain. Slowly, coherence came, and things dragged together in a logical manner. When his brain cells finally aligned, he hated himself for the conclusions he had so stupidly jumped to and for what he said to poor Abby. He had to find her and beg forgiveness but didn't have a clue how to start. Where would she have gone?

All the while he dragged on a fresh set of clothes, he searched the house for clues as to any friends Abby may have made while he had been away. Dianne - he remembered how often in her letters she had mentioned Dianne. Since he was near the study, he pushed open the door and strode across the carpet to the phone where he spied the open phone book and the screwed-up remnants of a well-used tissue sitting on the open page. The sight of the tissue wrenched at his heart. He scanned the listings on the open pages under the letter T and noticed an underlined number for the local taxi company. Of course, she would have rung for a taxi. Enquiries took over an hour but after he was passed from one person to another he was told Abby had been dropped off outside the local Anglican Church.

Ten minutes later he stood on the porch of the church but was at a loss as to what he was supposed to do next. In vain hope, he entered the open doorway and searched the inside with his eyes. The place was eerily quiet. There were a few nooks leading off the sides, so he wandered around to inspect every inch, including under and on the long wooden pews. At a noise from his right he twisted his upper body around but he remained silent in case it was Abby hiding from him.

'Can I help you,' asked a man who was, by the way he was dressed, obviously the minister.

'I'm not sure. I am looking for someone, a young woman. The taxi company said she got out here. I don't suppose you have seen her?'

'Ah, could you be referring to the golden headed mother-to-be who was so distraught I thought Noah was going to have to be resurrected to build another ark?' The minister's smile in no way eased the pain and guilt which gnawed away at Paul's insides.

'She was here?' Paul rushed over to the man with his hand held out in greeting.

'She was here.' The minister shook the proffered hand. 'I take it you are Paul.'

'Err, yes, but I'm not sure I like the way you said my name.' He didn't need any explanation; he knew damn well Abby would not have had one single decent thing to say about him.

'Well, young Abby was terribly upset and quite frankly from what she told me, I can't say I blame her. I rather got the impression you managed to break her heart.'

As Paul raised his closed eyes upwards with a painful grimace, his innards did an excellent job of tying themselves into a million very tight knots.

'I'm Reverend Brian Lee, rector of this Parish. Brian will do.'

'Sorry, Paul Sanders, contrite and incredibly sorry man of the moment. You can add decidedly stupid to my description. You don't happen to know where Abby is, do you?'

'I have a fair idea but is she going to want me to tell you?' One hand went to Brian's chin in a musing gesture as he stared at Paul.

He probably thinks I'm a prize idiot along with callous brute, Paul thought. And he would be right. 'If I were being honest, and the shoe was on the other foot, I would probably say, no. I imagine I hurt Abby a great deal by jumping to conclusions and not giving her a chance to explain. But seeing her pregnant was a massive shock. I had no idea and since we were not an item before I went away, I naturally assumed she had taken up with some other man.'

'But now?' The Reverend Lee dropped to the nearest pew and indicated for Paul to sit beside him.

'I had a phone call from her doctor who informed me I was the father of Abby's... err... our child.' Paul sat beside the Reverend.

'But if there was no... um... relationship, how could there be a baby on the way, unless of course, we are about to be blessed with another immaculate conception?'

'It's a long story but there was one and only one... um... occasion when conception could have taken place. Since Abby is over seven months into her pregnancy and she was a virgin beforehand, it seems a miracle did occur on that one occasion.' Paul's stretched his arms out along the back of the pew, more to give him support than anything else. He was certainly not in the least bit relaxed.

'And you want this miracle child of yours?' Reverend Lee leant forwards but kept his eyes on Paul.

'Oh, yes and even more, I want Abby. I love her and had intended to ask her to marry me after we had a chance to renew our friendship. You see I've been working overseas and...'

'Yes, I know, she told me the entire story except she didn't divulge the details of the one occasion. Something I didn't need to know.' He grinned at Paul, who didn't find this entire ordeal in the least amusing. 'It appears you have a bit of a problem. She was so full of heartache and despair last night. I feel it will take her a while to be amenable to humble apologies.'

'Last night? But she disappeared yesterday before lunch.' A long groan rumbled out as Paul dropped his hands into his lap and twisted around to face Brian better.

'Yes, so I believe. She hid in here for most of the day and I found her curled up on the floor, asleep, early in the evening when I came to lock the doors.'

A louder groan of despair tore from Paul's throat. 'I feel so bad about the way I treated her and have no idea how to make things better between us, how to get her to forgive me.'

'The truth often helps. Lying tends to make matters worse eventually. I suggest, if and when she allows you to speak to her, you simply tell her the truth from your point of view. She said she had written to you a couple of months ago, explaining about the baby.'

'I never received the letter. Mail in war torn areas is not at all reliable. In fact a lot of services are not very well organised. And even less now with the chaos which is going on at the moment. I was lucky to get out when I did. How I wish I had received all of my mail.' He searched the ceiling for inspiration. 'Can you tell me where she went? I would really appreciate it.'

'After we had discussed her options and Abby changed her mind more than once we finally rang a friend who came to pick her up and I believe has taken her in for a few days.'

'And does this friend have a name so I can begin to grovel and beg forgiveness?'

The Reverend released a shout of laughter. 'I like you and am sending a prayer to our good Lord I am not making a mistake here. I believe Abby needs the father of her baby. Does the name Dianne mean anything to you?'

Paul's face lit up. 'Oh, yes, Dianne is my cousin. A cousin who is not speaking to me right now but I was hoping it was where Abby went. Dianne was my next port of call.' Paul stood and faced the Reverend. 'You have no idea how relieved I am. I'm glad Abby found a safe place to hide in. Thank you, from the bottom of my heart.'

'I have a feeling you are not out of the woods yet. Abby was not what I would call, in a very forgiving frame of mind and your cousin was quite furious with you as well. But good luck and don't give up. Abby needs you and so does your child.'

The two men walked side-by-side until they reached the edge of the porch. After shaking hands, Paul stepped off the paved concrete of the porch and dodged the puddles still lying on the ground as he ran towards his car.

After what seemed to Paul to be an interminably long drive, but in actual fact took less than ten minutes, he slowed to a stop and hesitated before turning into the driveway of his cousin's house. Knowing the reception was going to be tense and icy cold, he pressed down on the accelerator as he swung from the road onto the gravel and slithered to a halt at the crest of the circular driveway in front of an imposing set of concrete steps which led to ornate double doors.

Half expecting to be thrown out without given a chance to discuss things with Abby, he was most surprised when Dianne opened the door to him. The supercilious look she bestowed upon him was as he expected. He had the good grace to look ashamed. 'Abby, is she still here?'

'What makes you think she is here?'

'I'm not in the mood to be playing games, Dianne. I know she came here.'

'And you expect her to be in the mood to want to see you? After what you did to her?'

'Actually, I wouldn't blame her if she never wanted to speak to me again but we really don't have a choice but to discuss things since she is carrying my baby.'

'So now you think the baby is yours? After what Abby told me I gathered you thought she had been sleeping around with all and sundry.' There was a definite sarcasm to Dianne's comments.

'Come on, Dianne. I had no idea she was pregnant and when I saw her yesterday it was a hell of a shock. What was I supposed to think? It's not as though we were having a physical relationship before I went away.' His attempt to enter the door was met by a solid, unmoving human wall of determination.

'Abby told me about the night in question and, I might add, she accepts the blame for what happened. She has had six months of hell fighting hard to keep this baby.'

Paul glanced at her. 'What do you mean?'

'She's had a very tough pregnancy. Several times she had break-through bleeding when she thought she was going to lose the baby. She spent around six weeks, all up, in hospital. She didn't write to you until she knew for sure she wasn't going to lose it. Your treatment of her yesterday was more than she could manage. I don't think she slept much last night but is now sound asleep. Poor girl is emotionally exhausted so is in desperate need of a solid few hours of sleep. How about coming back later?'

'Not going to happen.' Paul pushed past her and stepped inside while talking over his shoulder. 'I'm not going anywhere until Abby and I have discussed this whole mess. I will wait here. I want this baby and I want Abby as my wife. I don't care how long I have to wait.' Spinning around, he stared into Dianne's affronted gaze. 'Abby is worth every second.'

Dianne paused from her chase, a stunned look on her face. 'You want her?'

'Of course I do. I've wanted her since before I left here. It has been a damn arduous five and half months being stuck over there when all I wanted was to be here with Abby.' He grinned at the smile spreading over his cousin's face.

'You're in love with her aren't you?' Dianne said as she stepped right up to him, her eyes ending only inches from his.

'I'm crazy about her, but I would rather you don't say anything to Abby. This is between us. I need to convince Abby about my feelings and somehow get her to at least be amenable to the idea of a relationship between us. Plus now we have a child to consider. So please don't mention this to her? Where is she?'

'In the guest room, but don't wake her.' Dianne paused before adding, 'Look, I won't say anything but she is going to need time. She was pretty upset.'

'I realise this and I feel as guilty as hell but I have no intention of hurting her anymore.' He couldn't help the glance at the closed door of the guest room. He paused in front of it. 'I want to see her. I promise I won't wake her but I need to sit where I can watch her.'

Taking care to not make any noise, his hand turned the door-knob in a slow circle until he heard the click of release. With his heart jammed somewhere really uncomfortable he pushed the door ajar and sidled inside, where a fist wrapped around his heart at the sight of Abby huddled curled up on her side, a scrunched tissue clutched in one closed fist. Taking utmost care to not make a sound as he shut the door, he crept closer. The fist still around his heart, squeezed the life from him when he noticed her swollen eyes and tear-streaked face, the moisture now dried but her hours of distress were so blatantly obvious. An untidy halo of longer gold tresses fanned in all directions around the pillow, some of it lying in knotty tangles where she had tossed around in her grief. She still looked like an angel, but this time an incredibly sad angel. How he despised himself for inflicting such pain.

A delicate wooden rocking chair covered in pink and white gingham cushions, stood in the corner. With utmost care so as to not make any noise, he lifted the chair from the carpet and carried it to her bedside. After setting it into place he eased his body down, straining his arm muscles while he settled without disturbing the beautiful but desperately sad woman in front of him. The knowledge he had done this to her, gnawed at his heart while he watched, absorbing every nuance of her features. How he loved this beautiful creature.

Seventeen

At the very first sign of Abby stirring, Paul's muscles tensed. He had a strong urge to leap up, kneel by her side and envelop her in his arms. Instead he remained still, leant back in the rocker with his legs stretched out and his ankles crossed. He'd been there, apart from a brief foray to the bathroom and to coax a mug of coffee from Dianne, for three hours. While he sat, he played many scenarios through his mind on what he was going to say and tossed most of them away. It was all going to depend on how Abby was going to react to his presence.

The frown which creased her brow the moment her eyes focussed on him was not a good sign. 'Abby?'

'Go away.' The tone was bitter as she threw her body over to turn her back on him, her expanded belly making the manoeuvre ungainly and awkward but oh, so cute. His child lived in there, safe and snug, the thought turning his heart into mush.

'We need to talk.'

'We have nothing to talk about. You said all I need to know yesterday. Now go away.'

At the slight hitch to her voice, Paul felt sure she was fighting back a renewed bout of tears. 'I regret most of what I said yesterday and the little bump across your stomach tells me we have plenty to discuss. Why didn't you tell me yesterday the baby you are carrying is mine?' The sudden cessation of any movement from the covers told Paul she had heard his quiet words.

'If I recall correctly, you didn't give me a chance and besides, I wrote to you and told you.'

'I swear I didn't receive your letter, Abby. I had no idea you were pregnant. It was a hell of a shock when I saw you yesterday.'

'So how do you know you are the father? You accused me of being disloyal. Exactly like Jasmine – a lying bitch, in fact, I am sure you yelled at me.'

At the same time as a deep groan of regret rumbled from Paul's throat there was a choking sound from Abby. Paul knew the tears were flowing. He hated himself for being the cause of such anguish. He rose from the chair and crept around to the other side of the bed. 'Abby, please don't cry. I admit I flew off the handle and behaved like an inconsiderate oafish brute, but seeing you pregnant was a heck of a shock and since we weren't exactly sleeping together before I went away, what was I supposed to think? Not once in any of your letters did you mention our child so how was I supposed to know? I know apologising to you for how I reacted yesterday is not going to make one iota of difference, but I am sorry. I didn't mean to hurt you. I never want to hurt you.'

She flipped back over, probably so she didn't have to look at him. Abby swiped at the unstoppable deluge flowing from her eyes. 'What makes you think you are the father?' she managed to choke out.

'Several things. You are over seven months, which times it exactly to the night we met. I had a phone call from your doctor who was concerned as to why you didn't turn up for your appointment this morning and a charming Reverend and I had a little chat this morning.' He was about to move to the other side of the bed but his words had her spin back over and there was a spark in her eyes.

'How did you find me?'

He smiled at her fury; her angry independence was far better than forlorn tears. 'Finding you was the easy bit, you left me a trail to follow and I figured Dianne would be someone you would turn to.'

'How come it has taken you so long?' She sounded contemptuous and childish but he figured Abby wasn't convinced of his sincerity. After yesterday's outburst, how could she trust him? She glanced at the clock radio by her bedside, her widening eyes telling him she hadn't realised it was already afternoon.

He dropped to his knees by the side of the bed but Abby wriggled ungainly over to the far side in an unspoken but definite message for him to not touch her. His hands gripped the covers to prevent them from doing what they wanted of their own accord: to haul her body into his arms and hold her tight. Kissing her was high on the priority list but would be downright foolish.

'When I had a chat with your Reverend Lee this morning I had no idea how I was going to even begin to ask for your forgiveness. He suggested the truth would be the best way. Give my version of things, so here goes. In the past couple of months I have worked long hours pushing the teams of workers to complete the project ahead of time so I could come home sooner. In the end it was fortuitous I had pushed so hard and my side of the project was completed but it is a miracle I managed to get out before the Taliban entered Kabul and took control. There was utter chaos with thousands of expats and locals fighting to get out on the final flights. I was one of the lucky ones to get to Dubai where I had to wait for a flight home. When I finally arrived home I was exhausted but so excited at seeing you again I couldn't sleep on the plane. In fact I hadn't had any sleep for over thirty hours.'

When Abby sparked up, looking as though she was about to burn his ears in protest, he held up one hand in a conciliatory motion. 'I know it doesn't excuse the way I behaved but please give me a chance to explain. After I left the house yesterday I ran for several miles, feeling distraught, numb, devastated. In fact I was an emotional wreck, the same as you are right now. I guess being so tired didn't help things. I didn't, no couldn't return until my brain managed to sort itself out. So much turmoil went through my head as I tried to make sense of everything but couldn't. Not once did I think I could be the child's father. It didn't even enter my brain as a twinge. When I found you had gone, I went to your room, crawled onto the bed, buried my head in your pillow and wallowed in the scent of you. I slept until the phone call woke me this morning. I have been sitting in this chair for three hours waiting for you to awaken.'

'I still can't figure out why you were so vindictive towards me. Even if it was someone else's baby, you had no reason to be so nasty.'

Paul was about to respond but a weird expression crossed over Abby's face. She squirmed, wriggled and flung back the covers. 'Excuse me but I need the bathroom,' she mumbled as she struggled from the bed, staggered upright and fled from the room, her left hip still hitching but she managed to almost run.

Mesmerised by the ease in which she could now move, the only thing which entered his mind was the doctor's mention of con-tinued morning sickness so Paul rose from his knees and followed Abby, hovering in the passage a discreet distance from the closed bathroom door.

Dianne appeared at the far end of the passageway. 'Is everything all right?'

Paul turned at his cousin's voice and noticed the deep frown of concern on her face. 'Well I am still alive, which is a plus.' Realising sarcasm was the not the best thing to do at the moment, he altered his demeanour. 'Abby is in the bathroom. Do you think she is okay? The doctor said something about morning sickness.'

A smile hovered over Dianne's lips as she contemplated her cousin. 'Being over seven months pregnant doesn't leave a lot of room for a full bladder. She spends a lot of time in the bathroom at the moment. It's one of the pleasures of being a pregnant woman. I'll make her a cup of tea.' Dianne returned to the kitchen at the same time Abby opened the bathroom door.

'Are you okay?' Paul asked as he stepped towards her, but he paused mid-stride when he saw a look of fear wash over Abby's face. He winced as he took a step back, his hands dropped to his side in submission. 'Strewth, Abby, I'm not going to hurt you, I'm worried about you.' With a deep sigh he changed tack. 'Where do you want to go, back to bed, the kitchen, outside?'

He heard her sigh. 'I'm sorry. I didn't mean to react like an idiot. I know you won't hurt me. It's...' She paused. 'Bed. I need to lie down a bit longer.'

It took a moment for Paul to realise Abby was waiting for him to move out of the way, out of touching distance before she would take a step. A wave of all-consuming pain and self-disgust swept through him at how Abby was so afraid of him. To ease the tense standoff, he half turned. 'Dianne said something about a cup of tea. I'll fetch it for you. Go and lie down.'

By the time he re-entered the room, Abby was prostrate in the centre of the mattress with the soft gingham quilt pulled up to her neck, her eyes closed. She looked pale and there was a thin curved line of grey around her mouth. He settled the mug of so-called tea on the bedside table. It had so little colour, it was closer to boiled water. Paul noticed the same grey tinge in the area under Abby's eyes. 'Are you feeling all right?' he asked.

Abby swallowed, paused for a second or two before pressing her lips together even tighter and nodded her head.

Unsure as to what to do, Paul eased into the rocking chair and placed his own, much darker version of tea on the floor beside him. If he kept his distance it should ease Abby's distress. The ensuing silence was tense. They both appeared to be waiting for the other to say something – anything. 'Marry me, Abby.'

Abby jerked upright. 'What did you say?' Before she had the words out her face contorted and her hand flew to her mouth. In a flash, she shot from the bed and lurched across the room with the back of her hand pressed against her lips.

Alarmed, Paul shot up and followed to hear the sounds of Abby retching before he reached the bathroom door. Not caring about propriety or how Abby would feel about his intrusion, he strode across the hall, into the bathroom and knelt by Abby's hunched body. He didn't give a damn about how she would react when he placed his outstretched hand on her back and rubbed in gentle circular motions. There was no way he wasn't going to help her. Reaching out with his other hand, he grabbed a face flannel, soaked it under cold water and squeezed the excess moisture from it before placing it across her brow, ignoring the acidic stench when she heaved again. When she finally sat back on her heels, Paul wiped her face before reaching up to fill a plastic tumbler with water and held it to her lips. 'Rinse your mouth out.'

Fingers shook as Abby took the tumbler, sucked in a mouthful, swished, leant over the toilet bowl and spat it out. The next sip, she swallowed. 'Thank you.'

He smiled. 'I visualised several responses to my proposal but I didn't quite expect it to make you so ill.' At the first indication of a smile he had seen on Abby, he added, 'I figure since I am partly responsible for you having to suffer like this the least I can do is offer what little help I can. I only wish I had been here for all of your pregnancy. I feel tormented you had to suffer alone. How's the stomach now?'

'Better, I think.' She made to rise up but Paul was quicker.

Standing, he reached down and eased her upright. After pressing the button on the cistern, he swept one arm around her shoulders and the other under her legs and lifted her into his arms. The feel of her warm body against his chest was incredible. She still wore traces of the same floral perfume he had dreamt about so many times. He wanted to keep her in his arms but instead carried her back to the bedroom and within seconds she was back in bed. As he tucked the quilt around her, he stared into her gorgeous face.

'Has it been like this every day?' he asked as he perched on the side of the mattress while one hand swept away loose strands of hair from her sweat-dampened face.

'Sometimes not so bad, other times much worse.' She looked confused and he guessed she was.

'And I take it, you are not going to tell me about how it became so bad you were hospitalised – six times I believe.' He smiled at her shocked face.

'How did you know?' She paused. 'It wasn't always for morning sickness.'

'I know, you haemorrhaged several times. Oh, Abby, how I wish I had been here for you.' His hand stalled for a few seconds but finally dropped over her curled fist, entwining his fingers with hers. 'Are you going to answer my question?'

'What question?'

'Are you going to marry me?' He felt her body stiffen before she pulled her fingers free.

'Why get married?'

He laid one hand on the bulge hidden under the covers. 'This is our child. He or she deserves to be raised in a family environment. I want to be a father to our child – a full time, twenty-four hour a day father and not a distant male figure who only gets to see his child every second weekend. I want to be able to read bedtime stories and tuck them into bed, to be able to calm away nightmares, to be there for disturbed nights and walk the floor. I want to be there to clean and bandage scraped knees when they happen and to see every milestone as they occur. I couldn't bear it if you rang me to say our baby crawled for the first time three days ago or they smiled.'

Abby turned away and he wondered if it was so he couldn't read her expressions. 'We don't have to be married for all of those things to happen,' she said in a strangled voice.

A hollow sense of dread descended over him and wrapped around like a suffocating shroud. She doesn't want marriage, echoed through his brain. 'So what exactly do you propose? Do we live together – sleeping in different rooms? How long will such an arrangement work? Until you find a guy you fall in love with? Until you marry the guy and take our child away.' Frustrated and with his heart doing a grand job of tearing into a thousand pieces, Paul began pacing around the room, his hand combing through his hair in frustration.

'Well getting married for no other reason than giving the baby a family isn't going to work either. Maybe it will be you who falls in love with some woman.'

'Never going to happen.' He flung the almost inaudible words over his shoulder as he stalked from the room, afraid Abby would see the pain in his eyes he knew he couldn't hide. Abby didn't love him as he loved her.

* * *

Paul would never love her. Those few words confirmed her worst fears. Abby couldn't control the tremble of her lips. What was she supposed to do now? The appearance of Dianne in the doorway was enough to send her fragile emotions on a spiral. A new wave of tears erupted.

Dianne raced across the carpet. 'What happened? Paul barged out the back like the devil was after him.'

'He asked me to marry him?' Abby sobbed as she grabbed a tissue from the box sitting on the bedside table.

'I thought you wanted to marry him.' Dianne paused. 'You did say yes, didn't you?'

Incapable of words, Abby could only shake her head from side-to-side as she held the tissue to her nose.

'Why on earth not?' Dianne's arm wrapped around Abby's shoulder and drew her close in a warm but gentle hug.

'He only wants to marry me to give the baby a family. I can't marry a man who doesn't love me.'

'Personally, I think you underestimate Paul. After what happened to him before by the bitch, Jasmine, he would never take the chance of asking you to marry him if he didn't have feelings for you and you know damn well it's what you want. I can't figure you out.' Dianne stood and yanked the bedclothes down, indicating her frustration. 'Get dressed and come into the kitchen. Lunch is ready. I demand you two have a truce while we all eat. Do you think we can at least eat in harmony?'

Stunned at the imperious tone coming from Dianne, Abby nodded and wiped her face dry with a clean tissue she yanked from the box. Her eyes followed Dianne's back until she disappeared. Abby took her time to dress after a visit the bathroom for a quick shower. It was enough time to pull her fragile emotions under control. She could be civil, she could be nice, she could maintain a truce but she didn't have to like it.

* * *

While he stood on the far side of the pool fighting hard to not allow free rein to the unusual moisture spread across his eyes, Paul heard someone storming through the house.

'Paul, what happened?'

Dianne, damn. He turned away to hide his face. 'She refuses to marry me.' When his voice broke he paused until he felt as though he had control over his emotions before daring to turn around. 'Living together without marriage would never work but I want this baby, want Abby, want us as a family.'

'Why won't living together work?'

'I love her so much. How can I live so close to her and keep my hands off her? It would send me insane. But I refuse to be a part-time father to my child and I could never fight her for custody. What in heaven's name am I supposed to do?' He plonked onto the same bench from where he rescued Abby from the unwanted attentions of the drunk politician. It was the moment he realised he was in love with her. At the time he wanted to kill the man for daring to touch her. The memory of the night surfaced. He felt her in his arms dancing, recalled them swimming together and the way they got on so much better since, the growing love he felt for her, the laughter they shared.

'Why don't you give her more time to come around to your way of thinking? I feel sure it's what she really wants. At the moment her hormones are haywire. Her tears flow at the drop of a hat, even when she is happy. She's unwell most days and has to be careful to not overdo things in case she haemorrhages again. Right now she needs someone to be there for her all the time.' Dianne sank down next to him and swept an arm around his shoulder. 'Look, I asked her to put any animosity aside while we eat lunch, can you do the same?'

After staring at Dianne for a moment he agreed. 'I don't want to fight with Abby. I will do anything it takes to get her to agree to come home with me. I guess I will have to start from scratch to build a relationship with her again.'

'Could I suggest you leave her here for another day or so while she calms down. It will give her time to think. I can talk to her, try to get her to see how sensible it would be for her to stay with you, at least until the baby is born. It will be up to you to convince her you love her and marriage is the best thing.'

A long sigh escaped his lips. 'Okay, sounds reasonable especially since I don't have any other solutions or ideas.'

Paul came to a standstill in the entrance of the kitchen. He studied Abby's profile as she sat staring out of the window. Her elbows rested on the table with a mug of hot drink held in the air, both hands wrapped around it. He suspected it was the insipid excuse for tea she had such an avid hold of. She looked pensive but there was colour in her cheeks and the ashen rings had disappeared from under her eyes. His innards clenched and the breath caught in his throat at the sight of her. It took an effort to force his lungs to breathe. Go for it, Sanders, he thought and turned the corners of his mouth up into a smile as he stepped into the room. He wasn't sure if she heard him or sensed his presence but all of a sudden her head turned towards him. For a split second there was complete silence as though the world had stopped in a time warp, but her face broke out into one of her gorgeous smiles, lighting up not only her face but the entire atmosphere.

'Paul, it's good to see you.'

'Abby, you look so much better.' He knew he sounded trite but at the same time, he had no idea how keen she was to return home with him or what had transpired between the two women over the past couple of days. He felt as though he was stumbling along a dark, airless tunnel, fighting for a way out. All Dianne had told him over the phone was how Abby had agreed to return home with him.

'I feel heaps better and am desperate for some sea air again. Come and join us for coffee.' His breath huffed out when she released the fingers of one hand from her cup and pulled out the chair next to her.

Utter relief surged at the simple action of her asking him to sit next to her. He strode across the room and dropped into the proffered seat, taking care for their bodies to not touch.

With his tension easing, Paul became aware of other sounds in the room. Dianne had followed him and was at the granite bench preparing the offered refreshments. Somehow, he forced his tense body to relax. So far, things had gone much better than he had anticipated and all of a sudden he was hopeful. From what Dianne had told him during a private phone conversation, Abby's self-confidence had taken more of a battering than he at first thought. From their discussions he knew Abby wanted to stay with him but he also knew her trust of him was diminished.

Nothing was said while Dianne placed plates of cold cuts and salad in front of each of them. She looked wary as she sat across the table. Her eyes met Paul's a split second before she gave a slight nod of her head in Abby's direction. Figuring she wanted him to start the conversation he turned to Abby. 'How has the nausea been, Abby?'

'Better.' At first Abby didn't lift her face but she peeked under golden lashes and smiled. 'Much better.'

He smiled back. 'I'm glad. I hate seeing you suffer.' Even though conversation sounded a bit stilted it soon eased into friendly camaraderie during the light meal so by the time Paul suggested they leave, laughter was bouncing off the walls.

They were nearing home when Paul dared to broach something he had been concerned about. 'Would you mind if I moved you into the other guest bedroom?'

He dared a peek in her direction but stiffened when he noticed her shoulders heave as she sucked in a long, slow breath.

'Dianne suggested I should voice my thoughts instead of jumping to conclusion as we have both done more than once so am I allowed to ask why?' she said as she turned her head towards him.

'Dianne suggested the same to me. I am more than willing because I hate it when we are at odds with each other.' He gave her a quick glance and grinned. 'Now to answer your question, I was hoping you would agree to turn the room you had been using, into a nursery. I studied all the rooms in the house and figured it was the most suitable. It's bright and airy, is at the back of the house and hence quieter and the baby can be heard from the living areas which is where we both spend most of our time.' When he heard her gasp, he glanced at her again and smiled at her stunned look. 'You seem surprised.'

'I am a bit surprised. I wasn't sure you would want to go to the trouble of redecorating. I was under the impression it wasn't so long ago you refurbished the house.'

'Hey, Abby, there were no children on the horizon when I first renovated the house and I kind of like the idea of us creating a really nice environment for our baby. I was hoping we could work together on ideas; choose colours, furniture and anything else. I can do the hard, physical stuff and you do whatever you can manage without compromising your health.' He turned into the drive, switched the engine off and twisted his body around towards her. 'What do you think?'

Her hesitancy was obvious in the way she shuttered her eyes and gnawed on her bottom lip. He figured his whole attitude had surprised her but after a great deal of soul searching over the past couple of days, he was determined to show her he cared deeply about both her and their baby. 'Remember what Dianne said to us both. Talk about our thoughts and discuss any concerns. Don't bottle them up – get them out in the open. Please tell me honestly what you think.'

'Honestly? I love the idea but... umm, do you really want to do this? This is not only some...'

He figured where she was going. She still wasn't certain how he felt about the baby, or, he guessed, her. He couldn't really blame her. 'Can we get one thing straight? I am over the moon about the baby. I have always wanted a family of my own but after Jasmine, I put the idea of marriage on the backburner for a while.' He noticed her shoulders tense, her eyes close and one tooth grabbed her bottom lip again. He felt sure she didn't realise how her habit of gnawing the corner of her lip gave away her unease. Damn, but he shouldn't have mentioned marriage.

'Can I add something there? Your arrival in my life, has changed things a great deal. I still want to marry you but will not pressure you into something you don't want or feel isn't right.' He sensed a sudden increase of tension in the atmosphere. 'Let me apologise. I hadn't intended talking about marriage since you made your thoughts about it quite clear. As far as I can figure out, we both need time to see how things work out between us. And as for the nursery, it's something I really want.' Hoping he hadn't set a wedge between them again, he lifted the door latch and eased from the car but everything inside him tightened into a taut wire, ready to snap.

Abby was out the door and headed towards the veranda before Paul could reach her. It scared him when she paused for a moment at the bottom step, but delight blossomed when she mounted the steps with an ease he felt proud of. Even more so when she turned and grinned at him.

'I can't believe how much better you can move. Congratulations.' When he reached her, he snaked one arm around her shoulders and gave her a hug but immediately released his hold, determined to keep it to nothing more than a friendly touch even though he found it difficult to release his grip. What he really wanted was to wrap her in a tight embrace and never let her go. 'I often visualise the difficulty you had when we met with Simpson. I am proud of you, Abby,' he said over his shoulder as he turned to unlock the front door. After shoving the door wide he returned to the car to collect Abby's belongings.

He found her standing in the doorway of the proposed nursery. There was a look of deep concentration on her face as her eyes swung around the room. 'What do you think?' Dropping the case on the floor, he moved up beside her.

Before answering, Abby took one step back into the passage and stared towards the other spare room. He wasn't able to read her mind but waited patiently for her decision. When she turned and stared at his bedroom door he became concerned. 'Tell me what the problem is, Abby?'

'Do you really want me to tell you what I'm thinking?'

'Yes.'

'Even if you don't like what my thoughts are?' She finally turned to face him.

'Especially if you think I am not going to like it.' He knew he shouldn't do it but he couldn't resist lifting a finger and brushing it down the side of her face.

'Well, I think you couldn't have put me any further away from the baby if you had tried. Your room is right opposite which means you will hear him or her before me during the night. What am I supposed to say?' She glared at him. 'Actually, I hate the idea but logic tells me you are right. The end room faces the road and has a laundry and all its entailed noises close by. The study, with walls of inbuilt cupboards and shelving would require major renovations and I wouldn't expect you to move out of your room – after all it is your house.'

He was about to say something when Abby held up a hand to stop him. 'My underlying feelings of distrust wonder if your choice is deliberate but I know I mustn't think such negative thoughts because I know you are not a nasty person.'

He paused for an inordinate amount of time; her hand still held in the air an obvious indication he didn't dare say a word. He figured she needed to get everything out and besides, he had asked for it.

'I understand your reasoning and after all, it is your house.' She turned away suddenly and Paul noticed her body began to tremble as she headed for her new room. It didn't take a university degree to tell him she was fighting back those damn tears.

On a huff of breath, Paul grabbed the bag and followed. 'Abby, wait a minute.' When he reached the room, Abby was standing in the centre with her back to him, her stillness telling him she was fighting for control. 'It was only an idea. If you would prefer one of the other rooms all you have to do is tell me. If you want the main bedroom, I don't mind. Look, it's not as if we have to decide right now. We still have around six weeks and I figure it would take only two weeks at the most to redecorate, depending on the weather. If it continues to rain like this the paint may take a little longer to dry. It needs a certain temperature for the paint to set properly.' His heart sat somewhere uncomfortable as he settled the case onto the floor before moving to stand in front of Abby, smiling at her tense face. 'The last thing I want to do is upset you.'

'I'm not upset, truly.' A grin broke out on her face at the puppy dog look he bestowed upon her.

'You look as though you are about to burst into tears,' he said as he fought his arms from wrapping around her. She also looked as though the only thing she needed was to be held, but he didn't dare follow through.

'I was told my hormones make me laugh one minute and sob like it's the end of the world two seconds later. It's nothing you said or did. Can I think things over? Maybe we can discuss the nursery over tea, or coffee for you. I really don't mind which room I sleep in.' She glanced around as though taking in all the details. 'Apart from its position across the end of the house, this room is almost identical to the other guest room, probably even a little larger. The only other difference is the outlook.' Paul moved next to her as she stared out of the window on the end wall. It faced the road while the larger window on the longer sidewall gave a view of the side fence and bushland beyond the boundary. Together they moved to the other window. In the distance, Paul could make out glimpses of their nearest neighbouring house but it was too far away for there to be any intrusion of privacy. His three acres of land gave them more privacy than they needed but it was one of the reasons he fell in love with the place.

'So where would you like me to leave your bag?' Paul asked as Abby turned back around to give another cursory sweep of the room.

'Here, will be fine for now, thank you. I'll begin coffee.' Abby strode past him, headed for the kitchen.

For a moment Paul didn't know how to answer. Before he went back to Afghanistan, they fended for themselves but he was more than happy for them to do things together. 'Sounds fine,' he called after her. 'I brought in fresh supplies yesterday but let me know if there is anything in particular you prefer.' For the first time since he had returned home, hope centred in his brain as he followed her down the passage, but he continued on through the front door to park the car away in the garage.

There was still an uncomfortable tension while they sat opposite each other at the kitchen table, an atmosphere bordering on explosive. To break the ennui, Paul reached over to collect the cups. He could sense her eyes boring into him while he cleared the table and placed the mugs on the sink.

'Paul, can I ask you something?'

He filled the sink with dirty dishes, squirted in a dob of dishwashing liquid and turned on the hot water. 'Ask away,' he said, twisting his head around to catch her eye.

For a moment Abby looked at the floor as she swept one foot around and around in semi-circles. She appeared to be searching for courage. 'Abby don't be afraid to speak your mind. Nothing you say will offend me. I promise.'

She glanced up as she straightened. 'Okay, I was wondering if I could still use your car once in a while. It will only be for appointments, I promise.'

The hitch in her voice had Paul turn off the tap and twist his entire body from the sink. 'You sound as though you are terrified of asking me. I'm not an ogre. You simply need to let me know when and where and if I'm not using the car, I don't have a problem. If I am, we can co-ordinate times so I can drop you off and pick you up. When is your first appointment?'

There was quite a lengthy pause. 'Tonight, but I was wondering if you would come with me?' Her voice held an uncertain quiver. As though she was too scared to look at him she stared at an unseen spot on the floor.

'What's on tonight?' He moved closer, hooked one finger under her chin to lift her face up.

'My antenatal class,' she whispered.

Elation hit. He knew from past conversations with his married friends how husbands attended these classes with their wives. For Abby to ask him to join her, he knew, was a gigantic step for her. 'And you would like me to be there with you? Are you telling me you want me to be at the birth?'

It was obvious his question threw her by the startled look on her face. 'I had no idea you understood the meaning of antenatal classes.' Her eyes lifted as a hesitant smile crawled out. 'Only if you would like to be there.'

She became engulfed in his arms. He wasn't so sure how it happened. 'You have no idea how much I want to be there. Oh, Abby.' Overwhelmed by the sensations sweeping through his body, he was unable to say any more. They remained embraced with Paul resting his chin on Abby's head. 'I was going to wait a while before plucking up the courage to ask you. You have made my day. What time tonight?'

'Seven. I must ring Dianne. She's been coming with me up until now. Did you know she is also pregnant?'

Paul pulled away, holding Abby at arm's length. 'She never said. I'm thrilled. I knew they were having trouble conceiving and there were suggestions they might have to go on a fertility programme.'

'There's something else.' Abby stepped backwards, her eyes dropping again. Her actions had Paul stiffen, a sudden sense of foreboding swept through him. 'I have a check-up with Doctor Carstairs tomorrow morning. Will you come with me?'

He whooped out in delight. 'Will I? Try to stop me.' Unable to resist, he stepped towards her, lifted both of her hands up to his face and dropped a kiss in each palm. Afraid he had gone too far, he promptly turned away and sank his hands back into the soapy dishwater to complete the dishes. Damn, he had been reckless but he sent a silent prayer skywards to ask for Abby to not take umbrage.

He managed a quick glance over his shoulder, noted her stunned expression but at least she hadn't hightailed it to hide in her room. 'I'm sorry, but I was so delighted I couldn't resist.'

'Don't be sorry, Paul.' There was a pause before she added, 'I need to unpack and move all of my things into the end room.'

By the time he managed to dry his hands on a tea towel and turn around, Abby had vanished. He flung the towel over his shoulder, traipsed after her and managed to catch up to her halfway down the passage. 'Does this mean we redecorate this room for the nursery?' Desperate to see her face so he could read her true reaction he grasped her shoulder, turned her around and gently eased her through the doorway.

She smiled. 'Yes, it is the best room.'

'How are you feeling right now?' At the curious frown crossing her face at his sudden question he added, 'Do you feel well enough to drive into town with me this afternoon to visit the paint shop and begin looking for ideas? We could have an early dinner somewhere nice before going onto your class.'

Even though she fought to hide the elation from her face it was obvious but Paul could see how she did her darndest to control her features. He grinned

'Thank you, I would love to go,' she said so quietly but a tiny grin crept out at the same time.

Progress. It was one tiny step but the step was progress.

The moment she opened the pantry door after switching on the kettle, and found the shelves devoid of crackers, Abby knew the day wasn't going to be one of her best. Already her stomach had sent out waves of protest since she had become upright and walked along the entire length of the passage to reach the toilet to ease the pressure of a bladder which couldn't wait a moment longer.

Darn, what could she eat instead. She took her time to search the shelves, spied a loaf of bread, withdrew two slices and dropped them into the slots of the toaster. While she waited for the bread to brown she added the now boiling water to the mug containing a tea bag. The very moment the mug was full she flicked the tea bag out without waiting for it to brew, leaving an insipid pale brown in the mug. At the click of the toaster, she grabbed a plate from the cupboard and wrestled the two hot pieces of toast onto it.

Not game to venture any further, she carried plate and mug only as far as the sitting room where she settled the two items on the coffee table before easing her body full length on the sofa. While she lay statue still, she willed the nausea to abate, not even game to lift her head to sip on the tea. One hand reached out and felt around until her fingers settled on a slice of uncut, dry toast. She nibbled at one corner, chewed, swallowed and waited for it to settle.

Feeling a tad better, she bit off another corner and took her time to demolish the entire square of toast. At least she felt confident enough to raise her head far enough to be able to taste her tea. Only daring one sip, she lay down. Her stomach didn't swirl. She dared a second sip, followed by a third, lying out flat in between to wait for each mouthful to settle.

From the corner of her eye, she spotted a small pile of papers on a side table next to the recliner-rocker she knew was Paul's favourite. When she recognised them, a smile broke out. Paul must have sat up last night to study them. It hadn't been hard to figure how nervous he had been when they first walked into the antenatal class last night but he had been amazing. He asked so many questions, participated fully and been so supportive and incredibly gentle when they prac-tised breathing. Lying there with her eyes closed, she could still feel the rhythmic kneading of his strong fingers as they massaged her lower back, which sent sensuous pulsations along her nerves, and for the first time, eased the ache. If only he knew how much she loved having him there instead of being the only woman without her partner. Dianne had been great but it wasn't the same.

Certain it was now safe to sit upright, Abby wondered how Paul would react at the doctor's surgery today. She reached for the second piece of toast, took one bite but immediately dropped it on the floor as she felt the acidic bile rise. Unable to run, she fled as fast as she could, hitching her left hip, the dropping foot echoing in a type of rhythmic syncopation as she fled along the passageway. Flinging open the door, it bounced back from the wall with a resounding bang, which hit her on her backside as she knelt over.

Still on her knees, Abby tensed when she heard the door whoosh further open. She felt, rather than saw, Paul kneel beside her at the same time a cold, damp flannel brushed against her sweat-dampened brow. His other hand rubbed gently up and down her spine, the warmth from his hand sending a spiral of tingles all through her body. It took a moment before she could find her voice.

'You don't have to do this, you know,' Abby murmured as she sat back on her heels.

'Let me be the judge of what I can and will do. It's our baby causing you to be so ill. The least I can do is ease your stress. How are you feeling now?'

She paused for a moment while ascertaining whether or not it was safe to leave the vicinity of the hallowed white throne. 'I think I'm about done.' She took the flannel from his fingers, wiped it across her mouth with one hand while the other reached up to press the button of the cistern.

Before she had a chance to stand, Paul was behind her, his hands under her arms as he eased her to her feet. At least she didn't have to struggle with a protruding belly which played games with her balance. It was ridiculous how much she liked his help. He didn't let go until they were in the passage when he dropped his clasped hands behind her lower back and held her against his body in a comfortable embrace. It felt so darn good but she must have tensed for he paused.

'Relax, Abby, stand still until you're sure your stomach has settled. I'll make breakfast while you shower. What would you like to eat – if anything?'

She giggled. 'I tried tea and dry toast.'

'Which didn't work so well. What's second on the list of choices?'

She knew he was teasing by the feel of the rumble in his chest pressed up against her ear. Sweet mercy but he felt so darn good. 'What my pregnant hormones are telling me my body needs is chocolate ice-cream with sliced up banana.'

'Huh?' Paul stepped backwards with a stunned expression, while he held her at arm's length. 'You ejected sensible but bland weak tea and dry toast and you want to try chocolate ice-cream?'

A wide grin split her face. 'Well I can't get any sicker and besides my body craves chocolate ice cream. And don't forget the sliced banana,' she called over her shoulder as she headed for the shower.

'For you, Angel, anything,' he yelled through the closed bathroom door.

Behind the door, Abby stopped in her tracks. Angel? Where did the endearment come from? After searching through her grey matter she recalled a couple of times he had called her Angel before he went back to Afghanistan. The smile didn't leave her face the entire time she wallowed under the warm water, nor while she dressed in her room. Angel. She liked it. Maybe a little too much but hey, she would take anything she could get right now.

* * *

In the kitchen, Paul searched the freezer and withdrew four tubs of Neapolitan ice cream. After he struggled to open each he grinned at the contents. It appeared this was not the first time Abby had a craving for chocolate ice cream. One container was as yet untouched but the other three held mashed up remnants of pink and white where Abby had meticulously carved out the chocolate layer. Figuring he could be a little neater in uncovering the hidden middle layer he upturned the entire carton onto a dinner plate. With a carving knife, he sliced off the sickly pink layer and placed it back into the carton with a grimace at the thought of him being the muggins who would have to eat his least favourite of flavours or it was going down the sink. He lifted off the chocolate tier, plonked it into a large cereal bowl and upended the vanilla back into the carton. After he had tossed the cartons back into the freezer, he peeled and sliced a banana, arranging the pieces so they made a smiley face on top of the chocolate. While he waited for Abby to emerge, he kept the precious meal in the freezer and served himself a bowl of cereal with milk.

The moment he heard Abby walk down the passage, he removed her breakfast from the freezer and set it on the table. Without saying a word, she sat and wolfed the lot down. After scraping the last skerrick from the plate she even licked the spoon clean and sat back in her chair with a wide grin on her face. 'This was so good.'

'I discovered the remains of your obsession. Why don't you buy a whole tub of chocolate instead of macerating Neapolitan into an indescribable heap reminiscent of a Mount Vesuvius aftermath?'

'I couldn't find plain chocolate.'

'And who is going to eat the strawberry and vanilla?'

Abby grinned as she pointed to him.

'I detest artificial strawberry ice cream,' he replied. 'I can't believe you actually ate the entire bowl and have kept it down.'

'We'd better go shopping on our way home. It's usually the wee small hours of the morning when I get a craving.'

As response, Paul could do no more than groan but there was a grin on his face. This was the first time Abby had been so uninhibited in her actions and words. Hope flooded his veins. This step forward was huge.

Two hours later, they were ushered into the inner sanctum of Dr Carstairs' office. 'Paul, I presume. I'm Kelly Carstairs. Please take a seat.'

The handshake was brief, the doctor removing her hand from Paul's grasp to indicate a chair next to Abby. A bit taken aback by the haste of withdrawal and cool demeanour of the doctor; Paul took his time to ease into the chair while he tried to ascertain why he was treated with such perfunctory coldness.

'Abby, how are you? You look a bit pale.' The doctor sat with her eyes scanning Abby's face and obviously concerned about her wan cheeks. Paul was also concerned.

'I'm fine.'

The doctor laughed. 'You say the same thing every time you come in here, regardless of whether you are gasping for your last breath or bleeding litres of blood. Now how about the truth? You vomited this morning didn't you?'

A deep pink blush rose up Abby's face. She didn't have to answer in words.

The doctor frowned. 'I thought the crackers were working. What happened?'

Intrigued at the words, Paul sat forward. This was news to him.

'I ran out,' Abby mumbled.

The doctor's eyes blazed at Paul as though he was the sole instigator of Abby's malaise.

'Don't look at me. I have no idea to what you are referring. Abby said nothing to me about crackers but after she demolished an entire third of a litre of chocolate ice cream for breakfast I fail to see how crackers are going to help.'

'But she did have a bout of morning sickness this morning?' The definitely incriminating eyes fixated fair square on Paul.

'Yes – before the ice cream.'

'I suggest you ensure there is a ready supply of salted crackers at her disposal before she rises from her bed.' Kelly turned to Abby and smiled, her demeanour a complete about face. 'How about hopping up onto the bed? You have a sample?'

Totally confused, Paul watched as Abby removed a small plastic jar from her bag, the pale-yellow colour of the liquid telling him exactly what it contained. While Abby retreated behind a curtained partition, frosty Kelly Carstairs unscrewed the lid, stuck a paper stick in the jar and studied the resultant colour change before she emptied the contents down the sink and tossed the container in the bin. 'Stay here for a minute while I examine Abby. If she allows it I will call you in.' This time she managed a smile, which left Paul even more confused.

Five minutes later the curtain swished back and the doctor indicated to Paul to join the two women. It startled him to see Abby lying back on a raised bed, with her abdomen exposed and a cotton blanket draped low over her pelvis. Her T-shirt was scrunched under her breasts. For the first time he was able to study the extent of her abdominal injuries but said nothing. Pregnancy had stretched the still red scars. Sorry they were there but glad he had now seen them he moved to her side after a sweep of the doctor's hand told him where to go. He glanced at Abby but his eyes caught the movement of a sudden bulge sweeping across her stomach.

Mesmerised, he stared. All of a sudden he felt his hand grasped and lifted. Abby placed his hand on the bulge, spread her fingers over his to hold his hand in place. The sensation threw him into a spin, his chest cavity clenching like a vice as it flooded with warmth. A prickly sensation washed over his eyes and he knew he was close to tears again. 'So darn amazing.'

Abby's eyes took on an incredulous look as she stared back at Paul. 'You really do care don't you?' she whispered.

His eyes moved from where her hand held his, to her face. 'You doubted me? Angel, I care as much about our baby as I do you. Thank you. I can't describe how amazing it is to feel our baby move... hell, how do I explain? My heart felt as though it exploded. Knowing you are carrying my child felt like a pleasant dream before, but now it feels so real, so incredible. I am only too sorry I wasn't here when you felt the first movements. I regret I have missed so much.'

Heat rose when he noticed Kelly Carstairs watched the interaction between them. For the first time her smile at him was friendly. 'Would you like to see your baby?' she asked as she undid the top of a tube of gel and squirted a great dollop on Abby's stomach.

'See?' Confused, Paul withdrew his hand from Abby's stomach but kept his fingers wrapped around her hand. The steps forward were getting bigger and better.

'Yes, see. We do regular scans, especially in Abby's case. With all the breakthrough bleeding she's had we need to ensure the placenta is healthy. Watch this screen.' With one finger she pointed to a small monitor while the right hand waved the scope through the gel, spreading it out.

Gob-smacked, Paul stared as blurred images came into focus. He saw the beating heart, moving legs and a fist waving at him while Kelly positioned the scope in various places and paused before moving to the next position. 'Do you want to know what sex it is?' she asked quietly.

Paul dragged his eyes from the screen and glanced at Abby in an obvious but silent question but Abby merely shook her head. 'I don't want to know until it is born,' she whispered with a quiver.

Paul turned his attention to the doctor. 'It's Abby's decision. The only reason I want to know is because it would make our choice of colour for the nursery a whole lot easier. Whether it's a boy or a girl doesn't matter to me.' When he turned his attention back to the screen, he lifted a finger to trace the outline of the miracle in front of him. 'This is so awesome. I can't believe we created this tiny individual, especially given the unbelievable circumstances.'

Before they left, Paul insisted on an outline of all the details of Abby's pregnancy, all her likes and dislikes, what she should and should not do, what he should and should not do until he was satisfied. It amused him the way Abby blushed as he listened to the doctor, her instructions telling him Abby had kept more than a few details from him but he refrained from making a single comment. Only when he was completely satisfied with all the details, he placed his arm around Abby's waist and herded her outside.

Twenty

Abby stared out of the car window as they neared the house after the latest shopping spree. It was still raining and she was beginning to hate the rain. Redecorating had come to a standstill after three weeks of non-stop rain making it almost impossible to paint. 'The cold, moist atmosphere meant the paint wouldn't set,' Paul said after Abby had voiced her complaint about the halt to the painting. To fill in time between antenatal classes and visits to the obstetrician, Paul accompanied Abby while they searched baby stores for furniture, clothing and all the related paraphernalia required. She still couldn't believe how involved he had become in the entire process and wondered if it was his skills as an engineer which made him check every item of furniture for strength and safety features, rejecting any he felt were not up to standard for his child.

The only hitch to the friendly camaraderie had been when Paul discovered Abby had deposited regular amounts of rent into his bank account. She knew he had difficulty in containing his fury when he confronted her and there had been a bit of a cold standoff when he attempted to give her the cash equalling the entire amount. In the end he suggested they use the amount to purchase items for the baby, something with which she was happy. He was still unhappy about the situation, she was certain, but she didn't care. There was no way she would give him any reason to think she was in the same league as the dreaded Jasmine but she wasn't game to disclose her real reasons. Abby was happy with the result although she wasn't so happy Paul insisted on paying for every single item they bought for their baby.

It was both a relief and bliss to arrive home from their latest foray. Abby was exhausted but anxious to unpack her latest purchases. She was so excited she didn't wait for Paul to put the car away but instead, hurried to the nursery. She paused in the doorway of the half-completed room, and as always in the past week, surveyed the room in amazement. Paul certainly had a flair for interior decorating. The bottom third of the walls had a coat of cream paint and Paul had painstakingly stuck dozens of decals all the way around to create continuous flowing scenes of a magical storyland. The carpet had been torn up and the jarrah floorboards sanded and polished. The ceiling wasn't white but painted in a half tint of the cream with the cornice three different tones picked out from the pictures. It wouldn't matter if their baby were a boy or a girl - the room suited both. Still missing was the paint on the upper section of the walls. The cans of grey tinged green still sat unopened in the corner waiting for the first sign of a sunny day.

Eager to see how the mobile she bought this morning matched the room, Abby tore the packing away, scrunched it into a ball and stuffed it into the pocket of her flowing jacket which barely hid her growing bulge. Excitement shimmered as she unravelled the delicate sparkling ornaments depicting the Hey-Diddle-Diddle characters, Abby held it up in the air as she walked around the room to see where the best place would be for Paul to hang it. To get a better view, she dragged the small set of steps away from the corner where Paul had stowed all his work gear and set them up, checking the arms were locked into place.

She took utmost care to climb the four steps, ensuring she was well balanced before holding the mobile up to the ceiling. Not happy the mobile would catch the sun's reflections, she carefully moved down the steps and dragged it further to one side.

It took four different positions before she was happy. To mark the position, she descended the steps and searched amongst the tools for the carpenter's pencil she knew Paul used to measure a straight line around the walls. Pencil in hand, she climbed back up the steps, stretched to her fullest to mark a dot on the ceiling. Satisfied, she took the first step down, missed her footing and with the ungainly protuberance of her stomach acting as the centre of gravity, over-balanced.

The fall wasn't far in distance but she landed face first and on her tummy. She squealed in alarm while she was airborne but on landing every ounce of breath whooshed from her lungs. Paul is going to be mad, was her first thought before she forced her lungs to suck in a breath. Finally able to breathe, she tried to get up but a stab of acute pain shot through her. Too scared to move or yell for Paul, who said he was going to prepare afternoon tea, she lay still, her mind in panic mode. It was the sensation of warm stickiness between her legs which woke her from stunned shock.

'Paul!'

* * *

At the sound of the blood curdling, high-pitched scream, Paul dropped the teaspoon into the sink and ran, following the noise of the repeated scream of his name. Since he thought Abby had gone to her bed to rest, he shot past the open nursery door but came to a screeching halt when his brain registered the crumpled heap on the floor he spied as he raced past. Backtracking, he shot through the nursery doorway and dropped onto his knees at Abby's side.

'Abby, what happened?' He grasped her hand but recoiled at the puddle of fluid tinged with bright red blood. 'God, Abby, what happened?'

'I fell.'

His heart ceased to beat for a moment and pounded double time when he noticed the fallen steps. 'What the devil were you doing on the steps?' he shouted but instantly dropped his voice when he noticed the tears threatening to fall from Abby's eyes. He used a curved forefinger to sweep a single drop of moisture from her cheek. 'I'm sorry I yelled but you scared me. I need to get you to hospital – pronto. Don't move.'

Torn between staying with Abby and phoning for an ambulance, he hesitated a moment until logic took over. 'Damn it,' he muttered under his breath as he raced to his room across the passage, grabbed the cordless phone but wasted precious seconds to search for the piece of paper he knew he had with Dr Carstairs phone number on. A spurt of adrenalin sent his blood into panic mode as he tossed item after item from his bedside table onto the floor, cursing under his breath until he found the elusive piece of paper in the top drawer where he finally remembered he stowed it so he knew where it was when the time came.

Typical. For him to need it now really worried him. It took ages before the urgency of his call was finally understood and he was put through. Unable to answer all the doctor's questions he raced back to Abby to relay questions and answers but at the gasp and squeal from Abby when a strong contraction convulsed her body, Paul yelled into the receiver. 'Abby's in labour. It will be quicker for me to drive her to hospital than wait for the ambulance. I'll meet you there.'

He stabbed a finger on the off button, dropped the phone on the floor and scooped Abby up into his arms. 'Come on, Sweetheart, you will be fine.' But it wasn't what he felt. She wasn't fine. She was in freaking labour. He tore through the house, grabbed the car keys from the hall table with one finger but had to ask Abby to unlock the door, too afraid to put her down. It took too long to settle her across the backseat of the car and he had to waste more time to pelt back inside when Abby demanded he get a couple of towels. The last thing he cared about was the back seat but even more, he didn't want to upset Abby, so he obeyed. The hospital wasn't far away, only on the other side of town, but he pushed the boundaries of speed limits, praying there were no patrol cars around. Speed cameras he could deal with, the picture and fine came weeks later. He figured the fine was a small price to pay for the safety of Abby and his child. Within the longest fifteen minutes of his life, he eased Abby out of the car and onto a stretcher which was already waiting for them with a message the doctor had rung on ahead.

He was desperate to go with her but instead, he was instructed to wait in purgatory in the waiting room while Abby was examined. A torture chamber was preferable. He pounced from the darn hard, plastic chair the moment he saw movement coming from the door. Doctor Carstairs approached him.

'Abby has torn the placenta and is in full labour. Come with me. You need to gown up but if anything goes wrong, we may need to do an emergency caesarean section.'

Fear grabbed at his innards and twisted them into a torturous bind. 'Abby, is she all right? And the baby, is it all right?' Unable to think straight Paul felt sure he was garbling as he trailed after the doctor down the corridor with him sidling like a crab in an attempt to keep up with the woman.

'The baby is fine at the moment. Heartbeat is strong so it's not under any stress. Abby is naturally distressed but is in no danger.'

'But it's too soon. Abby has several weeks to go.' They turned into a room.

'The baby is quite large and well developed. A few weeks early is not so bad. I'll leave you in this nurse's care. She will show you how to clean up and put on protective clothing. When you are dressed come through the door over there.' Pointing with one hand, Kelly kept walking, leaving Paul standing in the middle of the room feeling completely bewildered.

After he obeyed the nurse's instructions and moved like an automaton he was shoved through the door fifteen minutes later wearing a pair of scrubs, a surgical cap, mask and bootees over his bare feet. Since he was such a tall man there was quite a gap between the hem of the trousers and the top of the ridiculous footwear but the moment he saw the ashen faced Abby lying curled up on her side, he forgot about feeling so absurd. His heart managed a tumble-turn as he strode across the polished linoleum. He slowed, grasped Abby's curled hand in his. 'Angel?'

Her fingers gripped so tight he didn't need her to tell him how she was feeling. 'I'm so scared, Paul. What if I harmed our baby?'

Although he felt as panic-stricken as Abby looked, he knew he had to show restraint in order to ease Abby's fears. 'The doctor said the baby is fine and not under any stress. How about you let me do the worrying while you concentrate on relaxing? Tell me what you want me to do.'

'Don't leave me.' The appeal was so heartfelt it wrung at his heartstrings.

'Not a chance in the world, Angel. I'm here for the duration.'

Apart from occasional visits to the bathroom, Paul was a good as his word even though exhaustion had taken a hold about ten hours ago. He had watched an overhead clock for fifteen hours while he massaged Abby's aches, lay spooned against her back when she dozed, murmured soothing words of encouragement when spasms contracted her muscles and had the blood squeezed out of his hand more times than he cared to count. He figured delivering mothers developed superhuman strength as he shook his arm to get the blood flowing again after the latest massive contraction. With the birth imminent, he had only managed a modicum of feeling in his fingers before Abby grasped them again.

'Push, Abby.' Dr Carstairs glanced at Abby's face but immediately dropped it to give all her concentration to the crowning head.

Abby pushed, unable to suppress her scream of pain while Paul sat behind her, supporting her tense body with one arm around her shoulders and the other squeezed numb. Inside his innards were in the process of being torn apart because Abby was in so much pain and even though he knew women went through the same endurance test every time they gave birth, it didn't ease his conscience to know it was his Abby suffering so much while she delivered the child he had created.

'We have a head. Now we need one more push, Abby. No, wait for the contraction and go with it.' The muffled words came from a hidden face.

Paul didn't need her to tell him when the next contraction came, he saw and felt the rippling tension of her abdomen. 'Come on, Sweetheart, only one more. You can do it.' Whispering in her ear he followed his words by planting a kiss on her brow. A brief glance from Abby told him she was surprised by the kiss but in an instant her face contorted as the contraction took control. Paul braced his body to accept her strain as she held her breath and pushed for all she was worth.

'We have shoulders, keep going, Abby.' There was a scary silence and a frenzy of movement before the silence was broken by a wail. 'You have a healthy daughter, folks. She's a little small but many full-term babies are smaller and she certainly has a healthy set of lungs,' Dr Carstairs called over the continual loud wails. 'Do you want to cut the cord, Paul?'

This was something they hadn't got around to discussing at antenatal classes and the question stunned him.

'Go on, Paul.' At Abby's words he glanced down. His heart went all mushy when he saw Abby's glowing face staring at him. When he glanced up again he saw all expectant eyes were on him.

'Sure thing,' he said as he eased his cramped body from behind Abby and stood on shaky legs. It was like walking on a metre of marshmallow as he moved to the other end of the bed where he was handed the surgical scissors. The nurse guided his hand to the right position. As he cut, an indescribable feeling of pure warmth and elation filled his body. Tears prickled his eyeballs as he handed the scissors back to the nurse.

He sniffed them back, not because he was ashamed of the tears but because he needed to show strength for Abby. Back at Abby's side, he bent over her and brushed his lips over her startled mouth. It wasn't enough so he lifted one hand to cup her face. 'Thank you, my angel, I can't begin to describe how incredible I feel right now.' He kissed her again and almost fell to his knees when he felt her kiss him back.

'Would you like to hold your daughter?' The voice came from beside his shoulder at the same time a gentle shove nudged his side.

He caught Abby eyes, staring at him as he straightened, turned to his side and accepted the tightly wrapped bundle into his arms. There was no way he could ever describe how he felt as open eyes stared up at him. A wodge of wood settled in his throat and his hand automatically lifted and brushed against the damp, soft cheek. 'She's beautiful.' His eyes caught Abby's. 'She has your gorgeous hair so now I have two beautiful angels. Here, our gorgeous daughter belongs in your arms now and I guess by the way her mouth is working, she needs her mother.' With a smile he had no hope of suppressing, plastered across his face, Paul eased their amazing daughter into Abby's arms.

While gazing at her daughter, Abby asked, 'Why do you call me angel?'

He looked down at her hidden eyes. 'The first night I saw you, when we... umm... created this little beauty, your mussed-up hair floated around your face. To me you looked like I imagined an angel would look, ethereal, golden and so beautiful. Even though your hair is longer now, you still take my breath away every time I look at you.'

The sudden silence in the room had Paul glance up. The other three people present were staring at him with gooey looks on their faces. His cheeks heated but he smiled, causing the doctor and two nurses to busy themselves with final procedures.

Twenty-One

The ensuing five days saw Paul at the hospital to eat breakfast with Abby and his daughter after late nights spent completing the nursery. Surprise spread across his face when he strode into the private room to find Abby dressed and huddled back in an armchair. It took his breath away to see his daughter nursing against Abby's breast. It had delighted him the first time Abby had settled the baby to her breast and she had asked him to stay when he turned to leave the room to give her privacy and it still gave him a feeling of wonder every time he watched.

'Our daughter needs a name, Paul.'

'What do you suggest?' Squatting on the floor beside the chair he brushed a finger against the downy cheek. 'She is so darn beautiful.'

'I want to name her after my mother. Her name was Susan so how about Susannah?'

'Susannah Sharpe, sounds pretty.'

'No, Paul, Susannah Sanders. I want her to have your name, and how about Grace as a middle name?'

Overwhelmed, Paul could do nothing but stare at Abby. 'You sure know how to bring a man to tears don't you?' His crooked finger hooked under her chin to draw her face upwards so he could catch her eyes. 'Mum will be delighted. She's back from overseas and will come over tomorrow as long as you feel up to having a visitor. Are you sure about the surname?'

'I'm sure. Now how about going to find the head nurse? She wants to see us before they release me.'

Before moving, Paul swooped his head down and brushed his mouth against Abby's lips in a gentle kiss. She hadn't protested last time he took the initiative and her wanting their daughter to have his surname gave him a whole lot of hope he despaired of ever having. But something held him back from speaking of marriage yet. Now was not the time, nor the place. Not game to linger, he pulled away from the embrace and stood. 'I finished the nursery last night,' he said but immediately turned to escape before Abby had a chance to comment on his kiss. It would hurt too much if she said anything negative so he wasn't about to give her a chance.

Half an hour later, he strapped the baby capsule into the back seat of his car for the first time, his heart doing wild palpitations around his chest. Ensuring Abby settled back and was comfortable, he folded into the driver's seat. 'I still find it hard to believe I am taking my daughter home. Hell, I even find it hard to believe I have a daughter.' He turned to Abby. 'Thank you for everything: fighting to keep her, putting up with months of sickness, the loneliness while I was away – everything. Which reminds me...' He leant over her and opened the glove box. 'Look what came in yesterday's mail.' He dropped the large, thick envelope into her lap and grinned before turning back to start the engine.

Abby stared at the package for a moment and noticed the address with at least seven different postal stamps decorating it. 'It's been all around the world.'

'It appears so. I read the contents over and over again last night. The photo of our little blob is going to go in a frame. I am more than sorry it didn't reach its destination months ago but thank you for being so frank and honest in what you wrote. I treasure every page. Now let's get you home.'

Abby shivered. 'Are you okay?' asked Paul.

'Sure, why do you ask?'

'You trembled when I mentioned home.'

A blush rose up her cheeks. 'I'm looking forward to taking Susannah home,' she murmured but looked away.

As he drove, Paul contemplated her words and actions and wasn't in the least happy with her explanation. He tossed around whether or not to ask her for a more thorough explanation but decided today was not the day to place any pressure on Abby. Desperate to keep the occasion happy, he changed tack. 'Since I've been back I've put a lot of thought into my job.'

He grinned as Abby jerked around. Now he had her avid attention.

'What do you mean?'

'I have decided to go out on my own but more as a consultant engineer and maybe some design for major construction.' He kept his eyes on the road but could feel Abby staring at him.

'Can I ask why?'

'With the money Dad left me plus years of savings from a highly paid job, I don't really need to work full time. In fact I can live quite comfortably on the interest I earn from investments but I would go stir crazy if I didn't work at all.' He glanced at Abby, smiling at her slack jaw and gaped mouth which had formed a huge circle.

'You look surprised.'

'More like stunned,' said Abby. 'I had no idea you were... sorry, but it's none of my business. I apologise.'

'So well off?' Paul turned into the drive and eased his foot on the brake to bring the car to a gentle halt. Nerves quivered as he turned the engine off before he twisted to face Abby. 'It is your business to know I can more than adequately support you and our daughter.'

'I don't expect... don't want... I can support myself.'

Reaching over, Paul settled one hand on Abby's clenched fist. 'I will support my daughter, Abby, and not because I have to but because I want to. I was only trying to point out I would never leave you in the lurch financially, especially while you are studying. But to get back to my work, I've decided to add a couple of rooms to the house. Another bathroom to start with and another room on the end which you can use as a study or office. On the other side of the garage I will build a large office where I can set up my design paraphernalia and work from home. My present office will revert back to another bedroom. In fact I have already sold out my partnership with my firm.

'You have?'

He smiled, turned back and eased out of the car. 'I have,' he added as he opened the rear door and set about releasing the seat belt holding his daughter in her safety cocoon. 'I still can't believe we created this beautiful tiny creature,' he added as he lifted their daughter from the car.

Before entering the house, Paul paused at the front door, his precious sleeping daughter snug in her capsule held in one hand. 'Before we go in, I need to tell you I changed the paint colour without consulting you. I hope you like the finished product. Our daughter deserved to have a bit of pink in her room.' He pushed the door open and stood back for Abby to enter. As he figured she would do, she headed straight for the nursery, the way she shoved at the door an indication of her wrath. Terrified of her reaction, his steps were hesitant as he followed her. 'I can change it back if you prefer,' he said quietly as he stepped into the open doorway.

Abby was standing in the middle of the room, her jaw hanging loose as she slowly spun around in utter amazement. 'Paul, it's gorgeous. I can't believe it.' His own gaze took in the soft rose pink he had added to the upper walls instead of the green. Across one wall he had hand-painted fluffy white clouds with two angels peeking from the wisps of white. Abby moved closer, her eyes agog. 'This looks like Mum,' she whispered.

'I copied the picture you had in your room. Now look at the other one.' He stepped beside her and slung his arm around her waist. 'I plan on painting a third one, much smaller but I need to wait until Susannah develops her facial features.'

'You painted me.' Seemingly stunned, Abby stared at the face of the second angel.

'Yeah, I did. Do you approve?'

'I never knew you were such a talented artist, but where did you get a picture of me?'

Paul chuckled as he settled Susannah into the cot to keep her safe. He took his wallet from the inside pocket of his jacket. 'I've had your photo with me since the night of the pool party.' Holding his wallet open, he held it front of Abby's face. 'I can't recall how many times I have run my fingers over your image. Right now I am an incredibly happy man but there is one thing missing to complete my happiness. You agreeing to be my wife would fulfil all my dreams.' With his nerves about to ping apart he shoved the wallet back into his pocket and placed both hands onto her shoulders. Her back was to him.

His nerves twanged when Abby dropped her head. They tightened even more when her body shook and Paul knew she was fighting to control her emotions.

'I can't, Paul,' she whispered.

Turning her around in his arms he drew her close. 'Can you at least tell me why you can't. I need an honest answer here so I can understand.'

With her face muffled against his chest her words were barely audible. 'Because I can't marry a man, any man, who doesn't love me. It wouldn't...'

'Doesn't love you? Where on earth did you get such a ridiculous idea?' He stepped back but kept his hands on her shoulders to ensure she didn't bolt from the room. 'Abby, I've been in love with you since before I went away. I fought it at first because I was afraid of being hurt again but my heart wouldn't let me deny my feelings for you. You remember the night of the pool party?'

'Yes.'

'When I saw the cretinous politician mauling you, I wanted to kill him for daring to touch you. It was pure jealousy and a desperate desire to protect you. It was the moment I knew I was in love with you. I wanted to tell you but was too scared because you told me you weren't interested in any kind of relationship. Oh, Abby, I'm crazy about you. Don't you know me well enough to know I would never contemplate asking a woman to marry me if I wasn't in love with her?'

Abby's head rose. Tears flooded from the corners of her eyes. 'Why didn't you tell me?'

He brushed the tears away with his thumbs. 'If I'd known telling you was all it was going to take to get you to agree, I would have. But you gave me no hint on how you felt about me. I was afraid of opening up my heart to be rejected again. I still don't know how you feel about me.' As he stepped back, his eyes searched Abby's face for an answer.

'I love you, Paul. It's the only reason I came back here to live. I couldn't bear being away from you. I was hoping you would learn to love me the same.'

She didn't get a chance to say another word for he dropped his head and devoured her gorgeous mouth in a long, sensuous kiss while he held her in a tight embrace. When he managed to take control of his soaring emotions Paul held her against his chest with his chin resting on her head. 'Does this mean I am going to get the chance to tell you how much I love you every day for the rest of my life? Please tell me you will marry me? Tell me we can be a real family.'

Reaching up, Abby placed a hand each side of his face. 'Yes, Paul.'

He swooped down once again and captured her mouth in another searing kiss. It was almost impossible but he managed to drag his mouth away but leant his forehead on hers. 'Can we get married as soon as possible?'

Abby blushed. 'Doctor Carstairs said I need about six weeks for my body to heal before I can... you know.' She dropped her eyes.

Paul grinned. 'Angel, I've waited eight long months for you and even though it has almost killed me to keep my hands off you, I can wait another six weeks.' He chuckled at her heightened colour. 'What say we make a date for six weeks from today? Or maybe it doesn't give you enough time. How long does it take to organise a wedding?'

'I've got no-one but me to attend so a big shebang would be wasted. What say we make it five weeks and two days from now?' Abby whispered as she reached up with both hands and drew his head down for another kiss.

His heart felt as though it wanted to explode as he settled into the kiss to show Abby exactly how much he loved her.